SIÂN JAMES was brought  rst
novel, *One Afternoon*, wc d;
her second, *Yesterday*, wc d;
and her fifth, *Dragons and* e.
Love and War is her eightl rs
she was married to RSC ac 1e
has four grown-up childrer

One Afternoon
'Siân James's first novel . . . is a quiet, gentle book, full of insight and truth, and she writes with grace, as to the manner born.'

Susan Hill

Yesterday
'The story of a marriage in the Sixties told with humour and detachment . . . tenderness and compassion shine out.'

Barbara Pym

A Small Country
'A psychologically sound, unshowy, well-ended novel of distinction.'

Financial Times

A Dangerous Time
'On the nature of friendship, of relationships of all kinds, Siân James is particularly good. A satisfying, intelligent book.'

Financial Times

'Siân James tells her story with humour and much closely observed detail. A well-written novel with much quiet wisdom.'

Daily Telegraph

LOVE & WAR

LOVE & WAR

Passions, long repressed, begin to stir...

SIÂN JAMES

PIATKUS

First published in Great Britain in 1994 by
Judy Piatkus (Publishers) Ltd of
5 Windmill Street, London W1

This edition published 1997

*A catalogue record for this book is available
from the British Library*

ISBN 0–7499–0259–0 (hbk)
0–7499–3018–7 (pbk)

Set by Datix International Limited, Bungay, Suffolk
Printed and bound in Great Britain by
Mackays of Chatham PLC, Chatham, Kent

To Mair, George and Bob

Chapter One

This was the dream: I was having a bath. I was in my own small bathroom; the blackout curtains were drawn, the water was none too hot and certainly not over the five inch limit, the face flannel in my hand was recognisably my own, the very one my lodger, Ilona Hughes, had recently made for me from a square of her father's old flannel shirt, blanket-stitched in pink at the edges.

The soap – a bar of liver-coloured Lifebuoy – was hard and gritty, but after I'd managed to work up a reasonably good lather, I set about washing myself as thoroughly and methodically as I do when awake.

To my dismay I found that my breasts had completely gone. My chest was worse than flat, it was slightly concave like the chest of a lanky thirteen-year-old boy. I stood up to examine myself in the mirror. My face was pale, my eyes dark, my chest ribbed as a corset.

I got out of the bath and started retching into the wash basin. 'I must be very ill,' I said aloud, waking myself up.

It was seven thirty. I was sweating, but not feverish as far as I could tell. At least my breasts were intact: one, two. I touched them tenderly: pretty breasts, on the small side but not insignificant.

I very rarely dreamed, that was the odd thing, though everyone else seemed to be dreaming extravagantly that year. Every morning in the staff room, someone would be relating the latest: how the Germans had landed on Pengraig sands and taken over the Teify View Hotel; how an Italian prisoner of war had gone up to the pulpit in Bethel,

1

leading the prayers in perfect Welsh.

Mr Talfan Roberts, our deputy head, once dreamed that his pilot son had been the first to fly the Channel without a plane. He showed us how he'd worked his arms up and down.

Mary Powell, Maths, whose fiancé was in Burma, was forever dreaming of his return or his death. She often asked me for dreams of Huw, but I never had one for her. Well, he'd been abroad so long, in Africa and Italy – where was he now? – I hadn't seen him for nearly three years. I couldn't even picture him very clearly. Rather plump rosy cheeks and dark brown eyes; I could get individual items but not the whole face. His breath had a lovely clean smell like fresh washing, his feet were small and narrow. I often wondered what he remembered about me.

It's Saturday morning, which means cleaning the kitchen and shopping. Ilona Hughes, my lodger, who works at the General Post Office in Bridge Street, is rushing over her breakfast. 'You are lucky to have Saturday off,' she says. 'You've even got some margarine left. How can I make a sandwich for my lunch-break without a scrap of margarine? I'll starve, I really will.'

I don't bother to answer her. She eats like a pig.

Anyway, I'm not happy, in spite of having a day off school and some margarine – and an egg and a rather hard slice of bacon, come to that.

I'm only twenty-four years old, but I feel forty. I'm so sensible, it's beginning to show. Such a good manager, stretching out my rations to last the whole week, and my work to fill my whole life. If it's Wednesday evening, I'm marking 5A's compositions. If it's Saturday morning, I'm doing my housework. If it's Sunday afternoon I'm teaching my Sunday school class, then home to write Huw his weekly letter. All the time, working and managing. And saving money for that bigger house – large enough for those three children we're going to have when he comes home.

As I sigh, my ribs stick into my heart. I'm getting much too thin; that dream was a warning. I'm as dried-up as last year's apple. *Dear Huw, I've turned into a school teacher. Love, Rhian.*

2

Huw and I got married three and a half years ago when he had his first leave from the army. I sit with my hands in my lap and think about him, letting my tea get cold. I still can't see his face.

We've only lived together for thirty days: two fourteen-day leaves, and one forty-eight hour. More of a honeymoon than a marriage, really.

We hoped for a baby when he was on embarcation leave. (If we hadn't been married, we'd probably have had one. There's been a lot of that going on. Rosie Williams had a little boy last year and I must say she seems very proud of him. He sits up in his pram in the front garden, looking very robust and self-assured. You can tell his father was a Yank.) We wanted a girl.

Of course, I'd known Huw for ages. He was almost four years older than me and when he first asked me for a date, I couldn't believe my luck. When he met me out of school in his father's dark blue van, I felt that life had nothing more to offer.

When I passed my Higher and got a place in college, people said I was sure to find someone else, but I never did. Well, I never looked for anyone else. Aber's only thirty miles away and he came to see me most week-ends, so I never went to the Saturday hops or anything like that. Perhaps I should have. Why did I say that?

Being reasonably intelligent and very hard-working, I got a good degree and after doing a year's teacher training, slipped into a vacancy at my old school. The war had been on for a year, by that time, and several of the young teachers had been called up.

Huw was a builder with his father's firm. He left school after getting his Senior, but his mother is always telling me how clever he was and how the Head begged them to let him stay on. 'But what's the good of college?' she says. 'It only makes people proud.' She'd have liked a different sort of daughter-in-law, someone content to live with them doing the housework while she got on with all the paperwork she's always complaining of. She's a small-minded woman, but quite kind in her own way. She doesn't have much time for me, but when I had pleurisy last winter, she was always up

3

here with little jars of this and that and running her hand over the ledges for dust.

It was Huw's father who gave us this house. It had belonged to his parents; his mother had lived alone in it until she was over eighty, so it was pretty dilapidated, but of course he could easily have renovated it and sold it. It was he who put in the bathroom for us, too – scene of last night's vivid dream.

I'm very fortunate, as Huw's mother so often points out, to have no rent to pay and a lodger for company. Not that she approves of Ilona Hughes. She says she's fast and that I shouldn't allow her to have men in the house. How does she know who Ilona has in the house? The fact is, she knows everything about everybody. I don't need the *News of the World*. She has it, but hides it under the sofa if anyone calls.

Dear Huw, I wish your mother would mind her own business and that your father wasn't so mean. Why couldn't he have fixed a few tiles on the walls of the bathroom? Even in my dreams, I'm ashamed of it. He only used that green distemper because he had it left over from the Town Hall. Love, Rhian.

On the whole, I quite like teaching, but beginning a new school term is like stepping into a tunnel: struggle, repetitive work, struggle, with examinations and the summer holiday in the far, far distance.

At college I felt immensely privileged. The other girls who were in school with me worked in shops and offices, while my work was to get to grips with great minds. 'A good book is the precious life-blood of a master spirit.' Occasionally I can sense a little of that idealism in some of my Sixth Formers, but on the whole, teaching is uphill work, thirteen and fourteen-year-old boys being as unresponsive to literature as an average herd of cows. In fact, you can recite poetry to cows and receive a flattering amount of attention; raising their large, mild eyes, they gaze at you without blinking or chewing the cud, while boys smirk and pass rude notes and anatomical sketches to one another. How do you make Shakespeare or Wordsworth relevant to great louts who want to be out in the fields playing? Or even lifting potatoes? For every pupil I manage to interest, there seem to

4

be ten or twenty who remain sullenly bored. They are marginally less hostile to the rules of grammar, but I can't spend all my time on parts of speech, punctuation and the comparison of adjectives.

I really don't think I could endure a lifetime of teaching. When Huw comes home, I'll probably have a family and become a full-time housewife, but this morning even that prospect fails to cheer.

There's something lacking in my life. Perhaps it's religion. This war has certainly strained people's belief in God. With so much death and destruction being doled out everywhere, He obviously doesn't care – so that He's not all-merciful – or cares but can't do anything about it – so that He's not all-powerful. I know I seldom feel spiritually renewed after a Sunday service these days. Of course, there's little of mystery and beauty about a Welsh chapel with its smell of Mansion polish and damp hymn books; even the singing lusty rather than uplifting. I often find myself studying the congregation instead of listening to the sermon and then, in no time at all, I'm thinking about clothes, hats and blouses and so on.

Why should I save all my money every month? I have a sudden urge to buy myself something new and frivolous. I'm so sick of my neat grey skirt and the hand-knitted jumpers and hand-sewn blouses I wear with it. What I want is a dress with a tightly fitting waist and a skirt that swirls. This very morning, before I change my mind, I'll go out and buy myself a really pretty new dress, perhaps with a bolero. I can do my washing this afternoon, can't I? Or even tomorrow morning instead of going to chapel? Why should I spend my whole youth being middle-aged.

My tea's gone cold, but with unusual abandon I treat myself to a fresh pot.

On my way to town, I call in at the Post Office to see Ilona Hughes. It's very quiet there, no one buying saving bonds or even stamps. She looks up as I walk towards her, sucking in her cheeks, trying to look hungry.

Taken item by item, I should be much better looking than she is. I've got thick, rusty-brown hair and pale grey eyes and a decent shaped nose and so on, while she's got small down-drooping eyes, a too-large nose and mouth and a very small chin. But when she's covered her freckles with make-up and put a lot of that shiny beetroot-coloured lipstick on her lips and Vaseline on her eyelids, she looks so pretty I could spit.

'I'm going to get myself a new dress,' I say.

She takes it in her stride as though it's quite an everyday affair. 'Go to Studio Laura,' she says. (She pronounces it in a very affected, foreign way; 'Studio LAWRA'.) Studio Laura – I couldn't go there. It's a tiny shop with nothing in the window but sand and pebbles and one hat. It's a shop for English visitors and it usually closes in September; it's remained open this year only because the owner's London flat has been bombed. The owner, by the way, is called Tremlett Browne and he wears a narrow satin ribbon instead of a tie.

I'd intended to go to J C Jones. They've got quite a good selection of clothes there, all the reputable makes. That's where I got the powder-blue dress and jacket I wore at my wedding and which I've worn to every school and chapel function since.

'What's wrong with J C Jones?' I ask her, but she only raises her eyebrows and turns her attention to a large, red-cheeked farmer who's just shouldered his way to the counter with a sizeable bundle of notes. She gives him an intimate little smile and nods her head at me as a sign of dismissal.

I wish now I'd given her a dab of my margarine.

I often wish I'd been born a Roman Catholic; the Catholic church looks dark and mysterious in its cobbled yard. It would be so restful to sit in there, quietly gazing at beautiful pictures and statues. Why not? I can't even imagine the smell of incense. What if it does dull the brain? I quite often find myself planning next week's lessons during Mr Roberts's long sermons; surely it would be more appropriate to be even muzzily thinking of God.

Of course, my mother is convinced that the Pope is the Anti-Christ and that all the Roman Church's rituals and ceremonies are mumbo-jumbo. She seems so *certain* of everything. Will my opinions have crystallised by the time I

6

become a mother? Is it part of the ageing process, like hardening of the arteries?

But I wish I could feel that my life contained some divine spark: 'A presence that disturbs me with the joy of elevated thought.' Why don't I have elevated thoughts? Even my infrequent dreams are pitifully down-to-earth.

I walk past J C Jones and down Marine Terrace.

'Well, Rhian.'

It's Gwynn Morgan, Art. He was the Art teacher even when I was a pupil: too old now, I suppose, to be called up. (I wish I didn't feel so awkward with him – never sure, for instance, whether to call him Gwynn or Mr Morgan.)

'What's the news of Huw?'

'I haven't had a letter for two weeks.'

'I thought you looked a bit peaky. Try not to worry, Rhian. It doesn't help him or anyone else. Got time for a coffee?'

Peaky. What a horrible word.

'I'm getting myself a new dress. From Studio Laura.' How dashing it makes me feel, even saying it.

'Come and have a coffee first. You rush about too much, Rhian. I watch you at school. Rush, rush, rush. It'll make you old before your time.'

Peaky and old. That does it. We turn into Glyn Owen's, walk past the queue at the bread counter and go upstairs. Several pairs of eyes follow us. What am I doing having coffee with a *man*? This will get back to my mother-in-law before I've taken the first sip.

Gwynn Morgan may be middle-aged but he's still very handsome; a long, lean face with curly greyish hair and rather wicked eyes which look sideways at you. He painted my picture when I was in the Sixth Form and it won a prize in some exhibition in Brecon.

'I've still got that painting I did of you.' he says, as though reading my thoughts.

'Have you? I thought you painted over your old ones.'

'I usually do. But that was one of my better efforts. My Renoir period. You were quite plump in those days. It showed very nicely even under your gym-slip . . . Two coffees and two buttered scones, please.'

7

'I had such a strange dream last night.'

'Nothing in the world bores me as much as other people's dreams. Even my own bore me.'

'I wasn't going to tell you, anyway. It was a bit rude.'

He leans towards me. 'I don't mind them so much if they're rude.'

He's got a really friendly smile which completely changes his rather melancholy face. I wish I saw more of him. His room is at the very top of the school and he keeps himself to himself.

'Are you Church or Chapel?' I ask him, my mind still hovering on the Catholic Church and the peace it seemed to promise.

'Is that always the first question you ask a man who invites you for a coffee? What if he doesn't intend any serious entanglement? Sorry, love. I was brought up chapel. Congregational.'

'Like me. But I've never seen you in Tabernacle.'

'Haven't been for years. Don't believe in any of it.'

'Really? *Really*? Do you mean you're an atheist? Like Shelley? How very interesting. I think you're the first atheist I've ever met. Do you mind if I stare at you a bit?'

The waitress, a girl from up our way, brings us our coffee. 'We've had quite a run on the sultana scones,' she says, 'but I've brought you some Madeira.'

Gwynn Morgan doesn't say anything, just looks sourly at the two yellow slabs of cake on the thick white plate.

'Thank you,' I murmur, 'very nice. Thank you.'

'Perhaps you'll sit for me again, sometime,' he says, after a moment or two.

'Oh no. How could I?'

'Do you mean because I'm an atheist?'

'Because I haven't got the time. I don't get any free periods this year. Not since Roy Lewis was called up.'

'You could always come to the house. You know where I live.'

'Oh, but I wouldn't want to do that. I couldn't – there'd be talk. Anyway, I'm not pretty any more.'

I wait for him to contradict me – I must be looking at him rather expectantly – but he doesn't.

'This cake isn't as bad as it looks,' I say, to cover my disappointment. 'Try some.'

He shrugs his shoulders, drinks some of the pale grey coffee and takes out a cigarette.

'I've been feeling depressed lately,' I say, 'and wondering whether what I need is some new, vital sort of religious experience.'

He looks at me with an expression I can't quite fathom. 'I thought it was a new dress you were after,' he says.

I consider this. It seems an important moment. 'Well, perhaps it is. I'd better go – Studio Laura shuts at twelve on a Saturday.'

'I wanted to ask you about your lodger,' Gwynn Morgan says, stubbing out his cigarette in his saucer. 'Ilona something, isn't it?'

'Ilona Hughes,' I say, sitting down again. 'What did you want to know about her?'

'Do you think she'd sit for me?'

'I could ask her. Do you really want me to? Do you think she's pretty?'

He seemed to give my question serious consideration. 'She looks like a Cranach painting. Little squashed face, small breasts, big hips.'

I almost smile. 'I'll ask her. I'll let you know on Monday.'

'Tell her I pay five bob an hour for a life model.'

I can feel myself blushing. 'Thank you for the coffee.'

As I get up again, I catch sight of the sea from the window; bathed in a stormy, violet light, its chilling beauty takes my breath away.

The window of Studio Laura has nothing in it but a twisted tree with hundreds of pink paper leaves and a very plain damson-blue dress.

I sidle into the shop, empty except for an oak chest of drawers with two brass candlesticks on the top. I find myself wishing I was at the great mahogany counter of J C Jones where Mrs Edith advises against buying ready-made. 'Run it up yourself, love,' she says, 'it'll only take three and a half yards at two and elevenpence. Think of the saving.'

'Good morning, Madam.' Mrs Edith would die sooner than call anyone 'Madam'.

'I'm looking for a dress, actually.'

I don't think I've ever said 'actually' before. 'I'm looking for a dress, actually,' with a clipped English accent. I suppose being called Madam has unnerved me.

Mr Tremlett Browne inspects me with head slightly tilted to one side.

'You've got a fine figure,' he says.

What a nerve. I didn't come in here for him to run his eyes over my body.

'I should think a size 36, Madam. Is that right?'

I make a little bobbing motion with my head, as ducks do when they know they're being watched.

'I see you in something very tight. You've got good shoulders. What does Madam think about the model in the window?'

Before I can say a word, he's got it out and is holding it up before me.

'I wanted something pretty,' I say feebly.

'Oh no, Madam. Nothing pretty. You want something . . . well, something like this. You take it through and try it on. You'll see what I mean.'

I look for a price tag, but there isn't one. 'How much is it?' I ask, but he's turned away and is staring at the pink-leaved tree and the sparkling sea beyond it.

Of course, it's a perfect fit and makes me look so different that I feel dizzy to see myself in the mirror. It's made of a thick, matt silk, so cleverly cut that it seems to reveal rather than hide my body; my breasts seem bigger and rounder, my hips and thighs harder, more sculptured. It's turned my brownish hair red as conkers. I don't think for a moment that I'll ever have the occasion or the courage to wear it, but on the other hand I know that to leave without it would be as difficult as leaving without my skin.

I go back into the shop.

Gwynn Morgan is there leaning against the door.

'Yes,' he says, nodding his head. 'Yes, that looks just right. Lovely. No need to try anything else.'

'How much are you going to charge her?' he asks Tremlett Browne, who mentions a sum which is almost exactly what I earn in a month.

10

'Nonsense,' Gwynn Morgan says. 'She can't afford that sort of money. She may look somebody in that dress, but she's only a teacher, man. Take half off and she may consider it.

'I do the window for him,' he tells me, 'so he owes me a favour.'

'You get paid.'

'Give her a discount, man. She's a friend of mine.'

They're still arguing while I change back into my grey skirt and green jumper and my navy-blue gaberdine.

In the end, Tremlett Browne takes almost a third off the price. It's still more, far more, than I've ever paid for anything else in my entire life, but I hand over the money readily enough.

After folding the dress very carefully and putting it into a shiny green and white striped bag with Studio Laura on it, Mr Browne hands it to Gwynn Morgan – rather odd, – who takes it without protest. And together he and I walk out of the shop and along the front.

'Did you really cut out all those hundreds of pink leaves?' I ask him, glancing back at the window.

'No. 2C did that part. But the grand design was mine.'

'Like God made the world.'

'That's right.'

When we come to the lifeboat station, we stop and look out at the lavender-coloured sea and the gulls wheeling silently overhead. Huge waves advance, one after the other, exploding and crashing and sucking the loosened shingle as they retreat. It's very cold.

Life is certainly strange. I've been bored to the bone for months and months on end, and suddenly I feel as though I'm conducting a great orchestra.

'Oh, bury me not in the senseless earth. But in the living sea,' I quote, my voice swelling with emotion, like someone on the wireless.

'I hope they don't bury you anywhere for a good long time,' Gwynn Morgan says, 'because, frankly, I enjoy looking at you.'

I try to say something, but fail. Behind the fury of the high January tide, I seem to hear the steady beat of a drum.

11

'And now I'm going for a pint. I don't suppose I can persuade you to join me?'

I smile and shake my head. 'My legs are still trembling,' I tell him. 'I'm no good at spending money. It's my upbringing.'

My whole body is trembling. Can it be the cold?

What a beautiful little town Llanfair is; three streets radiating up the hill from the market square, the posh houses on the front keeping out the rough sea winds. There are three chapels, two churches, eleven pubs and two licensed hotels.

The bigger houses are mostly Georgian, with flat windows, and doors with rounded fanlights. People complain that they're getting to look shabby, with no fresh paint since the beginning of the war, but I love the peeling grey-white of the walls and the peeling grey-greens of the doors and window-frames.

Chapter Two

For the rest of the day, I'm conscious of being surrounded by something heavy and threatening.

What an idiot I am. I can't get my little adventure with Gwynn Morgan out of my head. God, my mind is in a pathetic state, as well as my body.

But he was so friendly. What made him ask me to have a coffee with him? He really seemed to want my company, smiling so warmly. What made him come after me to Studio Laura?

To be absolutely honest, Gwynn Morgan was once my greatest heart-throb. Of course, I never thought of him as remotely connected with everyday life: other girls had crushes on Spencer Tracy or Robert Taylor, mine was on Gwynn Morgan, Art; it was in the same realm of fantasy. As they cut out glossy pictures from movie magazines, I cut out his picture – smudged black and white – from the local paper or the school gazette. I probably still have one or two somewhere.

I wonder if he remembers how I used to dote on him? He must, surely, have realised that something other than chance was responsible for our frequent meetings on the stairs and in the corridors. 'Well, Rhian,' he used to say when we came face to face for the third time in a morning, 'we really mustn't go on meeting like this.' How I used to envy Bethan Morris and Ruth Talbot, who took Art in the Sixth Form, monopolising so much of his time. I cultivated a friendship with Bethan, so that I could join her when she ate her lunchtime sandwiches in the Art Room. (Not that he was present on those occasions, but it made me feel close to him.)

His hair was black in those days.

My heart almost burst with pride when he said he wanted to paint my picture. I think it took about six sittings, two hours each, in the Art Room after school. He used to give me a bar of fruit-and-nut chocolate, I remember, and five minutes' rest after the first hour. He used to recite little verses to me when he thought I was getting bored, but I wasn't allowed to smile.

The finished picture was entitled 'Schoolgirl'. My parents didn't think it did me justice. 'He's given her a cast in the right eye,' my mother said, 'and it makes her look a bit simple.'

'It must have been all that sitting still,' my father said. 'She's got the look of a rabbit staring at a snake.'

It got a prize anyway, in that exhibition.

The only other time we were together was on Drama Club night. He was responsible for the scenery of the play we put on before Easter every year, but he took an interest in all of it: the preliminary discussions and the acting and directing. His interests and abilities were far more wide-ranging than any of the other teachers at our school; I remember being quite surprised, for instance, at how much Racine and Corneille he could quote. He spoke French well, too, with an enviable accent, someone said he'd once studied drawing in Paris.

I wonder if he really was more interested in me than in any of the others? Some days I used to think so and go to bed faint with happiness.

In my last year I played Rosalind in *As You Like It*. I remember Miss Eira Jenkins, our producer, getting rather annoyed because she thought he was getting too involved in what was, after all, her pigeon. But life could hold no greater delight for me than repeating those love-sick lines to him: 'I tell thee, Aliena, I cannot be out of the sight of Orlando. I'll go find a shadow and sigh till he come.'

I wonder if he knew that I was speaking directly to him? 'I cannot be out of the sight of Orlando.' I suppose he did.

Naturally, I got over all that high romance years ago – when Huw started taking an interest in me, I suppose. With

14

Huw, everyday life took over, and it was time it did.

So why do I feel this damp cloud all around me and settling on my chest? Perhaps I'm in for a cold.

Ilona Hughes approves of my dress. 'Well, it makes you look different anyway, and that's something,' but insists that I get a roll-on, now, to wear with it and some wedge-heeled shoes.

When I tell her about my meeting with Gwynn Morgan, she's even more interested. 'Gwynn Morgan?' she says. 'Yes, I know him quite well. He comes to the Ship most nights. I feel rather sorry for him, though. He's always got to go home after the one drink, he can never stay more than half an hour, he's very definitely under his wife's thumb.'

'Well, she's English,' I say, as though that explains a lot.

'No, she's not, she's French. Convent-educated and all that. Very religious.'

'Fancy that. And him an atheist.'

'Atheist? He's a Catholic, like she is. What made you think he was an atheist?'

'Are you sure?'

'Yes. Denzil sees them in Sant Ioan's. That's how I met him. Through Denzil.'

Denzil is her current boyfriend: Liverpool-Irish, a soldier stationed in Tonfaen.

I take my dress back upstairs and hang it in the wardrobe. When will I wear it? To Prize Day, in the summer? To Fflur's wedding, if she invites me? It seems altogether too worldly for chapel. Why ever did I buy it?

What a strange day it's been. A red-letter day, I suppose. Write a composition entitled A Red-Letter Day. 'I've never 'ad one of those, Miss.' 'Will one side be enough, Miss?'

A Blue-Dress Day.

Oh, but the way he looked at me when I came back into the shop wearing it. No one ever looked at me in quite that way before: admiring, almost deferential, but troubled at the same time. It set my pulse racing, I can tell you . . . And if I was completely honest, I'd admit that it was passion I felt in that look, not deference or even homage. 'The red rose whispers of passion, And the white rose breathes of love. Oh, the red rose is a falcon, And the white rose is a dove. But I send you a cream-white rosebud, With a flush on its petal tips . . .'

Rubbish, what absolute rubbish. What's the matter with me? Again I have to remind myself that I'm a respectable married woman, brought up to know the difference between right and wrong, between true and false, between doves and falcons. *Dear Huw, I'm a respectable married woman, but buying this new dress seems to have taken my wits away. I'm sorry. Love, Rhian.*

I make myself think of Huw. I go to the window, standing behind the curtains to look out: a moonlit night, the pavements gleaming, the sky pewter-grey but lighter at the horizon, the rim of the sea just visible beyond the huddle of the town.

Will Huw be feeling lonely on this Saturday night? Homesick for Llanfair? Somehow I don't think so; Huw is an extrovert, ready to make the best of any situation. As long as he's with his mates − his letters are full of stories about Nobby and Jock, Bill, Sandy, Ginger and Tich Gordon − Huw won't be too unhappy anywhere. I hope he isn't unhappy.

Will he like my new dress, I wonder. I can't remember his ever taking much notice of my clothes. How strange he'd looked in his hairy, khaki uniform, the little forage cap tilted over one eye. After the war, he'll wear ordinary clothes again and I'll have his Sunday shirt and his workshirts to wash and iron. How odd it will seem to have him living here instead of Ilona Hughes. Will it be better?

Why didn't Gwynn Morgan admit to being a Catholic? Fancy his having a French wife. Strange they have no children. When she comes to Prize Day or the Saint David's Day concert, she doesn't speak to anyone but the Headmaster's wife. The dress she wore last year was of some thick black material and much too long; I wish I could say she looked dowdy, but she didn't. She looked strange and different, but definitely not dowdy. She's quite striking-looking, I suppose. And French as well.

Ilona Hughes is having mackerel for her supper. She offers

16

me some, but I've got a piece of vegetable pie left from yesterday. I give her some rhubarb and custard which I'd intended for tomorrow and she eats it as though it's the only thing she's had all week. She loves custard, but she's never got any sugar to make any. She could easily learn to drink tea without sugar – anyone could – but when I suggest it, she almost cries. Sometimes I think she's not all there.

She finishes off the rhubarb and custard and then scrapes out the bowl and the jug.

'What are you doing tonight?' she asks me.

'I'm going to darn my stockings and listen to Saturday Night Theatre. It's a nice old-fashioned play with a butler.'

She sighs. 'Would you like to come to the pictures with Denzil and me?'

'Heavens, no. I mean, no thank you. I mean, three's a crowd, isn't it? I wouldn't want to spoil your fun.'

She looks relieved. 'But I don't like to think of you with a new dress and nowhere to go.' she says. 'If I see Gwynn Morgan, I'll ask him to call round to take you out for a drink.'

'I hope you're joking.'

'I can't see the harm.'

'I can manage my own affairs, thank you.'

'Can you? What affairs? Well, let me know if you change your mind. I don't suppose you could lend me some lipstick, could you? The Yardley cherry? I seem to have mislaid mine.'

I lend her my lipstick, but can't bring myself to tell her that Gwynn Morgan wants her as a life-model for five shillings an hour. I'm afraid she'll accept and fall in love with him, I suppose. I'd certainly object if she started bringing him back here every evening. I wouldn't be able to bear it.

Our minister gave a really good sermon this morning; I listened attentively for once.

Many of the older people don't like Mr Roberts because he hasn't got the eloquence of the great preachers they remember, but I like him the better for it. I'm suspicious of a sermon which grips you by its dramatic intensity rather than by its message. Perhaps the old-type preachers, whose voices

17

pitched and soared, whose hands fluttered like doves or stabbed home a point as though they were driving a nail into a wall, perhaps they had their own integrity. But I can't help thinking that even if they'd lost all belief, they'd still be able to build up an extraordinary edifice; emotive phrases, rising and falling cadences, rhetorical questions, alliteration and quotation around emptiness.

Mr Roberts is quiet and unemotive and his message is stark: hating the enemy, we sin against a loving God.

The congregation, many with sons, grandsons, brothers or nephews in the forces, don't want to hear about love and forgiveness but only of the noble fight against aggression, of defending the right to be free. Etc.

Huw's mother, for instance, thinks the minister is undermining her son's sacrifice. 'Is my Huw wicked to fight, tell me that?' she asks him on the way out.

'Your Huw is very bravely doing what he conceives to be his duty. I'm not trying to deny the great courage of our soldiers.'

'You're dodging the question, Mr Roberts.'

'Come along to Sunday School this afternoon, Mrs Evans, and we'll see if we can find some New Testament verses to enlighten us.'

'No thank you. I'll stick to my way of thinking and you can stick to yours.'

I'm having dinner with my in-laws and Huw's mother is still ranting on about poor Mr Roberts as we lay the table.

'To hear him carrying on about the Germans being God's children, only led astray, is deeply offensive, don't you think so, Rhian? Gwilym Martin, Horeb, isn't such a milksop, I can tell you. No, Mr Martin gets to the point quick enough, praying for the forces of God to smash the legions of Satan, and no nonsense about forgiveness either. I'd switch to Horeb in a minute, only Bryn's afraid of losing custom in Tabernacle. Rhian, I hope you won't let Huw know how disloyal Mr Roberts is being. I'm sure it would be no comfort for him to realise that his own minister is siding with the enemy. I hope their Padre – not that I like that name, very High Church it sounds – I hope he's at least on the right side.'

18

'I bought a new dress yesterday.' I say blithely.

I've long realised that's it's not a bit of use trying to alter or modify my mother-in-law's views on anything; all I can do is wait for one of her dramatic pauses and then seize the opportunity to change the subject.

She's astonished. 'A *new dress*?' Nobody can be as astonished as my mother-in-law. 'A *new dress*? Did you *need* a new dress?'

'I thought I did. Yes. I haven't had one for ages. Not since the wedding.'

'Well, well, well! A new dress!'

She lets the idea permeate into her mind as she mashes the potatoes.

'I wish I'd have known you were thinking of a new dress, Rhian. You see, I'd have offered to make you one. I've got a yard and a half of lovely pre-war material – beige – which would have been ample for the bodice. Such lovely quality. Two yards of some contrasting colour for the skirt, say a nice apple-green, was all you'd have needed to buy. About five shillings was all you'd have had to spend. And perhaps six pence for a packet of fasteners.'

'What a shame you hadn't mentioned it.'

'A new dress! Oh, I hope it didn't cost too much.'

'No, it was quite reasonable.'

'Where did you get it? At J C Jones?'

'No. I went to Studio Laura.'

'To *Studio Laura*? Oh Rhian, what a pity! Didn't I tell you about that Mr Browne who owns Studio Laura? Well, Mrs Watkins, Park Villa, is convinced he's a German spy. Yes, she saw him out very late one night when she was taking Mot for his last walk, and there he was, lurking in the shadow of the breakwater and staring out to sea with a pair of binoculars.'

'Great Heavens! I hope she reported him to PC Jones.'

'Don't make fun of me, Rhian. If he's not a spy, why isn't he in the army?'

'Well, I suppose he could be too old. I should think he'd be about the same age as Gwynn Morgan, Art, who seems to be a friend of his.'

She sighs again as she carries the meat to the table.

'That Gwynn Morgan. He's another fine one. Always has to be different, that man. Why doesn't he dress like a teacher, for a start? Probably fancies himself as one of these artists. And his wife is some sort of foreigner. It wouldn't surprise me to find that Gwynn Morgan is another of these conchies, like Mr Roberts.'

'Or a spy. I know for a fact that he's got a pair of binoculars.'

Huw's parents have an oppressively ugly house. It's crammed full of nasty new furniture: a three-piece suite and pouffe in cabbage-green velvet with bronze braiding, tables and chairs and an outsize sideboard in shiny, yellow wood and an Axminster carpet – A1 quality – in autumn's most vulgar shades. Every flat surface is covered with a display of glass and china ornaments which shiver when you shut a door.

To me, every object seems one too many, but Huw's mother cherishes each one, tenderly recalling its date of purchase and price, and dusting or polishing or blowing on it every day. Almost every week she's altered the position of something or other; the double-decker tea-trolley or the brown standard lamp or the large technicolour painting of Cader Idris, and I'm called upon to comment on the result. 'Oh yes,' I say, nodding my head sagely and fast to indicate that she's now got it to a T . . . And I'll be equally enthusiastic when it's back in its original place the following week.

Huw's father is proud only of how much it all cost. 'No one else in Llanfair has got things as expensive as these,' he says. 'Well, it'll all be yours and Huw's when we've gone.'

His wife frowns, none too pleased to be reminded of that day she'll have to leave even the A1 Axminster and the Royal Derby plates behind her.

The house where I was brought up is different, the poverty of generations of my farming family ensuring that nothing was ever replaced. Most of the furniture is scrubbed pine, centuries old, well-worn but still reflecting something of the skill and integrity of the country craftsman who made it. The floor is of blue flagstones.

After Sunday school, I write to Huw.

20

Dear Huw,

It's been another quiet week here.

I wonder where you are and what you're doing. There are so many rumours. Everyone seems to think we'll be hearing something as soon as spring comes, something momentous. The papers are full of phrases like 'the beginning of the end'. Whatever happens, you know that I'll be thinking of you and praying for your safety.

I bought myself a new dress yesterday, dark blue and quite plain. Well, I thought I needed something to cheer me up, I suppose. I went to the new shop on the prom. It was rather expensive, but luckily I'd happened to meet Mr Morgan, Art, when I was having a coffee in Glyn Owen's and he said he could get a discount for me because he does the window-dressing there. Anyway, he came with me and the owner, Mr Tremlett Browne, took a third off the price. Mr Morgan asked after you and sends his regards.

Mr Roberts's sermon this morning was on forgiveness. Your mother was, as usual, annoyed because he prays for all wounded soldiers instead of only ours. Mr Martin, Horeb, is much more patriotic, it seems. She wishes she could go to Horeb for the duration, but your father declares he couldn't share bed or board with a Methodist so she'll have to put up with poor Mr Roberts. Anyway, I like him. He may be a bit of a pacifist, but though people like to forget it these days, Christ himself had unfortunate leanings that way.

Your mother cooked a lovely dinner – lamb and mint-sauce [bottled].

I have no more news, so I send you my usual love.

Your wife,

Rhian.

I wish I hadn't bought it, that new dress. All is vanity, sayeth the preacher. I wish I could stop thinking of the way Gwynn Morgan looked at me when he saw me in it. All day I've tried hard to think of other things, serious things; war and death, oh, and the moral degeneration which is worse than death. But then I remember that look, that emotion encircling us, and happiness breaks in again. I can't seem to help myself.

Chapter Three

When I go home to the farm on Wednesday evening, I find my mother playing the harmonium to her POWs. The lorry taking them back to camp breaks down fairly regularly on the snow-bound hills, so they often have a happy half-hour like this.

At least, it's happy for my mother. The POWs have a tired, strained look; if it's appreciation, it's the sort too deep for expression.

They're a strange pair, Gino and Martino: quiet and rather sullen. I don't mean that there's anything strange about them being quiet and sullen; after all they are prisoners and hundreds of miles from home. The odd thing, I suppose, is that most of the others are usually bubbling over with mirth and friendliness.

My mother thinks her two come from a backward, rural area where there's very little culture. I suppose she'd hoped for a tenor and a bass who'd sing Verdi as they drove the plough; these two hardly talk, even to each other. She's desperately sorry for people who have neither music nor religion – Roman Catholicism being, of course, empty ritual and ceremony – so she tries to make it up to them by playing them Welsh hymns.

'*Buon giorno, buon giorno.*'

They turn their meek eyes towards me.

I try to ask them what sort of day they've had. Sometimes my terrible Italian raises a smile, but not tonight.

I kiss my mother's cheek. 'Don't stop because I'm here,' I tell her, knowing there's little hope of it.

'Well, I'll go on till the lorry comes. It shouldn't be many minutes.'

My mother has never had an hour's musical tuition in her life, but is able to play any tune as long as it's a hymn and sad. 'Why have we always got to be carrying the cross?' I used to ask her when I was a child. 'Why is it always our turn?'

It suddenly strikes me that my mother has become almost pretty again; she even seems to have put on a little weight. Of course her skin has been ruined by rough weather and rougher treatment, but her eyebrows are finely marked, her nose is straight and beautiful and she has a lovely delicacy of ear and jaw-bone. Strands of hair which have escaped from her bun are curling around her face in a way I would think contrived if I didn't know better. My mother is as God made her and it's not too bad.

It must be admitted that her Italians have been a great help to her. My father died during my last year in college four years ago and our helper, Dafi Blaenhir, who was about twenty years older, died early the following year.

I'll never forget how Dafi Blaenhir cried at my father's funeral. My mother and I were calm and tearless. I know I felt rigid with pain, as though all the normally soft and yielding parts of my body had been calcified, so that even to sigh made my lungs creak. Dafi Blaenhir cried for us like a hired mourner.

My mother, noticing his wet cheeks, had given him a large white handkerchief to take to chapel, but he must have forgotten it. Anyway, it would have taken a bath towel to stem the flow; his stiff Sunday collar and his flannel shirt-front were soon limp as dish cloths. He'd never got married; my father, I think, meant more to him than his closest relatives.

My father left school at fourteen but went on studying all his life. I think he bought every Welsh book as it came out, poetry, short stories, essays, criticism, and read them all, slowly and thoroughly. He was a poet too, as many farmers are in this part of the world; the long days of hard but repetitive work and the beauty of hill, field and sky, seeming to make a man eager to struggle with words and prosody. He

24

rarely came home to supper without having a new *englyn* to recite to us – only a four-lined verse, admittedly, but one of formidable complexity, with set rhythm, rhymes and alliterative pattern. Sometimes the completed verse wouldn't rise above the nature of an exercise: something to occupy the mind, something a man cobbled together when alone, finding the knack of it easier with practice. Often, though, it would soar; an englyn, like a sonnet, having some perfection of form which makes the sum of its lines greater than its parts.

When he'd finished, Dafi Blaenhir would gasp his appreciation and my father used to say that that 'Whew' meant more to him than all the prizes he won at local or national eisteddfod.

Gino and Martino get to their feet as soon as they hear the lorry arriving, and I can't say I blame them.

'Pasta for supper?' I ask them, miming extravagantly. 'Spaghetti? Macaroni?'

'*Bara caws*,' Gino says firmly.

'Ah, yes. Bread and cheese for us – pasta for you.' I'm smiling so broadly that it's beginning to hurt my cheeks. '*Buon noce.*'

'*Nos da*,' they reply as, grave and unsmiling, they make their way to the door.

'Well, Mam,' I say when they've gone, 'I don't know that a smattering of Welsh is going to do them much good when they get back to Italy.'

'You can be quite sure it'll do them no harm, anyway. It's a way of communicating with them, girl, pointing to this and that and offering them the Welsh word. I can't always remember the English, you know that. And they like people to make a bit of an effort. Old Hetty, now, she always stops for a chat, tells them the names of her thirteen children and where they're buried, poor things. They're always glad to see old Hetty.'

I'm restless again and make an excuse to go outside for a breath of air before supper.

The moon hasn't risen, but the snow casts a sharp, blue light on the track up to Rhydgaled. The hedges are bright with frost. There's no wind.

We hardly ever have snow in Llanfair; when we do, it never settles. But here, only fourteen miles inland and about a thousand feet up, it's a different world. I was often unable to go to the County School for a week or two at a time. I'd fight my way down the lane to the main road only to find that the bus driver had already turned back to town, deciding not to risk the last few miles. Stiff with cold I'd wait the required half-hour, then trudge home again to claim a second breakfast. To tell you the truth, I rather liked those days of unofficial holidays, sitting in the kitchen immersed in a book, a blanket over my knees, occasionally having to stop reading to minister to a tiny, half-dead lamb that my father brought in and thrust at me.

I was a dab hand with lambs. My father never let me have one as a pet, though. After a couple of hours, very occasionally a whole day and a night, it would be out again, roughing it with a foster-mother. There's no room for sentimentality on a farm. I understand that now.

I stumble against a dark, ivy-covered bush, waking some small birds taking shelter there against the long, cold night. They scold sleepily as hens do when disturbed. I realise that I've almost forgotten the smell of a hen-house. Perhaps I should have stayed in the country and married a farmer: a rich farmer.

I turn back towards the house and see all the fields flooded with snow. The evening star is bright. Everything is sacred.

But all's not well here about my heart.

There's still no word from Huw. And however hard I try, I can't stop thinking about Gwynn Morgan; whether it would be so dreadfully wrong for me to be just a tiny bit friendly with him.

In school today he asked me whether I ever went to the Ship in the evening. He knows very well that I don't, I've never been to a public house in my life.

I wish I could talk to my mother about him, but I can't. I love her dearly, but I've never been able to talk to her and she's never been able to talk to me. 'You know what I mean' is the nearest she ever gets to anything personal. 'She was a lovely looking woman, but ... you know what I mean.' 'They had one trouble ... you know what I mean.'

The supper is on the table when I get back; bacon broth with carrots and leeks, fresh, home-made bread. As I eat, I'm still fumbling for words. I've got an hour before the last bus to Llanfair.

I take a deep, deep breath. 'Do you remember my old art teacher?' I ask her. 'Gwynn Morgan from Nantgoch?'

'Of course I do, girl. He painted that picture of you, years ago. What about him?'

'Well ... he's been ... quite friendly lately ... you know what I mean.'

'You don't say. Whatever happened? Whatever did you do? And him with such a fine-looking wife.'

'The worst of it is, that I myself ...'

She looks at me with narrowed eyes. 'No, no. I'll never believe that. You've never done anything to be ashamed of.'

'Oh, I haven't. I'm talking about feelings.'

She sighs. 'I suppose there's no answer to feelings,' she says. 'We've all had those. But if I know anything about it, you'll come out on the other side with your love for Huw intact and strengthened. The important thing is that you don't ... you know what I mean.'

'You make it sound so easy.'

'No, no. Life isn't easy. I'd never tell anyone that life is easy.'

That seems to be it. She's spoken. Life isn't easy.

We sit silently then, thinking about wars and poverty and illness, about the shortness of life, the certainty of death. My father was old before he was fifty. How long will my mother last here on her own, carrying every drop of water from the pump outside, tending her fowls and her animals, digging the garden, making her own bread, working sixteen or seventeen hours a day like her mother and grandmother before her?

I think of the word delight.

Bus journeys are such a nuisance, all that jolting about giving you ... feelings ... you know what I mean.

It isn't right to be twenty-four and living like a nun.

I'm thinking about Huw, how it was for us. Very awkward, that first time. He didn't like to admit that he was inexperienced too; men don't, I suppose, especially when they're four

27

years older. Oh, it was pretty awful. If only we could have laughed about it, but that night it seemed the most serious matter in the world.

After the first few times it improved. Well, it had to, it couldn't have got worse.

After the first few times, I quite liked it. Having him on top of me, that weight. Oh happy horse, to bear the weight of Antony.

Ilona Hughes says that where sex is concerned, a woman has to take charge, but I don't understand what she means and I don't like to ask. Does she mean that a woman has to decide whether she wants to have sex or not? If so, I agree with her, of course. But once it's all started, I don't see how a woman can be much in charge. Oh, I'm so inexperienced. I didn't really like being turned this way and that, but I suppose it could have been wonderful. And how do you know unless you try?

Great Heavens, now I'm at least halfway to committing adultery with Gwynn Morgan, Art. And in that particular way I didn't even like with Huw. And, oh, it's quite thrilling. This can't be me – it's just my body being thrown about on this broken-down country bus. Only another couple of miles. I'm pressing my thighs together and my nipples are hard as peas.

A woman sitting in the front turns round and stares at me. Can she know what's going on in my mind? Oh, now I've admitted that my mind is also involved. Adultery is a frightening concept.

The little staring woman is lurching back along the bus towards me. I recognise her. She's Miriam somebody and she goes to our chapel at home. Miriam Lloyd, I think.

'Well,' she says, 'and how did you find your mother? I'd have come to sit by you straight away, only I didn't recognise you in your beret. It was the conductor, Wil Aberbanc, who told me who you were.'

I don't make any reply. I'm finding it as much as I can do to breathe slowly and evenly.

'She's much better at last, isn't she? It's taken her a long time, poor thing. Four years isn't it, since your poor father passed away and left her with those twenty-five acres and no

28

help. But now ... well, who can blame her, I say. I mean, it's been more than a decent interval, hasn't it?'

Gwynn Morgan slips away as I try to fathom what this round-faced, curly-haired little busybody is trying to tell me.

I confirm that it is indeed four years since my father's death and suddenly recall how much prettier and younger my mother was looking. Who can possibly be responsible? Who is there? I try to think of some middle-aged widower or bachelor somewhere in the neighbourhood, there's certainly no one in our chapel, and where would she meet anyone else?

'Tell me, now, have you met him, yet?' she asks me. 'Being a scholar, I suppose you'd be able to talk to him in his own language.'

Rather prettily, I disclaim all pretentions to scholarship, but decline to offer any other information. She'll get nothing out of me. Even if I knew anything, she'd get nothing out of me.

I think of Gino and Martino, docile as a pair of sheep in the front parlour. My mother did buy them a scarf each for Christmas.

'Well, here we are back in town,' I exclaim in a high artificial voice which I hardly recognise. 'I'm so glad you came to sit by me. I did enjoy our little chat.'

I smile brilliantly in her direction and hurry off the bus.

The depot is almost opposite the Ship and I've never felt so tempted to go in. I can't see that going to a public house is so sinful. Ilona Hughes and Denzil are sure to be there and there'll be people smoking and chatting, perhaps even laughing. People do laugh in Llanfair, though not usually when I'm around.

A tall man looms out of the darkness, comes towards me and takes my elbow. It's Gwynn Morgan. Thank goodness it's dark and he can't see how my cheeks are burning.

'Ilona Hughes said you'd been up to see your mother,' he says, 'so I thought I'd meet the bus and walk home with you.'

'Were you in the Ship?'

'That's right.'

'Oh, please go back there, Gwynn. I don't mind walking home on my own. Honestly.'

Why do I always have to sound so ungracious? Why can't I just say thank you and try to be pleasant? After all, he doesn't know why I'm feeling so hot and embarrassed.

'What's the matter?'

'Nothing. Why do you ask?'

'You seem on edge. I thought we were friends. Aren't we? Can't we be friends?'

'Oh Gwynn, I don't know.'

Great Heavens, now I'm crying. But if I just let the tears roll down my cheeks and into my collar, he might not notice. As long as I don't sniff. Thank goodness for the blackout.

'And now you're crying,' he says. 'Whatever's the matter? Come on, I want to know. Bad news at home? Look, I'm going to walk home with you. What's the harm?'

He's still holding me by the elbow. It's a great comfort.

I give one quick sniff. 'I met this silly woman on the bus. Miriam Lloyd. She comes from Tregroes and goes to our chapel. She told me some rotten tale about my mother.'

'Good Lord! What sort of rotten tale?'

'Oh, you know . . . she hinted she'd got some man-friend.'

There's a moment's silence.

'But what's wrong with that? Why shouldn't she have a man-friend? What could be more natural? Oh Rhian, are you against *everything*?'

'What do you mean?'

'You're a lovely girl, that's what I mean. You're very intelligent and . . . well . . . everything else. But you're not going to make anything of yourself, you're not going to realise half your potential, if you let your whole life be dominated by chapel rules. What's wrong with your mother having a man-friend? What's wrong with you coming with me to a pub?'

'Oh, you don't understand.'

'Then explain it to me. Why shouldn't your mother have a man-friend? Why should she have to be lonely for the rest of her life? She's still young, Rhian.'

'She's forty-seven.'

'That's not old. Five years older than me, and I'm certainly not ready for the scrap heap.'

'But why hasn't she mentioned him to me? She must be ashamed of him. Ashamed of *something*.'

'Not at all. Perhaps she just wants to keep him to herself for a while. Why can't *she* decide when to tell you? Why can't you trust her? You see everything in black and white, Rhian, and life isn't like that. Isn't it better to compromise about certain things? Isn't it better to be fairly good and fairly happy than to be entirely blameless and miserable?'

I pull away from him and blow my nose. My voice is thick with crying; there's no point in further pretence.

'Cheer up, Rhian. Are you any the worse for having had a coffee and a chat with me last Saturday morning?'

His voice is suddenly very gentle and smooth. I think of sin.

'Are you any the worse?' he asks again. 'Are you?'

'Yes, I am. You know perfectly well how I used to feel about you years ago – you must have known. So you should have realised how vulnerable I am. You shouldn't have led me on. Now I think about you all the time. And I'm miserable to have to do without you.'

'Oh Rhian.'

He puts his arm round my shoulders and propels me towards the high wall outside the Infants' school. We lean against it.

'I shouldn't have said that,' I whisper into his overcoat.

'Why not? Don't you think *I'm* miserable, to have to do without you? Yes, I did realise how you used to feel about me and now I feel the same about you. I think about you all the time, I watch out for you all the time at school. I know where you're going to be, I've worked out exactly when you'll be crossing the playground from one block to another so that I can look out and see you. Yes, I'm like an adolescent again. And you're the . . .'

'Go on.'

'You might not find this flattering.'

'I don't want flattery. My heart's racing already.'

'You're the object of my desire, Rhian.'

I let that sink in. It's certainly a very ungodly thought.

'But I'm married to someone else. Of course you are, too, but I expect you've become used to . . .'

'Yes? Used to what?'

'You know. To dividing your life up into fairly happy and

fairly good. So far, I've only been very good and, well, very bored.'

'That sounds as though you mean to change.'

'Does it? I don't know.'

All I know is that I'm very happy at this moment. I think I'll probably remember this moment for ever: the moon rising in white gauze, the tumbled clouds, the bruise-dark hills, the roughness of the wall behind my shoulder, the faint sigh of the sea in the distance. Will he kiss me? Do I want him to? No, I only want this cold peace, this clean truth and innocence we may not have again.

How long do we stand against the wall, quite still? It seems like several minutes. Or hours.

What will happen? Nothing. What can happen?

The town clock striking nine brings us back to some sort of reality. We sigh and set off up the hill; his house is in the same direction as mine, but a further ten minutes' walk out of town. We walk slowly, as though our feet are weighted.

We don't seem to have anything more to say to each other and in no time at all we're at my front door.

'Good night.' My voice sounds strained and despondent. 'Thank you for meeting the bus.'

Isn't he going to say anything in reply? How can I turn and leave him when he's said so much, confessed to feelings I wouldn't have dared dream of? Oh, I must have some final word. *Please*.

'Listen,' he says at last, his voice sounding harsh and as desperate as mine. 'Listen, my wife would like to paint you some time.' He takes a deep breath. 'Yes, she noticed you at the Carol Service. She's anxious to start portrait painting and she thought you had an interesting face. Do you think you could spare the time? To sit for her?'

I struggle to answer. I've no idea what to say, no idea how I feel about the prospect of meeting his wife; pleased or apprehensive – or both. 'I really don't know,' I say at last, trying not to sound as overwhelmed as I feel. 'I'm really not sure whether I've got the time this term.'

'Think about it,' he says.

'I didn't know your wife was an artist.'

32

'She hasn't been painting long. But I think she's going to be good.'

Tears sting my eyes. Oh God. French, and an artist as well. It doesn't seem fair.

'You love her.' It's a flat statement, not a question. My voice seems drained of all emotion.

'Yes. Oh, yes. We've been married almost twenty years. And you love Huw, I suppose.'

'Yes, I suppose so.'

Why does he want me to meet his wife? Is it something to do with being open and honest, not wanting me to go into anything with my eyes shut? Oh, what's it all about? What's going to happen?

'You must call round to meet her. Her name's Celine. You will, won't you? Shall I tell her you'll come?'

His voice is suddenly more relaxed. Something has been resolved, I suppose. He touches my hand. 'You will come?'

Of course I will. Life offers us opportunities and challenges we can't question or resist. Doors open and we go through them.

'Yes, I'll come.'

'Good. What about next Monday after school? Would that suit you? Perhaps you could come every Monday – I mean, till the portrait's finished. Could you? Do you think you could?'

'I suppose so. Shall I come straight from school? Or shall I go home to change first? Shall I wear my new dress? I've been wondering when to wear it.'

'Oh yes, the new dress. She'd be flattered. I told her about it. About my getting a discount for you.'

'Was she amused?'

I realise that we're now talking to each other in an affected, insincere way; better perhaps than talking like half-crazed lovers, as we were earlier.

I let myself into the house where I once, for about thirty days and nights, lived with my husband, Huw. I try to think about him, but I can't. I try to think of him with love, or even with pity or sadness, but I can't. He's out of my mind. I'm already deep in sin.

The fire is out and won't be revived, so I sit in my coat waiting for Ilona Hughes to get back. I boil some water on the gas and make myself a hot drink.

I'm going to his home. I'm going to meet his wife. I feel faint at the prospect. Why should I submit myself to such an ordeal? What if I start to tremble and she notices? She'll make mincemeat out of me. She looks terrifying, so bold and self-assured.

When Ilona gets back, my heart is beating so loudly that I can hardly hear her speak. I usually go to bed as soon as she comes in, but tonight I rush to make her a cup of cocoa. Perhaps she'll mention him. Even to hear his name will be balm.

'Did Gwynn Morgan meet your bus?' she asks me at last.

'Yes. Why did you tell him where I was? Why did you mention me to him? I told you not to.'

'I didn't. Not a word. He asked after you, came right out with it. "Where's our little Rhian tonight?" He's fallen for you, kid. He can't hide it.'

'Oh nonsense. He's only interested in me because his wife wants to do a portrait of me. She's an artist. She noticed me at the Carol Service and she's been desperate to paint me ever since. I'm going to their house after school on Monday. Yes, next Monday. So it'll be your turn to make supper.'

I've seldom managed to get the better of Ilona Hughes, but tonight I have. She stares down into the murky depths of her cocoa in the deepest perplexity.

'How was Denzil?' I ask her, but she shows no sign of having heard me.

After a minute or two, I get up, fill my hot water bottle and lock the front door. 'Good night, Ilona.'

'I don't like the sound of it,' she says at last. 'He's fallen for you, I know that much, I could hear it in his voice. So why is he taking you home to meet his wife?'

'Perhaps it's his way of fighting it.'

'I don't like the sound of it,' she says again.

34

Chapter Four

'You've got an unusual face,' Gwynn Morgan's wife says. 'Very nearly beautiful. Your nose is a bit too wide and your jaw is too square, but your cheek bones are good and your eyes are formidable. Formidable. Most Welsh girls are round-faced and pretty, but you're very nearly beautiful.'

'Sometimes I feel very nearly ugly.'

She studies me again. 'No,' she says. 'I may call the portrait 'A Young Woman Very Nearly Beautiful'. That is, if I get it finished. Perhaps you'll be too bored to come again. I shall probably need at least ten sittings. How do you feel about that?'

I smile uneasily.

She speaks with a faint but still distinctive French accent, enunciating every word clearly with slightly trilling r's. 'Would you like to see some of my work?'

I'm not sure that I would – as usual, I'm not sure of anything – but I follow her along the black-and-white tiled passage into a back room overlooking the kitchen garden.

'My studio,' she says proudly.

If Gwynn had said 'My studio,' the tone would have been ironic; the Welsh, insecure to a man, protect themselves with a large measure of self-mockery; his wife seems enviably self-assured.

She points at a number of watercolours ranged along the wall opposite the door; two are of a garden in summer, one is a woodland scene and there are three or four of meadows with hills in the distance. They all seem carefully planned and neatly executed, like paintings by a

35

retired infants' teacher.

'Don't say they're pretty,' she warns me.

'Oh, I won't.' But any other comment I can think of is either patronising or wildly untrue. Instead of words, I decide on deeply penetrating looks, moving close to the paintings and then backing away, nodding my head and biting my lower lip from time to time. And when, after this base little charade, I turn away, I'm confronted by a large oil-painting of Gwynn, blazing with power and vigour. I can hardly bear to look at it; he looks almost saturnine, the slight cleft in his chin is emphasised, his nostrils flare, his lips curl. The background is tomato red.

'Very 'orrible, yes?' his wife says.

Again I'm lost for words, but luckily Mrs Morgan turns it to face the wall, expecting none.

'I won't be so cruel to you,' she says.

I try to put it out of my mind, but I can't help feeling that she'd wanted me to see it, that it was meant as a warning.

The studio is bare of clutter, almost bare of furniture, a long narrow room with white walls and a big window facing the garden with a row of pine cupboards on the opposite wall. There are two kitchen chairs, one on each side of the bracken-filled fireplace; the room is heated by a small black oil-stove. Mrs Morgan fetches one of the chairs, puts it down by the window, sits on it and motions me to do the same.

'You're very tidy. I expected a jumble of canvasses, pots of paints and turps, brushes and old rags. The Art room in school is in a terrible state; the cleaners aren't allowed inside.'

'You don't teach Art?'

'Heavens, no. I can't draw at all, not even a rabbit. I go up to see the work occasionally, that's all. I teach English and Welsh. I did Honours Welsh.'

'I didn't know that Welsh was a University subject. I thought it was a dying language.'

'People do think that. They've been thinking it for centuries, but somehow it struggles on. My mother is doing what she can to promulgate a Welsh/Italian interest. There's already Welsh in Patagonia, Welsh and Spanish, but no English.' I talk a great deal when I'm nervous.

Mrs Morgan opens her eyes wide and examines me again. I wish she'd start working. So far, she hasn't produced even a sheet of paper or a stub of pencil.

As though reading my thoughts, she says, 'I want to discover a little about you before I start.'

'Of course.'

Great Heavens, what does she mean? What does she want to discover about me?

She studies me and I study her. She's a large woman with a large, very pale face. She looks as though she's never been out in the sun or the wind, let alone the Cardiganshire rain.

'You don't go out much,' I say. 'I've hardly ever seen you in town. You come to Prize Day and the Christmas concert, I know, and I know you go to Sant Ioan's on a Sunday, but I've never seen you shopping or walking about in Llanfair.'

'There is no one to know in Llanfair,' she says.

She's quite right, of course. Of people to know, we only have Mrs Harcourt-Williams and Lady Griffin and they're too busy nowadays with all their winning-the-war committees to hold garden-parties for the natives as they used to.

I search my brains for some social titbits. 'Mrs Wynne-Jones, the doctor's wife, told my mother-in-law a few weeks ago that she and her friends meet for coffee in the Dolphin every Friday morning. Do you know Mrs Wynne-Jones?'

'The Dolphin Hotel,' she says, as though with a sour taste in her mouth.

'I hope you're not going to be unkind about the Dolphin. It's a lovely place, I used to work there when I was a student.'

'What work did you do?'

'I was a chambermaid. The bedrooms are gorgeous, all huge mirrors and crystal chandeliers. Of course, it may be different now. I've never been there since.'

'I suppose you prefer to go to the Ship in the evenings?'

'I don't go anywhere in the evenings. Well, I go to chapel on Sunday, home to see my mother on Wednesday and sometimes to a school drama meeting on a Friday. That's about all. Other nights I stay in and save money. I don't like going to the pictures on my own.'

'You miss your 'usband? You're a very faithful wife, yes?'

'Of course.'

'Where is he now?'

'Abroad somewhere. He's been abroad for almost three years.'

She sighs and closes her eyes. 'My fiancé was killed in the last war. Jean-Pierre Lamarque. He was a violinist before he became a soldier.'

Her voice has become very sad and gentle. When she opens her eyes I see that they're not grey as I'd thought, but the washed-out green of old bottles.

'I'm sorry.'

'I wanted to become a nun, but I was only seventeen and my parents wouldn't agree to it.'

'How long was it before you met . . . Mr Morgan?'

She makes an effort to remember. 'I don't know. Oh, it was several years later. When I was twenty I came to England as a governess. I worked in Whiteways House in Surrey, a family related to the Devonshires. They were very good to me.'

The people at the Dolphin Hotel were good to me, too, but I don't bother to mention it. They weren't related to anyone, as far as I know.

'I was treated as one of the family,' she says.

In my experience, that isn't altogether a good thing. Treated as family in this part of the world means you work harder than hired help on no pay.

'They took me to balls at the big 'ouses and to Ascot and Henley.'

'And where did you meet Mr Morgan?'

She sighs deeply, not seeming eager to leave the delights of her past life. 'That was when I was back in France on my annual holiday. It was in Rouen – he was lost and I took pity on him. I think I was twenty-three or four then. We got married almost at once, though he was only a student and very poor.'

How soft and white she is. I can imagine her at twenty-three or four, very elegantly dressed, pale and plump as a white dove. How besotted the poor, simple art student must have been with her. Jealousy claws at my stomach, almost making me groan. How beautiful Gwynn must have been at twenty, his body slim and boyish, his curly hair black, his gaze straight and clear. Reader, she married him.

'Where is he this evening?' I ask, as soon as I can talk fairly normally.

'Oh, somewhere. Perhaps with his friend Mr Browne at the little dress shop. I never know where he is.'

He'd waited for me outside school to make sure I'd remembered my promise. *'She's expecting you. Don't be shy. I'll see you before you leave.'*

'I'm slow making a start,' his wife says. 'I suppose I should make a few sketches. Next time you come, I'll have the easel set up ready to begin. I think I'd like you with your back to the window, the hills as a background.'

'I will lift up mine eyes unto the hills,' I say, for no reason except that I often quote from the psalms. Our Sunday school teacher used to give us threepence for learning a whole psalm so I learnt them all. That's how I got my first bike.

'No, you have your back to the hills,' she says.

Well really! Of course, the Bible doesn't count for Catholics – only statues and incense and things like that. I think I'll stick to chapel; I love words even though I don't always trust them.

'How did you get your first bike?' I ask her.

'You can imagine me on a bicycle?' she asks, as she pulls out paper and charcoal from one of the cupboards.

No, not really. Not on a bicycle. I can imagine her being driven along Surrey lanes in a long black car. I can imagine her leaning back against a pile of cushions in a boat at Henley, gazing up at a fair-haired young man in shirt-sleeves and boater, who's keen on her, of course, but doesn't intend it to become serious, because though she's treated almost as one of the family, she's only a governess, and a Frog at that.

'Did you have many admirers in Surrey?'

'You've had little instruction in the rules of conversation,' she says.

It's absolutely true. Six years in the County School, four years at University as well as twenty years of Sunday school, and never a hint on the rules of conversation.

She relents. 'It was a very good time,' she says, but without answering my question.

39

'I can't imagine you without admirers,' I say.

'Even now? In this place?'

'Why not?'

'People don't have admirers in this part of the world,' she says firmly.

I'm not too sure about that. My stomach tightens as I think of my next visit home and my determination to ask my mother about her admirer. 'Miriam Lloyd tells me that you're courting,' I'll say in a firm, friendly voice. 'Is it true? Why haven't I been told?'

Who can it be though? I've refused to consider Gino and Martino. If my mother's having feelings, it's not going to be for small, mute men almost twenty years younger than herself.

'What's the matter? You're frowning. I don't want you to frown. It's not becoming.'

'Sorry. I'm thinking about my mother.'

'Your mother ... Yes, Gwynn says you don't approve of her having a friend. Why is that? You know, he may be a very rich farmer who'll take good care of her.'

'We don't have rich farmers in this part of the world. No, I'm worried because she hasn't mentioned him to me. And the woman who thought it necessary to tell me about him, implied that he was a foreigner – which I suppose means one of the Italian prisoners.'

'An American, perhaps? An American officer?'

'No. She mentioned a foreign language. I think he'd have to be an Italian.'

She's drawing rapidly now. A minute or two and I'm already fidgety, my shoulder feeling numb. Why am I doing this?

'Are there any penalties for fraternising with an Italian prisoner of war?' she asks me.

Great Heavens, I hadn't even considered penalties. I'd only been thinking of the difficulties, the heartbreak. 'What sort of penalties?' I ask her, my voice suddenly cold.

'In the last war, women who collaborated with the Germans were ... oh, but that was France. I'm sure you needn't worry about your mother. After all, she's not a silly schoolgirl, is she?'

She finishes the drawing, studies it for a few moments, then puts it in the cupboard without letting me see it. 'And now we'll go back to the drawing room and I'll make you a cup of tea,' she says. 'I'm sure you needn't worry about your mother.'

I'm quite surprised to find that it's already five o'clock.

Gwynn is in the drawing room looking very pleased with himself. He's laid the little round table by the window with a white cloth and pretty cups and saucers. 'I'll get the teapot,' he says.

When he returns, he's carrying a tray with silver teapot and water jug, and a plate with three large raspberry buns.

'Oh those cakes,' his wife says. 'Hard and dry and not worth eating.'

I can't even try to agree with her. 'I love raspberry buns. How did you get them? They've never usually got them in the afternoon.'

'That's my secret. Come on, help yourself. Take the biggest.'

'She can have mine as well. They're very nasty. Full of grease. And it's no great secret how he got them either. That Carys Edwards, manageress of the Teifiside Bakery, was one of his childhood sweethearts.'

Carys Edwards is a power-mad despot who marshals the bakery queues like a sergeant-major. She's got thinning sandy hair and warts on her face.

Gwynn winks at me and pours out the tea. It's dark and strong.

I have another very happy moment.

'I don't understand it,' Ilona Hughes says when I get home. 'I've heard of all sorts of strange goings-on, but this beats all.'

'What sort of goings-on?' I ask her, trying to change the subject. Me, I never hear of any. Llanfair is probably the most boring town in West Wales. Ilona Hughes comes from Brynteg in North Wales, where, according to her, life sizzles.

'There was an old couple in Brynteg, Charlie and Lil Hopkins. Nothing very special, he worked in the quarry, she scrubbed the front step, took in washing, chapel on Sunday; quite respectable. Only one trouble in their life, they had no family. Never mind, everybody said, you have more time for each other. It was true. I can see them now going for long walks on fine summer evenings, he with his check cap and his yellow corduroys, she tall and thin with grey hair pulled back into a little bun, always arm in arm, always in accord. Well, Lil dies, she's about fifty-something by this time, and only in the funeral we find out she was a man called John Arfon Rees.'

'Must have caused a bit of talk,' I say carefully.

'Not in Brynteg. Hardly a ripple.'

I can't help smiling, though, of course, I never believe a word she says.

She's remembered to make supper, fair play. It's potato and swede mashed with the top of the milk with grated cheese on top, and brussel sprouts. She eats twice as much as I do and then complains she's still hungry.

Denzil won't be in town again until Friday evening. He's stationed in Tonfaen and it's too far to get in to Llanfair except when they lay on buses on Friday and Saturday.

I can't get on with my marking while she's pacing about.

'Are you going to wait for Denzil if he's sent abroad?' I ask her.

She gives me a withering glance. 'Wait for *Denzil*? Whatever for? You can't think I'd consider marrying *Denzil*? Oh, he's bright enough, he's good for a laugh, but before the war he worked on a market stall. No, I'm going to marry money, kid. It's money that excites me. Oh, you'll be all right, Huw will have his father's business. I can see you now with a fur coat and matching toque and a Silver Cross pram.'

'And spending my evenings doing the accounts and sending out bills.'

'Saving up for a car and a holiday in Bournemouth. Buying Daniel Neal clothes for the children. Listening to their piano practice after school.'

'And then, suddenly, I'll be old, and I'll never have done anything to make it all worthwhile. "How then should sound upon Life's darkening slope, The wind of Death's imperishable wing?"'

'Don't start on Keats.'

'Rosetti. Dante Gabriel Rosetti.'

'You're in love, aren't you? With Gwynn Morgan. Am I right?'

Hearing his name makes my heart jump, but I'm definitely not going to confide in Ilona Hughes. She'll tease me cruelly and use it against me on every possible occasion.

'Aren't you? Just a bit? Come on, tell Auntie 'Lona.'

'He's married. I don't want to think about him.'

'A little bit? Just this much?' She holds up the tip of her little finger.

I burst out crying. 'Oh, Ilona, what shall I do?'

Ilona Hughes doesn't rush in with any trite solutions, I'll say that for her. She doesn't even smile. She sits quiet for a long time studying her hands, first the backs and then the palms, almost as though she's seeing them for the first time.

'Well, as far as I can see, there are three ways open to you,' she says at last. 'Only first of all, close your mouth. You look really stupid with your cheeks all blotchy and your jaw hanging open.'

I wipe my eyes and try to look intelligent.

'First, you do nothing. You face up to the fact that you find him attractive and do nothing except give him a fond look now and again, and even that could be dangerous. He's married – oh, he finds his wife a trial, I'm sure of that, but he'll never leave her, I'm sure of that, too. She plays on the fact that she's a foreigner in a strange, a *very* strange country. She doesn't choose to make friends, and with no friends or family, her dependence on Gwynn is that much greater. I suppose it's possible that he asked you home so you could work all that out for yourself.'

'She did seem to want to paint me.'

'Perhaps he managed to plant that idea into her head. You're quite pretty, I suppose, but you're not that special. You're certainly not the only pretty woman around here.'

'Who else is there?' I ask her.

She ignores me. 'Plenty of people, most people, perhaps, have a bit of a hopeless passion for someone at some time or another, but after a while it dies a natural death, I suppose, and they remember it, when they remember it at all, with a sort of wry smile.'

43

'How long do you think that takes? No, I'm not trying to be funny, I'd really like to know. How long does it take? From hopeless passion to wry smile?'

'The second way is to have a very careful affair. This is the way I'd choose. I could probably manage it, so could Gwynn perhaps, but I'm not sure you could. By a careful affair I mean that you'd only meet once a week or even once a fortnight, and of course, where no-one is likely to see you. It could be in this house. I've heard of people having careful affairs without even breaking their marriage vows. You can have a lot of erotic pleasure having a meal or a cup of tea together, thigh by thigh. You wouldn't, of course, ever turn up at his house unexpectedly or send him letters, or waylay him on the way to school. You'd always be perfectly controlled.'

'I can imagine what the third way is. An uncontrolled affair. The world well-lost.'

Ilona sighs. 'Yes, it sounds very romantic. The reality is likely to be that his wife finds out and insists on going to live somewhere as far from Llanfair as possible. He'd go with her, his tail between his legs, and you and Huw would be left here hating each other. Those are your alternatives as far as I can see. Over to you, kid.'

'I don't think I'd be able to manage the first way or the third – and certainly not the second. Oh dear. Anyway, I haven't got to decide tonight, have I? It's wonderful, I suppose, to have a decision to make. I mean, to know that he cares for me. Last week, I had no idea. Last week, I had nothing.

'Only Huw,' Ilona says, rather spitefully.

'Poor Huw.'

'Oh shut up. Don't ever be sorry for a man. They always end up having the best of it.'

At this moment, it strikes me that Ilona is far from being the light-hearted, free-and-easy flirt I've always taken her for. Something about the way she's looking at me makes it clear that she knows precisely what I'm facing.

'Who are you running away from?' I ask her. 'Why did you leave Brynteg and move to Llanfair?'

For a moment, I think she's going to confide in me, but her mood changes abruptly.

44

'Why, indeed. I think perhaps the good Lord sent me here to try and knock some sense into you.'

'Oh, Ilona, what am I going to do?'

'Don't start that moaning again. One way or another you'll make a mess of your life, just like everyone else. You'll do nothing and regret it or you'll do everything and regret it. Take your pick. And do you know what I'm going to do now? I'm going out for some fish and chips. I'm still starving.'

'I don't think I'm going to finish this marking. Not tonight.'

'Come with me, then. We can have cod and chips, a plateful of bread and butter and a pot of tea for one and six.'

Chapter Five

My mother is at the top of Pen Hewl Fach meeting me off the bus. She's got her Sunday coat on.

'I love these lighter evenings,' she says, 'with the snow almost gone. I couldn't stop in the house. I'm always restless in February, waiting and waiting.'

We pause at a five-barred gate to look down the valley at the sun setting in a blaze of pink. 'What colour is heliotrope?' she asks me. 'It's very fashionable this year, according to the *Western Mail*.'

'I think it's a sort of puce.'

'Is it really? Puce? Then I won't mind a bit not having a new costume of it.'

'You could buy a heliotrope blouse to wear with your grey costume.'

'I'd rather a nice rose-pink like that sunset, but I suppose I should stick to white. That does for everything, doesn't it; christenings, weddings and funerals. Yes, I may buy a new white blouse if I do all right with the lambs.'

Her voice softens. 'I used to meet your father here,' she says, 'when we were courting.' I squeeze her arm. The word courting gives me the cue I've been hoping for and I take a deep breath. 'Mam. I met that silly woman, Miriam Lloyd, on the bus last week.'

'Yes, she told me she'd seen you,' she says, very calmly. 'She said someone was meeting you off the bus as well, a tall pleasant-looking man she said he was.'

'It was Mr Morgan, Art.'

'Yes, I thought it might be.'

'He walked home with me, that's all. There's nothing wrong with that, is there?'

'I don't know,' she says. 'I don't know what I'm supposed to think.'

'And I don't know what I'm supposed to think about your – *friend*. That foreign gentleman Miriam Lloyd told me about. What am I supposed to think about him? Is it Gino or Martino she's seen you walking out with?'

Even in the fading light, I can see her smiling. 'I've meant to tell you for weeks,' she says, 'but I didn't want to worry you.'

'Is it anything serious, then?' I've broken out in a sweat.

'How can it be anything serious, girl, with him an Italian prisoner of war?'

My knees are giving way; I can't go on walking. 'Please, tell me about him. It's not fair to keep me in the dark. I need to know.'

'Don't get excited, girl, I'll tell you everything. His name is Fredo. Well, Alfredo really, but they call him Fredo. He's in charge of the others, a sort of foreman, I suppose. Not an officer, mind, they're in another camp, but he's older and he was a farmer himself, so he shows the others what to do. He works here for a few days with Gino and Martino, then works at another farm with another pair. He's a very good worker, too, the sort who goes at it without any huffing and puffing. Well, he can sometimes get away after supper when they're all supposed to be shut up in the camp. I don't know how he manages it, but I suppose it's something he could be punished for. He walks three miles to get here, so of course, I give him a bit of a meal, and we talk what little we can, me with hardly a word of Italian and him with next to no English. And after that he walks back.'

Why can't I think of anything to say? Because I'm terrified, that's why. My mother is so innocent and unworldly that she doesn't realise how violently her neighbours and friends might react. Even the mildest chapel people might feel outraged by her friendship with one of the 'enemy'. Italians aren't hated as the Germans are, but they're certainly not loved. What if she was ostracised from the community? Farmers depend on one another for help at the harvest and

48

in hard weather. What if she's snowed up? What if she falls ill and can't get out to feed the animals and milk the cows? And the man himself, what does she really know of him? If he was even a moderately decent man, would he be prepared to let her risk her good name? Perhaps he's a really sick man, wanting revenge, or money to escape.

'If you stayed tonight, you could meet him,' she says. 'That is, if he manages to get out. You could have a lift back in the post van tomorrow. You'd probably be a bit late for school, but you could say you'd missed the bus, which would be true enough, in a sense.'

'Is he married?'

'That doesn't come into it, girl. It's friendship I'm offering him, not a future. Rhian, I'm nearly fifty.'

'You're forty-seven and still very beautiful.'

'Very beautiful. Hark at her. Very beautiful, with my cheeks full of thread veins and my hair full of grey. If I was a hen, girl, I wouldn't be worth the boiling ... Well, he *was* married, but I think his wife is dead. At least, he's shown me a photograph of a big tomb with an angel on the top. He's a Roman Catholic, of course, but as you always say, Rhian, no religion has a monopoly of God. There, I'm getting quite tolerant in my old age, aren't I?'

'I don't know what to say. I'm frightened, I really am.'

'*Frightened*? Good gracious me, what is there to be frightened of? It's the war, isn't it, that's to blame for everything? If it wasn't for the war, he'd be home in all that lovely sunshine growing olives and those big tomatoes. And Huw would be home with you, and you'd have a baby by this time and another on the way, and not a minute to give a second thought to Mr Morgan, Art, or anyone else.'

We walk on in silence. I've never heard her talking so fluently.

'How did old Big Mouth get to know about Alfredo?'

'Oh, that was a real misfortune, that was. She'd called about a concert they're having in Saron, wanting to know if I'd play the piano, if you please. As though I'd ever play in public. Well, I gave her a donation, they're trying to raise twenty pounds for the Forces Comforts Fund, but do you think I could get her to go? She sat so long in your father's chair, I thought she'd taken root, and at last I said, "Well, Mrs Lloyd, I'll walk a step with you since it's getting so late." And as we were putting our coats on, Fredo arrived and let himself in, and that was that.'

'She'll tell everybody.'

'She promised not to tell a soul ... Oh yes, she'll tell everybody, no doubt, but will anyone take much notice? I shouldn't think so. I don't think anyone is going to take me for a dangerous woman, somehow. No, they'll only think I'm a bit foolish and leave it at that.'

'I don't know. People are stupid enough for anything these days. There could be a lot of bad feeling towards anyone who doesn't conform.'

'My family has never conformed, girl. My grandfather burnt his ricks rather than pay tithes to the English church. Why should I take the English side, now? The enemies of the English people are not my enemies. Why should I pretend they are?'

'I won't have an easy moment after this. And what would happen to him if they discovered he was breaking out of camp?'

'Come, come, Rhian, take a hold of yourself. What about Huw? Isn't he in far greater danger? Think of all the men, of all nationalities, who know they may be killed tomorrow or the next day or the day after that. The risk Fredo is taking is negligible, isn't it? But I suppose you're worried because you think he may be some sort of ogre. That's why I want you to meet him. Once you've met him, you'll understand ... you know what I mean. Come on now, I've got a nice piece of sparerib in the oven and some parsnips and roast potatoes. In a way, it's a new lease of life for me.'

When we get into the house, I can see that it is. Her eyes, always her best feature, are soft and glowing. With love, I suppose.

Alfredo arrives at about nine o'clock. He's small and wiry, his skin dark and shiny as acorns, his dark hair turning grey: an attractive man, lively as a terrier.

My mother is blushing as she introduces us.

He says I am *bellissima*. Then he says, I think, that he knew I would be. And my mother blushes again.

I've been upstairs to my old bedroom and found an English/Italian dictionary which we're soon passing back and fore to one another. Alfredo seems delighted by this new and more exact way of communication.

I ask him whether he has children. He has three sons, he says, and my mama, three daughters. He can hardly believe it when I tell him there's only me; he felt sure my mother had held up three fingers when he'd questioned her. I try to tell him that one daughter is worth three sons but he fails to understand me.

'Don't try to be clever, Rhian,' my mother says sharply. 'Why must you always try to be clever? Talk slowly, and don't put on that English accent either.'

Chastened – and indeed subdued – I have to sit and listen to her giving him a list of my shortcomings; in particular, pride, waywardness and stubbornness.

Then he, pointing to the occasional word in the dictionary, says I must not have care, because he knows I am gentle, true and radiant, as my mama has told him already much times. Then, suddenly, he understands my earlier weak attempt at a joke and laughs rather a lot.

Then he takes out the snapshot of the large tomb with angel, and yes, it is the grave of his beloved wife, who was as beautiful and virtuous as my mama, though not alike in outward, except regarding gait and industry.

After that, I leave the talking to him and my mother. Leaning back in my chair, I let their simple, halting sentences wash over me and even without following the words, recognise their grave commitment, and recognise also that there is nothing I can say or do which could cancel it.

There is absolutely nothing I can do. The tension slips away from my shoulders as I accept this fact. My mother has always, quietly and steadfastly, gone about doing exactly what she's decided on, how could I have considered myself capable of influencing her in any way?

'Your girl is happy, yes?' Alfredo says, noticing, I suppose, my change of mood. I rearrange my face, careful not to agree too readily. After all, I'm not happy, only a little less unhappy.

All the same, I can't help liking him. He seems so lively,

51

trying so hard to communicate and understand. And now that he and I are both silent, I'm aware of something else too; a quiet dogged strength, very like my mother's, very like my father's; perhaps the strength of all small farmers struggling against nature, but taking a certain pleasure both in the struggle and the occasional victory.

'My father was a poet . . . *una poeta*.' The word comes to me from my one term of Italian.

'Ah, yes,' he says. 'Is good, poetry and music is good for peoples.'

'And religion,' my mother adds, rather sternly. 'Don't forget religion, whatever you do.' She turns to me. 'By the way, Rhian, Fredo is very worried because I haven't got a picture of the Virgin Mary on the mantlepiece and I don't want him to think I'm a heathen, do I?'

'I'll get one for you. I'll bring it with me next time I come.'

'It's only for his sake, of course.'

'Of course.'

My mother cooks him liver and bacon and fried potatoes which he eats very quickly and delicately. And then he smiles a lot at both of us, shakes our hands and leaves.

'He never stays later than half past ten,' my mother says. 'He knows I need my sleep, and so, of course, does he. He won't be back at that camp until well gone eleven as it is, and he's got to be up at six.'

Chapter Six

The post van is early and gets me to school in time. In spite of this piece of luck, I feel worried and rushed all the morning; with so much on my mind, I slept badly last night and for the first time my marking hasn't been done.

Angela Pugh, 5B, whose aunt lives in Tregroes, asks after my mother. I'm very short with her. 'She's quite well, thank you. Why do you ask?'

She gives me a wounded look. 'I know you go home on a Wednesday evening,' she says, 'that's all.'

I search her face and decide that she's innocent. 'I'm sorry. I've got a headache this morning.'

She's prepared to forgive me. 'Shall I get you an aspirin from Mrs Lewis?'

'It's all right thank you, Angela. I'll struggle on.'

In my Welsh lesson with 2A, we're reading a story set in the last war. An elderly Welsh couple hear that their only son is being sent abroad on active service. '*Lle mae'r hen abroad 'na*?' the frightened wife asks her husband. 'Where is that old abroad?'

'Somewhere ... somewhere beyond Wrexham,' he answers.

This morning the story constricts my throat and brings tears to my eyes. I blow my nose, but the girls are nudging one another.

'It isn't right is it, Miss?' Arthur Williams asks. 'Sending our boys to fight for the English?'

I'm determined that this lesson is not going to turn into

another political debate. Arthur Williams's father is in prison for his pacifism; the majority of the class think he's wicked or mad. 'He's helping Hitler, isn't he, Miss?' 'It's cowardice isn't it, Miss?' This morning I'm not capable of maintaining fair play.

'War is a great tragedy,' I say sternly, 'and we'll say no more about it. Go on reading, Carys.'

I'm more than ready for the dinner break and the first to reach the staff room. Gwynn Morgan, who never usually comes near, rushes in after me, closing the door behind him.

'Where were you last night?' he asks, his voice unrecognisably harsh. 'I waited for your bus. I was worried out of my mind when you weren't on it. Where were you?'

'I stayed with my mother last night. I didn't arrange to meet you. What's the matter with you?'

He comes right up to me and grips me hard by the shoulders. 'You *knew* I'd be meeting you. You knew I'd be waiting. Don't you care a bit about me?'

I shake him off. 'Leave me alone, somebody will see us. You didn't ask to see me. I don't owe you any apology.'

'Rhian.' Suddenly he looks old and dejected.

'I'm sorry. I didn't realise you'd be meeting me. I had so much to think about.'

'We must talk, Rhian.'

'I know. But not here, someone will come.'

'Come to my room later. I'll send everyone out.'

'No. I'm worried about being in your room. Come to see me tonight, at eight o'clock tonight.'

He looks surprised. 'All right,' he says. 'Yes, that will be better. Eight o'clock.'

He leaves and I find myself trembling again.

Mary Powell, Maths, comes in to find me staring out of the window, trying to compose myself. I turn towards her, making an effort to smile.

'Rhian, what's the matter? Your face is a terrible colour. Have you had bad news?'

'No, I'm all right. It's only, you know, the time of the month, that's all.'

'Thank goodness for that. I thought it was . . . Have you heard from Huw?'

'Not for three weeks.'

'And that doesn't help. It's hard, isn't it? It's not fair that we have to suffer like this. I haven't heard from Alun, either, not this week or last. He had a few days in hospital last month, he had something called prickly heat. It sounds awfully painful, doesn't it? He burns terribly in the sun, even in Llandudno, he's so fair-skinned, you see. He should never have been sent to Burma.' She turns her engagement ring round and round as she talks. 'I wonder if he'll come back safe,' she says. 'I'm afraid to listen to the news these days. Those Japanese are worse than the Germans. And there are more of them, too.'

We take out our sandwiches and make a pot of tea. Most of the staff go home or have school dinners, so we're on our own.

'Do you ever think, Rhian, about that telegram coming? We regret to inform you . . .'

'I don't let myself think of it,' I reply, rather harshly.

'Don't you really? Oh, you are brave. I think about it all the time, seem to think of nothing else.'

'For goodness' sake, Mary, don't be so morbid. You're not helping Alun by spending your time rehearsing his death. Write to him as often as you can and try to keep cheerful, that's the only way you can help him.'

She doesn't seem to hear me, but carries on in a high, wavering voice, like someone in a fever. 'You hear about women who don't stay faithful to their men when they're overseas. How can they bear the guilt when that telegram comes? Don't you think it would drive them mad?'

'Mary, if you're not careful, you'll be the one who'll go mad and Alun will come back and find you in Brynglas Asylum.'

'Oh, that's cruel.'

'I was only joking, girl. Look, we'd all go mad if we spent our time dwelling on all the terrible things that could happen. Everyone has got somebody they're worried about; son, father, husband or friend. You're not the only one.'

'I know. Why can't I be reasonable and calm like you? I've lost my faith, that's the trouble, I think. I can't even pray any more. Religion has always been such a big part of my life and now it means nothing.'

'You should go to see Mr Roberts after school. He's so understanding about doubt and weakness. He'd really help you.'

'Do you mean, Mr Roberts, Tabernacle?'

'Yes.'

'Oh, I couldn't, Rhian. You see, he's Congregational and I'm Baptist.'

'He won't mind. You remember how Christ was always ready to associate with sinners and publicans? Well, Mr Roberts is like that even with Baptists.'

She manages to smile – and Mary Powell doesn't often smile. She looks very like the young woman in the *Radio Times* advertisement, the one so badly in need of Parkers' little pink liver pills. Perhaps I should get her some.

'I must go back to my room now,' she says. 'I've got some Form Three boys coming in to do their corrections.' Her voice becomes shrill. 'And if they don't finish them this dinnertime, I'll keep them in tonight until they do. There are some evil boys in 3C.'

Mary Powell can't keep any sort of discipline, poor thing. She should never have become a teacher. The sooner Alun comes back and takes her away, the better for all of us.

When I tell Ilona Hughes about Gwynn Morgan coming to the house, she says she's off to the pictures, which is very decent of her. It's a double feature programme; Esther Williams swimming in one and Dick Haymes singing in the other; she'll be bored out of her mind. I give her some of my sweet coupons.

She goes at ten past seven and then I don't know what to do with myself. I can't imagine why I suggested he should come to this house. What could I have been thinking of? What if my mother-in-law decides to call on me? She doesn't come often, admittedly, but what if she happens to be at a loose end and takes it into her head to come up to criticise my new dress? What if she can't resist calling to ask if I've heard from Huw? We've got an arrangement that if I get a letter before school, I call to tell my next door neighbour, Sam Jones, a retired railwayman, who'll immediately go down to let her know, but I don't think she trusts me to remember. Every time she happens to see me in town she asks whether I've had any news. You can't blame her, I suppose; he's her only son, the only fruit of her womb. And besides, she remembers him when he was sitting up in his pram, clapping his hands and gurgling. I try to think about him, far from home, trusting me completely. It's shocking, but I can visualise Ilona's Denzil more clearly. Huw seems like someone I used to know in a previous life.

I wash up, tidy the living room, make up the fire and brush the hearth, all the time trying not to think of the sin I committed: marrying without love. It's Gwynn I love – and that's another sin. All day, while pretending to be anxious about my mother, what I've really been suffering is an anguish of love. And now my heart is aching again, my breath laboured.

Can I live through the next half-hour until he comes? What else can I do to use up the time? I can't settle to read the paper or write a letter. I've brushed my hair, put on some lipstick and rubbed it off, changed my shoes, washed my hands for the third or fourth time, gone upstairs again to look out at the road he'll walk along, counted to five hundred and recited the long psalm.

And then, just as I'm telling myself that if he doesn't come in the next four and a half minutes, he's going to be late, there's a knock at the door. And as I'm warning myself not to rush, to keep some semblance of calm, I'm there opening it.

When I see him, I know at once that things are not going to be easy. Suddenly I feel cold and quiet.

'I shouldn't have come,' he's saying, as he comes in.

'I shouldn't have suggested it. It's my fault.'

'No, it's mine. I shouldn't have behaved so wildly. I'm older than you, years older, and should know how to keep a grip on myself. I'm sorry to have embarrassed you.'

When he sits down, it's on the very edge of the chair.

'I didn't know you intended to meet the bus. You didn't mention it.'

'I was afraid you'd tell me not to.'

'I suppose I would have. But, of course, I would have wanted you to come. Oh Gwynn, I'm torn in two. All the same, we mustn't meet like this – I know that much.'

'You're too young. You've got too much to lose. Good God, I was your teacher – and Huw's too, for that matter. How can I let you risk breaking up your marriage?'

'Why would it be a risk to my marriage, but not to yours?' It's not that I want to argue with him, but I need to understand his reasoning, because I know I'll be going over his words again and again when he's gone.

'My marriage . . . Oh, my marriage is a very settled thing, Rhian. Yours is new and full of hope.'

'Why did you ask me to your house? Was it so that I should see for myself how lonely and vulnerable your wife is?'

He looks hard at me for a moment or two. 'Not really,' he says at last. 'Nothing as complicated. When I asked you to let me paint you, you said no. I thought – rightly, as it turned out – that you might come to sit for her. I need to see you occasionally, need to talk to you, it's as simple as that. Was it difficult for you? Did you dislike it?'

'No, it was interesting. And of course, I enjoyed having tea with you afterwards. We'll have that time, at least, won't we? For the next few weeks?'

'It's not what I want, Rhian, but it's as much as I can have.' He looks into my eyes again. 'Come on, ask me what I *do* want. Won't you?'

I shake my head. 'How can I?'

I can't look at him. I can't ask him what he wants, because hearing it would bring tears to my eyes, and where would that lead us? If he makes a move, takes me in his arms, it must be his decision not mine and he mustn't regret it afterwards. I can't look at him because I'm aware – angrily aware – that I'm not as much in control as he is.

He's completely in control again. 'You asked me whether my wife was a good artist,' he says now, 'and you may decide that I misled you. I'm afraid she's only a beginner. I hope you won't mind.'

I can hardly bear to think of his wife, but I have to. 'I thought the portrait she did of you was very impressive.'

'She hasn't done a portrait of me, Rhian. That's a self-portrait. How could you have thought it was hers?'

'It was with her other paintings. I took it for granted, I suppose.'

58

'You should be able to recognise my work by this time.'

'I'm sorry.'

'No, I'm being arrogant as usual. Why can't I accept that I'm not an artist, only a teacher in a small school in a Welsh backwater.'

'You've had your work exhibited. You've won prizes.'

'Rhian, don't patronise me.'

'You should be proud of your work.'

'I'm a conceited ass and if I had any sense I'd go before you throw me out.'

'I won't throw you out.' The simple words sound like a declaration of love. I feel as though I'm blushing; my cheeks are warm and my lips feel soft and swollen.

'Would you like a cup of tea?' I ask, in what I hope is a brisk no-nonsense voice.

'I would, please,' he says, very quietly.

When I go out to the kitchen to put the kettle on, he follows me.

'Pretty house,' he says, 'much as I'd expected. I love these small, artisan cottages.'

'Then why do you live in that great posh house?'

'God knows.'

'I was only joking. It's a beautiful house.'

'I'd like to live here with you.'

'Oh, Gwynn, don't.'

We're both stunned by this second lapse.

He takes the cup of tea from me and we sit one on each side of the table in the kitchen. We don't say a word for a long time.

'I didn't intend to marry her,' he says at last. 'I honestly didn't. I had no money, no prospects; I certainly didn't mean to be a teacher in those days. She invited me to a Sunday meal at her home and because I accepted, her parents took it for granted that we were engaged and immediately started planning the wedding. They lived in a small town, about seven miles outside Rouen. I expected them to be worldly and sophisticated, I thought all French people were worldly and sophisticated, but they were more narrow-minded and provincial than the people round here, all lace curtains and genteel poverty and dressing up in their best clothes to walk to the nearest couple of shops. And every evening we endured excruciatingly boring visits from grandmothers and aunts and great aunts and cousins bringing very ugly wedding presents. It was a horrendous time.'

'You must have been very much in love.'

'I suppose I was. Oh, of course I was. But I'd never, for a moment considered marriage. My God, I was only twenty-one, a diffident Welsh art student, very proud of having won the attention of this elegant French woman of twenty-five, but intending only a relationship for my six-months' stay in France. Not for ever.'

'I can't imagine that you struggled very hard to get out of it.'

He sighs. 'No, I don't suppose I did. She was very *gentille* and, yes, quite a lot more, too. She'd been engaged to a young lad from the next village while she was still at school and he was killed in the war and her family was resigned to the fact that she'd be on the shelf for the rest of her life. I think they felt ashamed of her – she became a governess and they were looked down on, you know, and treated very badly.'

'She told me that the people she was with were very good to her.'

'I don't think so. You tend to remember the good times and forget the humiliations.'

'So you got married in France?'

'Yes. In September 1924.'

'I was only five, then.'

'Yes. Just starting school, I suppose. Big dark eyes and little fat bottom.'

'I wish I could have seen you when you were twenty-one.'

We sit for another half-hour, I think, hardly speaking. When he says he should go, I jump up to open the door for him.

'Good-night.'

'Good-night, Rhian.'

I would have gone with him to the edge of the world.

Chapter Seven

Poor Mary Powell is in trouble. She banged some boy's head against the classroom wall – one of those boys in 3C she was moaning about last week – and his mother comes up to school to complain.

She declines an invitation to the Headmaster's office, preferring to confront him in the corridor, where, the time being exactly ten to nine, she has the largest possible audience of pupils and staff. Cynrig Williams, the Head, has to spend a considerable time saying how sorry he is, explaining about the fiancé fighting in Burma, and how she, Miss Powell, is yet another casualty of war. Complete strangers might think he was quite a compassionate man.

The boy's mother is a thin, acid woman with royal blue turban, long grey coat and a magnificent voice which she hoists up and down like a banner. 'Miss Powell's fiancé is nothing to me, Mr Williams, wherever he is and whatever he may be doing for his country. But my boy has ringing in the ears, and if it leads to something serious I'll sue Miss Powell and you and your school with every means at my disposal. I'm taking him to Dr Oliver at ten o'clock this morning. You shall hear from me again, Mr Williams.'

'Strictly forbidden, Miss Powell,' the Head says in the quiet of the staff room after she's been persuaded to leave. 'Physical violence by any member of staff is strictly forbidden. You should have sent the boy to me, Miss Powell. I'm allowed to administer the cane quite freely as long as it's entered in the corporal punishment book – the cane, as you all know, is not physical violence but permissible chastisement. And now I want everybody in Assembly as soon as possible, please. The children are already agitated and excited.'

'I can't go, Rhian,' Mary says as soon as he's left. 'Everyone will be looking at me. I'll faint, I know I will. Oh, I'm so ashamed. How could I have done it? Oh, and I've done it several times, if I'm honest. I just lose control of myself, something seems to snap inside me. They're evil, those boys, the things they say, the way they snigger. What can I do? I certainly can't go to Assembly.'

'Then I won't go either. I'll stay and make you a cup of tea.'

'Don't worry, Mary,' Jack Jones, the boys' PT teacher says as he goes out of the room. 'I know that Alfie Morris – all the little bugger wants is a morning off school. He'll be back, bright as a button, this afternoon. I've laid him out before this. He's a little devil, but he doesn't bear grudges.'

'What if his brain is damaged?' Mary asks when everyone's left. 'What if he has to go to hospital? What if he dies?'

'He'll be all right, I'm sure. You can't have hurt him much, you're not strong enough. It's you I'm worried about, Mary. You need some time off. You should go home for a week or two, the doctor would give you a certificate.'

'I can't go home. I don't get on with my step-mother or my step-sisters. Even my father seems to have turned against me. All I've got in the world is Alun and he'll probably be killed . . . Oh, I think I'm going to faint.'

'No, you're not. You drink this tea instead, it's got two spoonfuls of sugar in it, it'll do you a lot of good. What lessons have you got this morning?'

With a judicious mixture of bullying and cajoling, I calm her down and eventually get her to her feet and ready for her first class, a double with 5A. 'I'll see you at break,' I say in my most cheerful voice. Great Heavens, she depresses me.

As I'm gathering up books for my first lesson, a prefect taps at the door and tells me the Head wants to see me. I shall probably be reprimanded for missing Assembly but I can't say it worries me. I rehearse a drawling apology as I go downstairs to his study.

'Come in, Mrs Evans. Sit down, please. I noticed that you

stayed in the staff room this morning with Miss Powell. That was kind. Just what I would have expected of you. Let me tell you what's on my mind. I'm worried about Miss Powell. So are you, I know. As you're aware, I like my staff to be on top form and at the moment Miss Powell is not on top form.'

His huge smile seems to bulge out of his face. He's a large man with enormous energy but little imagination. He waits a moment or two for a comment from me, but as I remain silent, he continues.

'I don't go out of my way to flatter my staff, Mrs Evans. Hard work and total dedication are things John Cynrig Williams takes for granted, but since we find ourselves here on our own, I'll take this opportunity to tell you that I find your work – and conduct – entirely satisfactory.'

Again he smiles his sudden, over-sized smile. I incline my head a fraction.

'But of course I didn't send for you to tell you that. No, I'm asking you to do the school a favour. Would it be possible for you to take Miss Powell as a lodger? I think it would be the making of her. She is all nerves and wild imagination. You would give her a calm centre. Because you are solid, Mrs Evans.'

I hope he recognises the venom in the look I turn on him.

'No, I'm afraid it wouldn't be possible, Mr Williams. I'm sorry, but I already have a lodger.'

'Yes, I'm aware of that. A Miss Hughes, I believe, from North Wales. You seem surprised? Ah, but I consider it my duty, Mrs Evans, to get to know something of the private lives of the young people on my staff. In that way, I can help them tackle any problems they may have before they prove insurmountable. For instance, when I discovered that young Mr Roberts seemed unable to get his weekly teaching forecast finished on time, I was able to convince him that it wasn't due to any lack of mental prowess, but solely to the fact that he was spending just a little too much time every week in the town Billiard Hall. He felt, of course, immensely relieved at my confidence in him, and his work improved almost at once.'

I grit my teeth for another smile, but on this occasion his large mouth remains in a frog-like, down-drooping curve.

'As you're aware, Mr Williams, I have one lodger and I'm afraid my cottage is too small for another. I'm sorry.'

'Thank you, Mrs Evans. That will be all.'

I leave the study trembling with anger at the thought of being spied on out of school hours. And I'm not *solid*, I growl to myself. And the thought of having poor dopey Mary Powell as a lodger instead of Ilona Hughes appals me.

I come face to face with Gwynn Morgan in the empty corridor and for a moment I stand gripping one of his large strong hands in mine. He looks surprised but pleased. 'The Head's been checking up on me. I'm absolutely furious. He says it's his duty to keep an eye on his young staff.'

'Come up to my room at break,' he says. 'Let's make his day.' His voice is playful, but his eyes are dark and serious, so beautiful that my throat aches.

'Shall I?'

'Do. It'll make my day, too.'

And mine.

Last week, the thought of being alone with him in the Art Room frightened me. Today it seems only a minor irregularity. How smoothly and imperceptibly one slips into sin. Only we won't be doing much in the sinning line, I have to assure myself. A little gazing and sighing, perhaps, and what's the harm in that?

I give the Upper Sixth a terrific lesson on Paradise Lost, Book IV. Things I'd hardly understood myself about the nature of love and temptation, fall into place; I feel that I'm speaking with the tongues of men and of angels. I hope they're getting it all down.

Ilona Hughes has never met, never even seen, Mary Powell. I try to describe her: 'She's not exactly fat but she's all weight, somehow, you know, really heavy on her feet. Even her eyelids seem heavy. She shouldn't have become a teacher because she has a lowering effect on everyone and the last thing a Maths class wants is to feel tired as well as bored. But what else could she have done? I'm really worried about her.'

'It's you I'm worried about. You haven't done your ironing tonight or your marking and you've just used half your butter ration on that toast.'

'I was rude to the Head as well, and late for my Welsh class with 2B because I stayed too long in the Art room with Gwynn Morgan.'

'Great Heavens,' Ilona says, 'whatever were you doing?'

'Discussing *Paradise Lost*.'

'Hm. Well, I'm going down to the Ship, I need some cigarettes. I'll just have one drink with old Lizzie and then come back.'

'If only there was a vacancy at your place, Ilona. Mary Powell would be just right behind the counter in a Post Office. She's wonderful with figures and she'd be so earnest and conscientious. Do you think you could mention her to Mr Gruffydd?'

'No. We've got enough dreary people there as it is.'

'If only you two could change places. You'd love the boys in 3C. Mary Powell thinks they're evil but they're only dirty-minded little scruffs. Do you know, I think I'll walk down with you and call in to see her. She's got digs in Marine Place.'

I'm surprised to find Jack Jones, the boys' PT teacher, with Mary. I suppose he's worried about her as well.

'Well, I think I'll just have to make us a pot of tea,' Mary says. 'You're both being so sweet to me.'

Her voice sounds foolish and flirtatious; she obviously thinks Jack has at least some degree of romantic interest in her. Perhaps he has.

Jack Jones is a big, broad, tough-looking man, not in the army because he had to have his right arm amputated a few years back, after a rugby injury. 'I bet you'd like to be a soldier, Sir,' the boys say, giving him every opportunity to indulge in some heroic fantasy. 'Not on your life,' he says. 'I know when I'm well off.'

Tonight, he's telling Mary about all the boys he's thrashed and left for dead, all the mothers who've threatened to sue him.

'Oh Jack,' she says at last, her voice still sugary, 'I don't believe a word of it. People like you and Rhian don't lose control of yourselves. You're born teachers, both of you, but I'm a complete failure.'

65

'Why don't you try to get a job in a bank or a post-office?' I find myself asking. 'With your Maths degree, you'd be bound to get on.'

She looks at me bravely, blinking back tears. 'You see, Jack, Rhian thinks I should give up teaching. Thank you, Rhian, for being so honest.'

'Well, I don't,' Jack says. 'I definitely think you should stick it out. That little bugger was back in school this afternoon, cheeky as ever. You were quite right to fetch him one.'

She gives us very weak tea and soft biscuits that smell of cupboards. Why is she so dreary and hopeless about everything? Her bed-sitting room is hideously depressing, dark brown rexine and varnished wood with tired-looking mats and cushions. I know there's a limit to what you can do in a furnished room, but she could at least have taken down the pictures: sepia reproductions of some Roman battle scenes, strewn with Roman corpses.

'Where do you live, Jack?' I ask him.

'I've got a couple of rooms at the top of Graig Road. Been there a few years now. Quite comfortable. Furnished with old washing-stands and octagonal bamboo tables, but at least the landlady is no bother.'

'My landlady is a friend,' Mary says breathily. 'I don't know what I'd do without her. She lights this fire for me before I get home and brings in my washing when it's raining. I have my evening meal with her and my Sunday dinner.'

'Oh, I wouldn't like that,' Jack says. 'I like to come and go as I choose.'

He yawns and looks around him. He has a wide mouth and a big bony nose. He's very shy as a rule; I've hardly spoken to him till now.

'I like my independence,' he says.

I break out in a sweat. What made me so eager to forgo my independence? Younger than either Jack or Mary, I'm already tied. Ilona Hughes can talk and flirt with anyone in the pub tonight; she can begin an exciting new relationship with anyone who catches her eye. She's free, but I'm trapped.

Do all married women feel like this from time to time? Or only those who've married the wrong men?

66

'What's the matter?' Jack asks.

'I was thinking about . . . about all the marking I've got, I can't seem to settle to it this week. So I think I should be going home now. Thank you for the tea.'

Mary seems ready, almost eager, for my departure. 'I'll consider your advice very carefully,' she says as she shows me out. 'Thank you for being so honest. I've been thinking along the same lines myself. Some other job. I'm definitely not cut out to be a teacher, I know that.'

'For God's sake,' Jack says, 'don't start that again. You're doing fine. You're not a saint, but who is?'

I leave him there, still comforting her. I wonder, briefly, what Alun Brooke would make of the situation and decide that he's too upright and noble-hearted for anything as degrading as jealousy.

My mother has a poisoned finger – the middle finger on her right hand – and is feeling very low. She can't do the milking or any housework, she can't cook, can't even cut bread and butter. I try to do some chores for her, but watching me only makes her more irritable. 'Good gracious, you can't even squeeze out a cloth properly.' 'That's not the way to sweep a kitchen, girl, that's the way to sweep a yard.' 'Don't hold the loaf like that or you'll cut off your thumb.' 'You have to be gentle with that drawer, it won't open unless you coax it a bit.'

She has no modern appliances, not even a carpet sweeper. Every carpet and mat has to be swept or taken up and beaten. She hasn't any electricity or gas, not even a water tap in the house.

'I'm not worrying about the housework, girl – it's just that I hate feeling out of sorts. I've told Alfredo not to come again till I'm better. I must go to bed early and try to sleep.'

I think she's got a fever; her skin feels hot and dry.

'I'll come up again tomorrow night and bring you some of that iron tonic.'

'I've got some iron tonic here. But why should I waste it, girl, when it's only my finger that's bad?'

'It's not only your finger. The poison has got into your blood stream by this time.'

I rummage in the medicine cupboard. 'Mam, this tonic is almost ten years old. It's the one you bought for me when I had glandular fever that time.'

'It's all the better for being old. You only get coloured water these days. Gracious me, are you sure I should have as much as this? Well, it will do me a power of good, I'm sure. It was the most expensive one they had in Albert Lloyd's. Now, don't worry about me any more, I'll have another dose when I get up. And thank you for bringing me the holy picture. I don't think you ought to leave it in the middle of the mantelpiece, though, in case the minister calls. He may come this week because I didn't manage to go to chapel on Sunday. Put it on the dresser, behind the cups. That's better. And fancy the artist being an Italian. They're very clever people, no doubt about that. Will you help me up to bed now?'

She leans against me as we go upstairs. It's the first time I've ever known her ask for help.

The polished wooden floor of her bedroom slopes like the floor of a ship. It has the same smell as I remember from childhood; beeswax polish, clean washing and dried rose petals. The pink and white quilt on the bed was made by my great-grandmother; the lace cloth on the chest of drawers is even older and the silky white rug at the bedside was brought back from China by my sailor grandfather. The water-jug and basin – and the chamber-pot under the bed – are a bright, turquoise blue. This is the only pretty room in the house.

'Let me bring you a cup of tea and a biscuit. You hardly had any supper.'

'That would be a treat.'

She's sitting up in bed reading the Bible when I return.

'Do you still read a chapter every night?'

'No. It was your father who used to read a chapter. It's just five verses I read, I never have time for any more. I'm a slow old reader.'

'Doesn't that mean you finish in the middle of a story?'

'Yes, but I always know how it's going to end, don't I? Always in the same way. The wise men always find the stable, Jairus's daughter is always raised from the dead and the prodigal son always comes home.'

'And Christ is always crucified in the end.'

'Only that's not the end, girl. That's the beginning.'

She smiles at me, then closes the Bible and sits back against the pillow to drink her tea. She looks pale but pretty, a white shawl over her shoulders.

I was born – and conceived – in that wide bed. When I was ill I was allowed to sleep in the warm valley between my parents, one soft and one bony.

When I wasn't there between them, did they sleep enfolded together, their limbs entwined? Though I never saw them kiss or even hold hands, their eyes often sought each other's and their relationship seemed warm and close. Does she miss him still, miss him with her body?

'Rhian, why are you looking at me in that strange way? Are you unhappy again, Rhian? Oh, I'm worried about you, being on your own all these years.'

'And I'm worried about you. Listen, I'll be up again on Friday and I'll stay the night.'

'But what about your housework, girl, and your shopping? You only have the Saturday.'

'I'll manage. Ilona Hughes will help me. Goodnight, Mam.'

'Goodnight. It'll be lovely to have you here, as long as it won't put you behind. Take the lamp down with you and leave me the candle. And don't forget to put Flossy in the barn.'

Flossy barks when I put her in the barn and then stops dead. We both listen. I've become a town girl; the mare clanking her chain, a cow coughing, a mouse rustling in the straw, any noise or no noise at all disturbs me.

I hurry down the long, narrow lane to the bus stop, from time to time flashing the torch in front of me.

Gwynn Morgan is meeting the bus and we walk up Hill Street together as though it's the most natural thing in the world. I tell him about my mother's poisoned finger, about her pretty bedroom, about all the noises of the quiet farm.

Chapter Eight

The next morning, I have a letter from Huw – the first for over a month.

He never tries to tell me where he is or what he's doing. He could easily put in a few Welsh words to confound the censor, but he's always too cautious and careful. In my last letter I wrote: *Have you come across Rho Wybod*? Rho Wybod sounds like a fat, slightly stupid country lad, but it's actually Welsh for 'give me news'.

But he still hasn't; doesn't seem prepared to try. Instead he goes on yet again about Ilona Hughes whom he's never even met. *I know you think my mother is old-fashioned, he says, but I agree with her about this one thing. I don't think it's right for you to have a lodger who goes to pubs every night in the company of soldiers. I'm quite sure you don't do anything like that yourself, but people might think you do. In people's minds, birds of a feather flock together, and if your lodger leads that sort of life, they'll think you do too, and I can't bear that people should think badly of my wife. I'm sure you could get a decent, clean-living woman to keep you company, one who wouldn't harm your reputation or our family's. Please do what I ask, love. My mother would be so pleased. Believe me, I want everyone to think the best of you. I think of you constantly and look forward to being home with you. I don't feel it will be too long now. With all my love, Huw.*

Of course I'm very pleased to hear from him, relieved that he's safe and well, but soon my strongest emotion is indignation at how small-minded and overbearing he is.

To calm myself I write a note for my next door neighbour,

71

retired railwayman Sam Jones, to take down to my mother-in-law.

> *I've just had a lovely letter from Huw. He's very well and feels confident that the war will soon be over. He asks me to give you his love and to tell you that he's longing to be home. He's very pleased with our letters; to know that you two are well and that I still have Ilona Hughes for company.*
> *Love from Rhian.*

I feel much better after writing it. I suppose I'm small-minded as well.

The portrait isn't going well. Gwynn's wife hardly talked at all during today's sitting and frowned when I did. I'm still not allowed to see it, though Gwynn is. He said, this afternoon, that it was at a tricky stage and gave it as his definite opinion that it would improve next week. He picked up a paintbrush to demonstrate something about tonal values, but she snatched it from his hand, saying, 'It's *my* painting, *mine*' sounding like a six-year-old.

I felt I really deserved my tea and that half-hour in the front parlour which she calls the *salon*.

I wonder if Gwynn lays the table as prettily when I'm not here? I know the Chelsea buns are for me, but sadly, they're the one incongruous item: too large, too vulgar and sugary for the delicate china, the white lace and the silver.

'I had a word with Jack Jones this afternoon,' Gwynn says, when his wife has poured out the tea. His hand grazes mine as he passes me my cup.

'What about?' I ask, trying to keep my voice steady.

'About that silly girl, Mary Powell,' Mrs Morgan says. 'Feeling sorry for a silly girl is one thing, but living with the consequences for the rest of your life is quite another.'

She knows everything that goes on at school; Gwynn tells her every smallest detail. I'm sick with jealousy at the thought of the hours and hours of conversation they have, while he and I have so little. He feels something for me, I know that: some twinges of desire, some love, perhaps. Oh, but she is his lawful wife. She sleeps with him every night. If she wakes from a bad dream she can put her hand on his chest, feel the warmth of his lovely body, the steady beat of his heart.

My misery is so sharp, it's a kind of ecstasy.

'She's a man-eater,' Mrs Morgan continues. 'She's so insecure and so unattractive, poor thing, that she makes a grab at whatever's offered, even in the way of friendship. She exaggerates whatever happens, too and makes a mountain out of it.'

Gwynn observes his wife with what looks like tender exasperation. 'When she first came here – before you arrived, she was the only youngster on the staff– she seemed so lonely that I once asked her over for Sunday tea.'

I have another pang of jealousy.

'And I found that she'd told Miss Walters – who was the school secretary at that time – that I'd taken her out for some birthday celebration. I didn't even know it was the silly girl's birthday, her twenty-first as it happened. I wasn't even aware of it.'

'And Gwynn has some taste,' Mrs Morgan says. 'He has some standards.'

'What about Carys Edwards?' I ask, throwing in the name of the balding bakery manageress, a childhood sweetheart, in an effort to appear light-hearted.

Mrs Morgan looks at Gwynn and gives him a small, intimate smile.

I have a moment's panic: she knows all about me too: Gwynn tells her all about our affair – which is no affair – as he tells her about everything else in his life. For a moment I see a mother bird, sitting fat and serene on a nest, while her mate flies back to her with some little wriggling creature in his beak.

'I don't think it means anything,' I say firmly. 'Jack is –

'A man,' Mrs Morgan says.

I ignore her. 'He's very lonely. He's always been a man's man, but now that all his friends are in the army, he wants Mary as a friend. He feels sorry for her because she's such a dead loss as a teacher and because her fiancé is abroad. Their relationship is quite platonic, I'm sure.'

Of course I'm not as sure as I pretend. Like everyone else, I've been uneasily aware of their sudden closeness. He's been trailing after her during school hours, carrying her books, waiting for her at the main gates when it's time to go home. Only today Mrs Lewis, History, reported that she'd seen them on the prom together on Sunday afternoon.

Mrs Morgan studies me. She's wearing a dark grey dress in a heavy, shot-satin material, shiny as a trout's belly. She always looks as though she's in an elegant form of fancy dress; the flounced smock she wears when she's painting looks like an artist's smock from a musical comedy. Even in my best Studio Laura dress, I look ordinary beside her. What if I had to sit here in my gathered skirt and my lumpy, hand-knitted cardigan?

Her pale eyes are still focused on me as though she's interested in far more than my words; as though she's trying to suck in every thought from the deepest recesses of my brain.

Gwynn notices her absorption in me, and comes to my rescue. 'Anyway, I had a word with Jack this afternoon,' he says again.

She turns to him. 'What did he say?'

'I hardly like to tell you. Not in front of Rhian. It made me feel . . . well . . . rather upset.'

He examines the crease in his trousers, pulls the legs up a fraction to ease the strain of the material over his knees. He's enjoying the way we're both looking at him.

'It was in confidence, of course.'

I jump up. 'I'll go,' I say. 'I don't like secrets.'

'He told me to bugger off and mind my own business,' he says with a delighted smile.

'Well, really,' Mrs Morgan says. 'That's shocking. To speak to you like that, when you only meant to be kind.'

'I'd have said exactly the same,' he says, 'if anyone dared advise me on a personal affair. What about you, Rhian?'

'I'm afraid I'm another who doesn't take very kindly to advice. My mother says I'm stubborn as an old donkey.' I tell them about Huw's letter and the note I sent my mother-in-law.

Gwynn smiles again.

'This Ilona Hughes I don't know,' Mrs Morgan says, 'but I don't think I approve of her either. Oh, these conventions are so boring, I know, but they can save a lot of trouble and 'eartache in the end. You know this young woman, Gwynn?'

'Yes, we have a chat in the Ship occasionally. She's all right, perfectly all right. You must come to tea one Sunday afternoon to meet her.'

As soon as I've said it, I wish I hadn't. I can't visualise Ilona and Gwynn's wife together and my front room is very ugly, not much better than Mary Powell's bed-sitting room. And I haven't got any decent china. I had a pretty tea-set as a wedding present, but Ilona keeps breaking the cups and bringing me some of her grandmother's as replacements.

'Rhian's cottage is lovely. You'd like it,' Gwynn says.

'I didn't know you'd been there,' she says, quick as a cat with a mouse. 'When was this?'

'I know it well. Ted Rowlands had digs there before he got married. Most of the houses in Hill Road have been ruined with bay windows and glass front doors, but Rhian's is much as it always was.'

'Only it's got a bathroom,' I say.

'Only it's got a *bathroom*,' Gwynn says, mimicking me.

'We didn't have a bathroom at home,' I tell him. My mother still doesn't. She has to pump every drop of water and boil it in the kettle, or in the boiler in the back-kitchen on washing day. And on Friday nights for baths.'

'So what,' he says. 'I was brought up exactly the same. It doesn't make us worse – or better – than anyone else. Tougher, perhaps.'

'Can we please stop talking about these baths and bathrooms?' Mrs Morgan says. 'Can we perhaps think of something more interesting to talk about?'

She's getting bored with me. I dredge my mind for a tasty piece of gossip but come up with nothing.

'I haven't seen Ilona's boyfriend lately,' Gwynn says. 'The curly-haired chap. Has he left Tonfaen?'

'Yes. For the South Coast, I think. She hasn't heard from him yet. She seems to miss him, though she always said it wasn't serious.'

'These soldiers don't want anything serious,' Mrs Morgan says. 'They want to kiss and run. This girl should be careful about who she sees.'

I take a deep breath. 'Denzil wasn't like that. He seemed

very fond of Ilona. He seemed very nice.'

'Well, he was Catholic, for a start,' Gwynn says, 'and they're always a cut above the rest, aren't they, Celine? He used to be at Sant Ioan's every Sunday morning.'

'There *was* a small group of soldiers, yes. Very good boys they looked – but soldiers always look serious and good in church.'

When tea is over, Gwynn announces that he intends to walk home with me; the heavy rain, I think, has given him an excuse. I've got a mackintosh with a hood, but he insists on holding his large black umbrella over the two of us. We walk closely together; I can feel his hip bone hard against mine.

'How's your mother's finger?' he asks me.

'Much better. The district nurse came on Friday and lanced it. She's supposed to be calling today to change the dressing. I'll go up there again tomorrow after school.'

'How's the Italian foreman?'

'Oh Gwynn, I'm too nervous to think about it. He came again when I was there on Friday evening. Because she's ill, he's beginning to take charge of everything – and she's letting him. What's going to happen?'

'Don't worry. When the war's over, everything will be fine. He'll stay in this country and they'll get married.'

'Oh yes – when the war's over. Everybody's talking about when the war's over, but it may go on for years and years.' I splash through a puddle, lose my balance for a moment, feel his hand gripping my shoulder.

'It will be wonderful for you when Huw comes back.'

'It won't, and you know it.'

'Perhaps we'll go away together.'

'If only we could. Where would we go?'

'Somewhere far away. Scotland.'

'The tip of Lleyn. Aberdaron. A tiny cottage. You could paint and I'd cook mackerel for our tea.'

'Isn't rain wonderful?'

'I love rain.'

He comes with me as far as the door. Retired railwayman Sam Jones, my next-door neighbour, nods at us from his front window as we say our chaste goodbyes.

*

76

When Ilona comes home at six o'clock, she brings Jack Jones into the house with her. 'I found him on the doorstep,' she says, 'like a stray. We've introduced ourselves.'

'I hope you don't mind my coming to see you uninvited,' Jack says. He seems very ill at ease, Ilona's presence being perhaps the last straw. He's a very shy man. I manage to get him to sit down; his eyes search the room as though locating a possible escape route.

'Of course, I know your husband,' he says, catching sight of Huw's photograph in the middle of the mantelpiece. 'We were in the school rugby team together years ago.'

'Were you really? I didn't realise you were at school in Llanfryn. How is it I don't remember you?'

'I'd probably left before you started. I'm thirty this year, a few years older than your husband. Have you heard from him lately?'

'I had a letter today as a matter of fact. He seems quite well.'

'Longing to be home, I'm sure.'

'Yes.'

He takes another long, searching look at Huw's photograph. 'I didn't know him well, mind. I didn't come across him much in school, we were in different forms, but he was a good rugby man.'

'He enjoys rugby and cricket.'

In the long pause that follows, I find myself studying him, wondering what Ilona will make of him; she's studying him, too. He's moderately good-looking; mahogany coloured hair and pale skin with still a sprinkling of faded, almost yellow, summer freckles, a large beaky nose. What's he doing here? What does he want to tell me? He's still looking nervously about him.

'I suppose Mary must have spoken to you about her fiancé, Alun Brooke,' he says at last.

'Yes. What about him? I mean, he's all right, is he? He'd been in hospital, last I heard.'

'Yes, that's right.'

'I'll make us a cup of tea,' Ilona Hughes says, obviously aware that whatever Jack's got to say will take some time.

I try to help him along. 'Poor Mary gets very worked-up about him. Is she particularly worried at the moment?'

I can hear Ilona filling the kettle and rattling cups and

saucers on to a tray. We've got a casserole in the oven, I hope she remembers to turn the gas down.

'He doesn't exist, Rhian.'

'What do you mean, he doesn't exist?' I find I've lowered my voice as though talking of the newly dead. 'What can you mean?'

'He never did exist. She imagined him, that's all.'

'*Imagined* him? Are you serious? Do you mean she invented him?'

'I suppose she did, in a way. Yes. She cut out a picture of a soldier from a newspaper and gave him a name.'

'Great Heavens! And a family, too. And took him over. And got engaged to him. Great Heavens, I can't believe it. Dreamed about him every night. Carried his letters about with her. Where did those letters come from? Jack, she used to read me great chunks from his letters. How he looked up at the sky and saw ... Oh dear, I don't know whether to laugh or cry.'

'What's the matter with you?' Ilona Hughes asks from the doorway. 'What have I missed?'

'Don't laugh,' Jack says, very quietly. 'Please don't laugh.'

'Oh, why not?' I feel anger welling up inside me. 'Oh Ilona, you'll never believe this.'

'Think of all the shyness and loneliness and insecurity behind it,' Jack says. 'Please don't laugh.'

'If I promise not to laugh, will you promise not to ... Oh, she's sick, Jack, and I'm very worried about you, everyone is. You mustn't get involved with her.'

'She's not sick.' His voice trembles. 'Oh, it's all very well for you. For you and your friend. You're beautiful and easy-going and you're both spoilt because you've never known anything but a chorus of admiration. You've always been surrounded by boyfriends, you've always been popular and sought-after.'

I'm trying to concentrate on what he's saying, but Ilona, who has no idea what the real issue is, is incensed.

'Are you talking about *me*?' she asks. 'I'm spoilt? Oh, no I'm not. Nor beautiful either, come to that and neither is Rhian. And I work hard to be popular. Yes, I'm sought-after because I always try to be friendly and sociable. I could be lonely and shy and insecure if I allowed myself to be. Anyone could, it's the easiest thing in the world. I often think that lonely, shy and insecure are only other ways of saying selfish, self-regarding and self-engrossed.'

Jack shakes his head as though someone's hit him. 'I'm sorry,' he says. 'I didn't mean to offend you. I was making a bid for your sympathy, that's all. No, I won't stay for a cup of tea, Rhian, thank you. I said I'd get back to Mary. She wanted you to know, but she couldn't bring herself to tell you.'

I'm not surprised. 'Jack, don't go. I feel so mean-spirited. I do feel sorry for Mary, of course I do, but I can't help feeling even more sorry for you.'

'Don't be sorry for me. I've always liked Mary, always felt protective towards her. Over several years, in fact. And now, well we've – we've fallen in love, I suppose. I might as well tell you the truth, Rhian, I've asked her to marry me and she's accepted. She's giving in her notice tomorrow and she'll be leaving school at the end of term. We're planning to get married in the Easter holidays. She wanted you to be the first to know.'

The news sinks down into my mind like a stone. 'In that case, I can only offer you both my best wishes.'

'Poor deluded man,' I say over and over again when he's gone. 'Poor man.'

'Come on, come on, what did I miss?'

I tell her; give her all the details. But of course no sort of abnormal behaviour takes Ilona by surprise. Besides, I've been the one constantly cajoled into worrying about this big, boyish, fair-haired, star-gazing, romantic, God-fearing second Lieutenant Alun Brooke. Who doesn't exist.

'I've even prayed for him,' I mutter through clenched teeth when I'm washing up after our evening meal.

'Serves you right,' Ilona says. 'You shouldn't take those liberties with people, Rhian, when you hadn't even been introduced.'

'Ilona, don't try to be superior. Just try to help me understand this woman. Is she quite mad, or what? Jack thinks I should feel sorry for her, but I just feel I want to hit her.

Ilona, what do you make of it? Don't you think there must be something terribly wrong with someone who can go to such lengths to deceive people?'

'There's something wrong with everybody. Don't you ever tell lies?'

'No. Well, not whopping great lies, anyway. Great Heavens, she's even told me all about his parents – his mother who had rheumatic fever when she was eighteen and who's had a weak heart ever since, and his father who was always winning prizes for his camellias. They had this acre of garden and a big mansion with wisteria over the front door.'

'And you believed it all?'

'*Everybody* believed it all. She had a huge emerald and diamond engagement ring from him; she was always going on about how much it must have cost. Did she buy it herself? Can you imagine going to a jeweller's and buying an engagement ring for yourself? If she was really mad, I suppose I'd have to try to feel sorry for her, but I think she was quite aware of what she was doing. She did it for the advantage it gave her; so that people would take more notice of her, I suppose.'

'It probably started off as a harmless daydream. All her friends were getting engaged and married so she pretended to have a boy-friend, too. She probably mentioned him to someone, the whole thing took off and she couldn't control it anymore. You often hear of people like her. There was a woman in Brynteg who used to . . .'

'Please don't tell me about her, Ilona, I couldn't bear it. Tell me about someone who's normal. Why can't people be truthful and honest with one another? Oh, it's Jack I feel sorry for. He's going to be sucked into this great whirlpool of lies and deception.'

'Well, he's only got himself to blame. He was at her digs when you called there that night and you told me how attentive he's been to her ever since. He shouldn't have been hanging around with someone else's fiancée.'

'He was only being kind to her when she was so upset about Alfie Morris's mother coming up to school.'

'Rhian, don't waste your pity on a man. He's big enough and tough enough to look after himself.'

*

80

At school the next day, Mary and I smile carefully at each other. I know she'd love to talk, if I let her, but I can't bring myself to have anything to do with her at the moment. Anyway, she's got poor Jack now. She can pour out her heart and soul to him.

I wonder what the Head will say when he hears about them? Of course he'll be delighted to accept Mary's resignation. Perhaps she'll tell him that Alun was killed in action. It would certainly be a hero's death. He'd die while rescuing a badly wounded private – a fellow Welshman probably – and you can bet your life they'd have a few quiet words of prayer together, too.

I'm beginning to feel quite unhinged. Why can't I stop thinking about him? I can see his face so clearly; the band of peeling sunburn over his nose and cheeks, his sweat-streaked blond hair curling slightly on his neck even after the severest army haircut, the broad, six-foot-two-inch frame. My hold on reality seems as weak as Mary's. I repeat Huw's army number under my breath! 14405196. Why can't I see *his* face? I take out his letter from my handbag and re-read it; my anger floods back, so I suppose he must be real, too. But why can't he write sweet, poetic letters like Alun Brooke's? Stop it. What's the matter with me? Perhaps it's the effect of the times we're living in: life and death, fact and fantasy, truth and lies, wild impossible events and ordinary day-to-day happenings all swirling round together in this mad cauldron of war. I'll blame it on that, anyway.

After my lesson with 2A, I'm summoned to the Head's room again. What does he want now? I'm beginning to think I'm some sort of special chum.

'Come in, come in,' he says in his most hearty voice when I tap on the door.

He waits for me to sit down opposite him.

'Well, you've got more sense than I have,' he says. 'Yes, indeed. A woman of sound sense and judgement.' He gives me quite a pleasant, unforced smile which seems only an inch or two wider than other people's.

'You saw through her,' he says. 'I didn't. I confess that I was taken in by her. And I'm not often taken in, no, indeed. John Cynrig Williams is not often deceived by people.'

That's how he talks.

It doesn't seem worth trying to tell him that I was taken in by her too – even to the extent of being envious of her handsome, steadfast sweetheart.

'Well, I've insisted on her reporting sick for the rest of the term. I can't have any more of her lies and hysteria. Lies and hysteria disrupt a school more than any number of absent teachers. Colleagues can cover for absent teachers – I know you won't mind taking over some of her first-year classes, Mrs Evans – but no one can undo the effects of lies and hysteria. Yes, I'm sending her home by the midday train today and she won't be returning. If Jack Jones chooses to follow her to Fronilltyd during the Easter holiday, that's up to him. I've strongly advised him against it, but unfortunately I have no power to control a teacher's out-of-school activity, except in so far as it affects his school work. If he chooses to get himself involved with a lying, hysterical woman, I can do nothing about it, though one would think he'd consider the loss of an arm enough of a liability. However, these last few weeks of term may give him the opportunity to reconsider his position.'

I don't respond because I can't bear the thought of being in any sort of agreement with him. In fact, he's succeeded in making me feel a little more sympathetic towards Mary and a little less worried about Jack.

The interview seems to be over so I get to my feet.

'I'm very pleased with you, Mrs Evans,' he says, 'very pleased to have you on my staff. You're doing well here. Mrs Evans, I've been disappointed in Miss Powell. Don't let me be disappointed in you, Mrs Evans. Do I make myself clear?'

I meet his searching little eyes. Great Heavens, how much does he know about me and Gwynn?

But what is there to know?

Chapter Nine

This morning Gwynn received his call-up papers; a catastrophe I hadn't anticipated since he's already over forty.

We have a quarrel in the Art room at lunch time. I'd thought he was a pacifist, as I am. He says he is in principle, but that he still intends to join up. He says, yes, he's quite aware of the power of propaganda, thank you, is quite aware that the Germans are not all savages nor the Allies all avenging angels, but he also believes that the Germans were the original aggressors, that it would be better for the world if the Allies win and that, in any case, he'd be proud to help liberate France.

I've been a Welsh Nationalist and pacifist almost since I can remember. I believe that an independent Wales would be neutral like Switzerland, Ireland and Sweden, but since she is legally part of Great Britain, then individuals who think as I do should follow their conscience and refuse to join the English army.

He says my concept of Wales is over-romantic, that the Welsh way of life I talk about is no different from the way of life of any poor, radical, non-conformist section of society in any part of Britain.

I say that our language and literature make us a separate nation so that we are set apart from any other section of society. We are a nation with a national culture and if that's an over-romantic idea, I admit to being over-romantic.

He says that no man is an island, that Wales, whether a separate nation or not, is part of the main.

I say that war is never right and that he's capitulated to

the propaganda of the English press.

He says my outlook is narrow and parochial.

I say that he's a moral coward, afraid of the scorn of small-minded, English-oriented people.

He says I'm over-emotional and that it's time for me to grow up.

It's our first quarrel. When the bell goes for afternoon school, I march out of the room, slamming the door behind me.

My first lesson is Welsh with 2A.

Arthur Williams's father is in Swansea jail. Most conscientious objectors are allowed to work on the land, but he wouldn't accept that alternative.

It seems the right time to show my hand. 'How is your father, Arthur?' I ask him as the class leaves.

'I don't know, Miss. My mother is only allowed to visit him once a month.' My interest gives him courage. 'He's not a coward is he, Miss?'

'No. I think he's a very brave man.'

He's a large, unattractive boy with bright red hair and flailing arms. He gives me a delighted, wide-eyed look before rushing out. For a few minutes I watch him chasing and clouting some smaller boys in the playground.

Behind the hills, the sky is a mild spring blue. Fourteen miles away my mother is doing as much work as she can manage with a still-bandaged finger. The little double daffodils are already out in the sloping garden and there are hot-scented gillyflowers in the shelter of the house. She hasn't much time, and even less money to spend on flowers, but by saving the best seeds and some judicious planting – 'I try to imagine where I'd be happy' – she's always got something in bloom. She's got one rose bush with lovelier roses than I've come across anywhere else; deep pink, sweet smelling, perfectly round and fading to the palest lavender when fully open. She calls it Mary's rose, not after the virgin or the queen, but after the woman who gave her the cutting years ago. Of course it's much too early for roses now, but the pale primroses are out in profusion, their faint wet smell the breath of early spring. When I was little, I used to pick so many bunches of primroses that we had jam-jars full of them even on the outside window sills. I knew where to get the rare white primroses, too, and the pale pink ones. I think I could find them still.

On Palm Sunday, we used to make a primrose wreath for my grandmother's grave. My mother used to say it was much prettier than the shop wreaths on some of the other graves, but I loved the big arum lilies shaped into crosses, used to promise faithfully that I'd always get one of those for her. Death seemed natural and not too frightening on those spring Sundays. Even those graves where the earth was newly-turned and raw failed to terrify me, then.

I was alone a great deal as a child, but I never thought of myself as lonely; never felt the lack of friends. I had friends at school and that seemed enough. Home and school were two different worlds with a two-mile stony track between them. At home, I had my mother and father and Dafi Blaenhir and a little house in the barn where I played with my doll, Grace, in wet weather. And later, I had books.

On fine summer days I used to hide away with the book I was reading, pretending not to hear them calling me in for meals. I had a little green den, formed by the bindwind which hung like curtains from the branches of the hazel trees by the brook, and the pages of my book were dappled with green. And no idiot-boy or sex-starved stranger ever lurched up to destroy the idyll; I can't recall any really frightening experience. I had wasp stings and bee stings, of course, and was often caught in summer storms; thunder and lightning and torrential rain. I almost stepped on a snake once, but though momentarily alarmed, I recognised it as a harmless grass snake and stepped aside to let it pass; I remember being surprised by the rasping papery noise it made as it slithered along the path. Usually my solitary hours and long mountain walks yielded nothing worse than the stench of a decomposing animal, a rabbit or a fox.

I was brought up to be unafraid. My mother used to impress upon me that there were no such things as ghosts or witches. And no wicked burglars either, at least not in Wales. And any tramps I met were poor harmless fellows who I was welcome to bring home for some bread and cheese and a night in the barn.

I was brought up to think well of people; every man, not exactly a blood brother, perhaps, but certainly of the rank of cousin or cousin-in-law or second-cousin-once-removed. Land of brotherhood. Poor people help one another. We couldn't manage the harvest on our own, neither could our neighbours, so we formed a self-help society. In the larger farms that employed two or three servants, it was almost unheard of for the year's contract to be broken; far oftener they would remain with the family, as part of the family, for a lifetime.

Now I'm in a town of landladies out for themselves and charging too much money for a bed and a breakfast. There seems to be something about the sea air that makes people greedy. In the hills we're kinder to one another; our roots go deeper, I suppose.

Jack Jones comes into my room bringing me a cup of tea. I've been too agitated to go to the staff-room and he's noticed. As a reward for his thoughtfulness, I ask after Mary.

He says she's been very depressed after a bout of 'flu, but that he'll be seeing her in the Easter holidays. He doesn't mention their marriage and to my surprise doesn't seem over-eager to talk about her.

I begin to drink my tea, expecting him to go, but he stays at my side looking out of the window. There's a friendly detachment about him which I find comforting after my bruising contact with Gwynn.

'Would you join up?' I ask, 'if it wasn't for your accident?'

'I wouldn't have any choice, would I? If it wasn't for the arm, I wouldn't have any choice.'

'Unless you were a conscientious objector.'

'Oh no, I wouldn't be one of those. I don't like the idea of war – who does? – but I'm not a pacifist. Why do you ask?'

'I would be one, that's all.'

His face registers mild interest but no real surprise. 'Does Huw know?'

'Yes, but he doesn't take it seriously. He doesn't take me seriously at all. Huw thinks all my strange ideas are a part of my being a woman. He, a man, doesn't have any strange ideas – or any ideas at all, come to that. I didn't even try to talk Huw out of joining-up. I suppose I realised how futile it would have been.'

'Most men would be the same, though. I mean, most men join up when they get their papers, don't they? I think perhaps women are more concerned about the sanctity of life because they produce life.'

'Do you like women? I mean, in the way you like men? I don't think Huw does.'

'Of course he does. Well, I know I do, anyway. In the past, I've always been more comfortable with men, but that's only because I've always been very shy with women – I had five brothers but no sister, I never got to know any girls. But as far as *liking* is concerned, yes, I think I like them better than men.'

I'm moved by his words and by the slow, serious way he's speaking, by his courtesy in giving my foolish questions such grave consideration. I wait for him to continue, and after a moment or two he does.

'For one thing women don't boast as much as men do. Huw was a bit of a show-off, I remember that much about him. I shouldn't have mentioned it, though, because he's probably grown out of it by this time. I mean, he was only sixteen, seventeen when I knew him.'

'The worst thing about Huw is that he's so sure he knows best about everything, so sure I should accept his judgement without question. For instance, his mother has written to him – several times, probably – telling him that Ilona Hughes is not a suitable companion for me because she goes to the pub with men. So he imagines he's got the right to tell me to get rid of her and get a decent-living lodger, my feelings and my judgement counting for nothing.'

'I liked Ilona Hughes. She seemed very . . . very straight.'

I smiled as I remembered the way she'd shouted at him. 'You're right,' I said. 'She is straight. Oh, she's very impatient and outspoken and she loves to shock people, but you're quite right, she's entirely straightforward and honest.'

'And perhaps people round here need to be shocked. All the chapel people who think they're virtuous because of all the things they *don't* do. I don't think there's much real harm in them, but I sometimes think goodness is a bit more positive than that.'

What he says is not original in any way, I know that, but

I've got a feeling that he's thinking it out for himself, that he's rarely talked seriously to anyone before; everyone says he never talks about anything but rugby.

'Do you know, I've never in my whole life been to a pub,' I tell him. 'That says something about my mentality, doesn't it, the way I've clung to all the negative principles. Thou shalt not.'

'Come out and have a drink with me tonight,' he says, suddenly cheerful again.

'That wasn't what I meant.'

'No, I know. But come anyway. Half an hour's chat and half a pint of beer. How about it?'

'All right.'

'Good. I'll call for you at nine.'

I find myself staring at the hills again. In the last ten minutes they've become a darker blue, a more sombre violet.

'I shouldn't have married Huw,' I say, almost in a whisper.

'Rhian, you don't mean that.'

'I didn't mean to say it. I've never admitted it to anyone else, hardly even to myself. Don't let it upset you, though, Jack. Forget it. People make mistakes all the time. And have to live with them for the rest of their lives.'

'Are you trying to warn me off marriage, Rhian? Because if you are . . .'

'No, I'm afraid I wasn't thinking of you and Mary. Only of Huw and me.'

'Try not to be depressed, Rhian. When Huw comes home I'm sure it'll all seem different.'

'I don't know. I don't think so. He seems so domineering.'

'Perhaps all men are the same once they're married. I know I've often been embarrassed by the way my friends treat their wives. I mean, they go out every night while their wives stay in with the children. It's a fact of life. So much about marriage seems unfair. Men always seem to have the best of it.'

'I don't have any married friends.' Or did Gwynn and his wife count, I wondered.

'I suppose being on my own, I've had time to notice,' Jack says.

'I don't think Gwynn Morgan is like that. I've been to his

house a few times and he always seems very thoughtful. Of course his wife is an exceptional woman, isn't she? I mean, French and all that, very sure of herself. I don't suppose anyone could take advantage of a woman like that.'

'Well, you'll have to become a woman like that, won't you?'

His voice has changed, becoming suddenly cold. I shouldn't have mentioned Gwynn.

'She's painting my portrait. I've been to their house a few times.'

'I know. He's told me about it.'

In spite of Jack's obvious disapproval, I can't resist talking about Gwynn. 'And Gwynn is exceptional, too. Because he's an artist I suppose, and a thinker.'

'Don't get too fond of him, Rhian, for all that. Mrs Lewis says she's worried about how often you're up in his room.'

'Great Heavens! Haven't we got some busybodies on this staff?'

'Mrs Lewis says that every young teacher has a term or two when she spends every available moment in the Art room with Gwynn Morgan.'

My throat is burning. 'In that case, why is she worried about me?'

'Because you're married, I suppose.'

'That should make it better, not worse. We're both married so we're both safe.'

'I hope so.'

The bell goes, Jack smiles at me rather sadly and takes my empty cup back to the staff room. I'm quite surprised at how much I like him. At least I've got one thing to thank Mary Powell for; I'd hardly spoken to him before we met at her digs.

As Form 3C – the noisy lot that gave Mary Powell such trouble – surge into my room like a battalion of not-so-light infantry, I scribble a hasty note.

Dearest Gwynn,
I'm sorry for all the harsh things I said. You're right. I am immature and over-emotional and too much in love and too fearful of your safety. Please forgive me,
    Rhian.

*

Of course I'm ashamed of my complete capitulation. I still think I could sacrifice a great deal – my career, for instance – for Wales. But to fall out with the person I love is another matter and altogether impossible.

I put the letter in an envelope and ask Mali Vaughan, the girl sitting in the front desk, to take it to Gwynn.

'I said I'd go out to the pub with Jack Jones tonight,' I tell Ilona Hughes after supper. 'Will you come with us?'

She gives me a look I can't quite interpret.

'He's a very nice man, Ilona, very decent and thoughtful. What's the matter? You always say I should go out and meet people instead of stagnating here every night.'

'Why is it all right to go out with Jack, someone you don't care about, but wrong to go out with Gwynn? It seems contrary, that's all.'

'How is it that you don't understand? It's obvious. I feel safe with Jack. Because I'm not in love with him, I suppose. Even if someone told my mother-in-law I'd been seen with him, I wouldn't mind. He's a colleague of mine, I'd tell her, and there's nothing wrong with my seeing him from time to time. She could think what she liked as long as I knew it was innocent.'

She gives me another long look. 'Or perhaps you intend to paddle in shallow water for a while before you take the plunge . . . Something like that. Yes, I'll come with you. I've got nothing better to do.'

'He's coming round at nine. Apparently he's going to see Mary in the holidays, but perhaps he's beginning to see sense because he didn't mention getting married.'

How was I to know that Ilona would bring up the subject within about half a minute of his arrival?

'Well, Jack, are you getting married in the Easter holidays, or not?'

'No,' he says, 'as a matter of fact, I'm not.'

'Why not? Did you decide against it, or did she?'

'It's all right, Rhian,' he says, noticing, I suppose, the way I'm glaring at her. 'Don't worry, I was going to tell you sooner or later.'

'So you may as well tell both of us,' Ilona says blithely,

'because she'll tell me everything eventually.'

'It was her father,' he says.

There's such a long pause, then, that I get my coat on, thinking it's as much as he's going to say. It was her father who had ... advised postponing the wedding, perhaps.

'What about her father?' Ilona asks. 'What exactly did he say?'

Jack sighs. 'It's a long story.'

'Well,' Ilona says, settling down more comfortably into her chair, 'let's have it. It'll do you good to get it off your chest.'

Jack looks at each of us in turn, seeming none too anxious to unburden himself.

'What does her father do?' Ilona asks. 'Start there. What does he look like? How old is he?'

'Works on the railway. A clerk, I think. Quite ordinary-looking. Short and thick-set. About fifty.'

'And the mother?'

'A step-mother. Quite ordinary-looking, too. A bit younger.'

I try to help him. 'I remember Mary saying she didn't get on very well with her step-mother.'

'She seemed all right. She seemed concerned about her. There are two step-sisters, too, about seven and eight. But I only saw them for about ten minutes and then they were off to bed. There's a dog as well, nearly blind. A big yellow dog. Carlo.'

'Let's get back to the father,' Ilona says in her most patient voice. 'He seemed quite a nice chap, did he?'

'Yes. He took me out to his local after supper. I deserved a drink, he said.'

'Did he mention Alun Brooke?' I ask.

'Don't take any notice of that girl,' Ilona says. 'She's obsessed with Alun Brooke.'

'Mary hadn't told them about Alun Brooke. They didn't know she was engaged to him. They didn't even know of his existence.'

'He didn't *have* any existence,' Ilona says, her eyes turned to the ceiling. 'That's the whole point.'

'But the Head had sent them a telegram asking them to phone him at school, and he told them about him – I mean Alun Brooke – and about Form 3C and about me and how he was convinced she was having a mental breakdown. And a lot more, it seems – Alfie Morris and so on.'

Jack looks very upset.

Even Ilona seems a little downcast. 'Yes,' she says, 'I get the picture. The father, Mr Powell, this rather old, quite ordinary-looking man, thanks you for being kind to his daughter and advises you to hold your horses until she recovers her mental stability. Something like that.'

'Something like that,' Jack says. 'Yes, that's right. Something like that.'

There's another long silence. The small fire, which we've decided to let out, collapses quietly into the grate. For a time, we stare at the dying embers.

'Well then, we'd better go,' Ilona says. 'They shut at ten.'

I don't feel at all like a first visit to a pub, but I dare not say so.

'The thing about a pub,' Ilona says as we sit down at a small round table in a rather dark and very crowded room, 'is that everyone is here wanting to talk, to escape some stress or forget some trouble. No-one is here for any grave or serious purpose. That's what's good about a pub. People talk and argue but it's not a debating society with voting at the end. It's nothing at all really, but a pleasant way of wasting time.'

'They've sold out of beer,' Jack says. 'There's only this stuff. Drink up, Rhian, it's good for you.'

It's dark and unpleasant, not unlike the ten-year-old iron tonic I recently found for my mother.

'It's stout,' Ilona tells me. 'A bit of an acquired taste. Leave it if you don't like it, I'll finish it for you.'

Some men are singing a hymn in the other bar. A superb counter-tenor orbits the last verse, but the general feeling in our bar is that he's showing off. 'It's that Ieuan Harris again' someone mutters. A pub is obviously not the place for choir practice.

After about five minutes, Ilona gives Jack money for

another round. It's not the thing, she tells me, for women to go up to the bar.

Apart from us, there are only two women, with about twenty-five or thirty men, and none apparently in the other bar.

'Of course, they'd like it to be men only,' Ilona says. 'Welshmen are always happiest without women around. Even at funerals they try to keep us away. They pretend it's because we're not up to it emotionally, that they want to protect us, but of course it's not that. Even death is more bearable in a black huddle of men ... With the women in floral overalls seeing to the food.'

We watch Jack pushing his way through the smoke with two more glasses of stout.

'Take Jack, now,' she continues, 'I bet he's never brought a woman to the pub before tonight.'

'No, I haven't,' Jack says. 'And now I've got two.'

'He doesn't look too miserable.'

'No. I feel happier than I have for a long time. Except that Gwynn Morgan is just coming over, look, so I've got the feeling I'm going to lose at least one of you.'

'Drink up,' Ilona tells me.

Gwynn sits at my side without a word. My heart is thumping so loudly, he must be able to hear it. Ilona lights a cigarette. Jack stares at his drink. I can't think of anything at all to say.

I suppose this is what I'd intended all along. After all, wasn't I well aware that he comes to the Ship most nights?

'How's the wife?' Jack asks, after what seems an interminable time.

'How's the portrait going?' Ilona asks. 'What do you think of it? Is it good?'

Words start to flow. I try to listen to them, even to add a few of my own. Soon the room is thick with words and smoke. Gwynn's knee is pressed hard against mine.

'*I bob un sy'n fyddlon*' starts up from the other bar. For a few moments we listen to tenors and basses exhorting us to enlist on God's side against the Devil. After a verse or two, Jack joins in.

93

I smile tenderly at Gwynn.

'Such a pleasure to see you here,' he whispers, after the thorough trouncing of Satan's legions. 'Now I've got everything I want under one roof.'

I clutch his arm. 'Wine, women and hymns.'

'That's right,' he says.

When we leave, it's very dark and the sea is loud and rough. The four of us stand for a while clutching the cold railings, listening to the waves crashing on to the rocks. The singers, still in good voice, have started on an anthem and the wind accompanies them as they walk up Marine Terrace.

'It's too cold here,' Ilona says. 'I'm going home. Are you coming with me, Jack?'

'We're coming, too,' Gwynn says.

They lead the way and we follow. Ilona has taken Jack's arm, but in spite of the darkness, I'm not so daring.

'What did Celine say about your call-up papers?'

'She didn't make such a fuss as you did.'

I can't see the expression on his face, but his voice sounds as though he's rather proud of it; the fuss I made.

'It came as such a shock to me.'

'You think of me as an old man, do you?'

'I suppose it must have been that. A venerable old man. Far too old to go to war.'

'Too old, too old for anything,' he says, his voice still full of pride and tenderness.

I want him to crush me in his arms. My mouth is dry. My flesh and my bones desire him, but I'm too nervous even to take his arm.

Ilona turns back towards us. 'Jack and I are going for some fish and chips. What about you two?'

'No, I've got to get home,' Gwynn says. 'Will you go with them, Rhian?'

'No, I need to get back, too.'

He and I walk up Hill Street on our own.

'I had quite a shock to see you in the pub,' he says. 'Will you come again?'

'I expect so.'

'And another shock to see Jack with Ilona Hughes. How long has that been going on?'

'There's nothing going on between those two. No, Jack's accounted for. He's seeing Mary Powell again in the holidays. Though they're not getting married. Not at the moment, anyway.'

'I know. He told me about her mother.'

'About her mother? He didn't tell us anything about her mother.'

'Her mother died in an asylum, it seems. She became ill when Mary was born and never recovered. Mary's father took Jack out to a pub and put him in the picture.'

We don't speak for some minutes. The hill seems steeper than usual.

'But that doesn't mean anything, does it? Mary doesn't have to be insane because her mother was.' My voice is shrill.

'No, I know. All the same, no-one could say that she's altogether normal, could they? No-one could describe her as well-balanced.'

Poor Mary. I'm ashamed of my anger and impatience towards her; I should have been kinder. I look up at Gwynn. 'How cruel life is.'

'I know, love, I know. Life seems pretty terrible for everyone at the moment.'

'That's true.'

I find I'm almost pleased about it; the way it evens things out. 'It'll certainly be terrible for me when you go away. I won't be able to bear it.' I put my hands over my ribs to steady the sudden thumping of my heart.

'And I thought you were still angry with me,' Gwynn says.

'No. Didn't you get my note?'

'No.'

'I sent you a note by a little girl from 3C. Mali Vaughan. Third period this afternoon.'

'I didn't get it. I was in my room all afternoon.'

'Where the devil did she take it? She certainly took it somewhere. She came back looking very pleased with herself.'

'She probably took it to the Head. She's not very bright, Mali Vaughan. What was in it?'

'Nothing much. A few words of love, that's all.'

If he's worried, he doesn't show it. As we reach Sea View, he puts his arm around my shoulder and pulls me towards him. For a second or two, I can feel his breath on my cheek; I can smell his skin.

Chapter Ten

The Easter holidays. Ilona Hughes goes home to Brynteg for the week-end. She's been tired and irritable for the last few weeks so it may do her some good to get away. She has a perm before she goes. She looks different. 'You look different,' I tell her. 'Different better or different worse?' 'Just different.' Why do I have to be so honest? It cost fifteen shillings. Telling a little lie wouldn't kill me.

Gwynn takes his wife to Anglesey where he's got a brother, a sister-in-law and nephews and nieces. He promises to send me a postcard. When I ask him whether he'll miss me, he becomes angry. 'Don't flirt with me. You know how I feel towards you, don't trivialise our love.' I go over and over the words in a sweet daze. He's got his medical a week after he gets back.

As soon as he goes, I'm as miserable and lonely as if he'd already been sent abroad. He says he and Celine are nothing to each other now, nothing but friends. But people get closer on holiday. I keep thinking of them walking arm in arm along quiet Anglesey lanes.

The Allied invasion of France is expected in late spring or early summer, but surely Gwynn won't be involved in that. At his age, he'll surely be stationed in this country or in England. I suppose Huw is bound to be in the fighting; every night I try to pray for his safety. The anger I felt towards him seems to have completely gone. What I feel now is a despairing kind of affection; he seems someone I knew and cared about a long time ago; I don't love him, I shouldn't have married him. I know I'm going to hurt him, but at least

I won't do it lightly.

All in all, I'm in a turmoil of love and anxiety and guilt. 'How are you?' my mother asks when I get home. 'Me? Oh, I'm fine.'

My mother is well again and very busy with six calves, thirteen piglets and several broods of chicks and ducklings.

Alfredo has forged ahead with his English by this time, reading and understanding newspaper headlines and talking well. Unfortunately it's much more difficult for him to get out in the evenings; the friend who covered for him having been transferred to another camp. However he seems to find it necessary to give Gino and Martino some help and advice several times a week, so we still see him fairly often.

On the Saturday after Easter, I watch him and my mother mending a fence. He's several inches shorter than my father was, but he has the very same way of tackling a job, the same unhurried way of walking round, studying the problems from every angle, the same economy of movement when he gets started, the same easy grace. Every time I see him I'm reminded of my father.

When the fence is finished, my mother goes to feed the calves in the upper field and he comes up to the house alone.

I offer to make him a cup of tea but he says he wants only my company in talk.

'The war is over already in six months,' he says, 'and then I must go to my country to see my sons.'

'How old are they?'

'In between boy and man. Not old enough for the army.'

'Do they work on the land?'

He shrugs his shoulders. 'I have no letters for many months. Perhaps they work, perhaps not.'

'They'll be very glad to see you.'

He frowns. 'Glad? I don't know glad.'

'Happy. They'll be happy to see you.'

'Yes. Also, they'll be happy and glad to see your mama.'

Does the poor deluded man imagine that my mama is going to go with him to Italy? She's never been out of Wales except on a day trip to Shrewsbury. Which she didn't enjoy.

'Is she going with you to Italy?'

He smiles at this ridiculous notion. 'No, no. After the war

98

is all over, my sons will come here.'

'Good.'

'To see my wedding and my home.'

Gwynn was right. He said they'd marry when the war was over.

'Of course. Very good. Perhaps one of them will stay here with you?'

'No. I think this country is too cold for young men to be happy and glad.'

'But not too cold for you?'

He lifts his chest and throws out his arms. 'But I have a wife and much work, I think.'

'I hope you like my idea,' he says then.

'Oh, I do.'

I go for a walk in the afternoon. It's sunny, but the wind is cold. The buds on the sycamore trees are shell-pink and almost ready to burst open. The hedges are a faint delicate green and there are violets and celandines everywhere.

I feel as emotional as I used to when I was fifteen. Then, I knew that the word for the mood threatening to overwhelm me was 'yearning', but what I was yearning for, I was never quite sure. For love I suppose; I certainly never wanted adventure or travel or money or to get away from home. Now at least I know why I'm so close to tears; I love Gwynn and can't have him. I bang my fist against the trunk of a tree. We could be happy together. We're well-suited, with similar backgrounds and ideas and ideals. We're moved by the same things. The same things make us laugh.

He says he loves me. Perhaps it's a love a man feels for a younger woman when he's been married for twenty years, something essentially trivial which he'll indulge in just as long as it doesn't threaten his marriage. I don't think so. When he says, 'I love you. You love me,' there seems a weight of truth in his words. I choose to believe in his love, but I must also accept that he can't leave his wife. Ay, there's the rub.

I know I could leave Huw, but that's different, because he's young enough to start a new life. I'm sure that I'll never live with him again. That makes me sad, too; sad and angry at the mistake we made, at the sheer stupidity of it all; the way we let one day and another day follow a first almost unconsidered meeting, until the stranglehold of all those days led to our marriage. I've felt bitter about it often enough, but here on home ground, in the shelter of this round-backed mountain, I feel at my lowest ebb.

Last term, I contrived to see Gwynn for a few moments every day; his loving glances sustained me. We had a longer time together every Monday after the portrait-painting and every Wednesday evening he met my bus and walked home with me. It was something – a great deal – though much less than I wanted. I wanted to risk an out-and-out affair with him, I admit it, but I accepted that he had more to lose, and of course, admired his loyalty even while suffering for it.

Next term, he'll be in the army and I'll lose contact with him. It will be his wife he'll write to, and how will I bear it? I close my eyes against the sudden dazzle of tears.

My self-pity sickens me and I make an effort to switch my thoughts to my mother's affairs, to get some pleasure from the fact that her life now looks full of promise; Alfredo seems hard-working, warm-hearted and uncomplicated. If only his prediction – that the war will be over in six months – comes true. Everyone is waiting for news of the invasion. Ilona has a school-friend living in Worthing who says the whole South Coast is swarming with American soldiers.

Down by the brook, the ferns are unfurling their golden-green and a robin sings a full-throated courting song.

When I walk home the wind has dropped and the rain is full of melting sunshine.

We have bacon and eggs for supper. Rationing, for my mother, means going short of tea and sugar, which we'd always gone short of because of the cost. Of eggs, butter, cheese and meat she has plenty and plenty of home-grown fruit and vegetables. She gives me little quick, sideways glances as she eats, but as usual, says very little.

'I like Alfredo,' I say, when I realise that she's not going to broach the subject. 'He's a good worker and he's interesting and lively.'

'Your father was an exceptional man and a poet,' she says,

as though to bring the conversation to an end before it has a chance to begin.

'I know that. That's not in question. I knew him for years.'

She closes her eyes against my flippancy.

'I know he was,' I continue, more seriously. 'But Alfredo is exceptional too. For instance, he's learnt English very fast.'

She frowns at this, as though what she wants from me is greater loyalty to my father. 'He already knew more than he admitted to you, girl. You made him nervous, that first time.'

'I must say, I'm quite taken by him. But of course, if you're not, that's the end of it. You're the one, after all, who's got herself involved with him.'

I finish eating, lay my knife and fork neatly together as she likes me to, and try to look as though the conversation is now closed. 'I'd like a piece of cheese, please. Or is there pudding?'

'When did you or your father ever go short of pudding?'

'Never.'

'Rice pudding, bread and butter pudding, rhubarb fool, egg custard, Eve's pudding, jam sponge, blackberry tart and cream.'

'Your blackberry tart! That alone is worth coming over from Italy for.'

'Whatever are you talking about, now?'

'Those sons of his. He said something about them coming over on a visit.'

She flings her head back. 'That's all a lot of nonsense. When the war is over, the man will go back to his own country where he belongs.'

'Yes. But he intends to come back here afterwards. He may find there's more for him here than in his own country.'

She goes to the pantry to fetch me some bread and butter pudding left over from our midday meal. It smells of vanilla and eggs.

'It's your cooking he'll come back for,' I tell her. 'My bread and butter pudding tastes like soggy bread and butter, but yours is angel food.'

She doesn't eat pudding – she never has – but enjoys watching me eating mine and doesn't speak until I've finished.

'On the other hand,' she says, 'I don't think your father would want me to be lonely for the rest of my life.'

'He wouldn't. When he was ill, he was terribly concerned about all the extra work you had to do.'

'He was concerned about you, too. Don't ever forget that.'

'I won't.'

'And don't scrape your plate like that, girl. It's not good manners.'

'Why not? It shows appreciation.'

'It seems as though you're hinting for more.'

'I am.'

'Tch, tch, tch.' She loves it when I behave like a child.

'Also,' I say, 'he wouldn't like the thought of the farm being neglected. How could you possibly manage here on your own when Gino and Martino go back to Italy?'

She doesn't answer, but studies her small work-worn hands.

'I couldn't get married in a Roman Catholic church,' she says after a long silence. 'That's definite. It's something I couldn't bring myself to do. It wouldn't be a marriage for me.'

'You wouldn't have to. You could get married in chapel.'

'Oh no, I don't think chapel would be a proper sort of marriage for a Roman Catholic.'

'I'm sure it would. You might both have to go to his church for some sort of ceremony afterwards, but that wouldn't kill you. Not if you were already married. Properly married.'

'And I suppose he'd have to go to confession, too, because of marrying a Christian.'

I look hard at her. Yes, she's completely serious.

'It's been a lovely day today, anyway,' she says. 'Spring again after so much death and destruction. And Gino planted two rows of potatoes this morning and Martino carried manure and dug a trench for the runner beans and the new hens have settled and we'll be able to let the calves out now that the fence is mended. It seems silly to live in the future when April is here, and all May untouched.'

*

102

After washing-up, we go out to watch the resident owl.

People who claim that it rains every day in Wales may be fairly accurate, but they never comment on how fine the evenings are, when the clouds open and the hills are bathed in a warm apricot light and oak and alder and ash are claret and copper.

'Mam, shall we call the new calves, Claret and Copper?'

'No, no, they're Meg and Daisy. Claret and Copper indeed.'

We watch the owl gliding, silver-white and silent, against the sickle moon. We watch him pouncing on some little creature and rising up again in one continuous movement. 'Look. Now he'll go onto that ledge on the cowshed roof and watch, now, how he's shifting the mouse from his claws to his beak, so that he can make a tidy landing back in the nest. There. Beautiful. It's a funny thing, but he doesn't mind me one bit. I could climb up the ladder and have a good look at his wife and chicks, but if you went near he'd probably have your eyes out.'

'You've been telling me that for years and I've been telling you for years that nothing would induce me to climb up to see his old nest.'

'That's all right, then.'

We come into the house again, blinking and shivering. My mother sits by the lamp mending stockings for an hour and then goes to bed.

I stay up until eleven – very late by country standards – and when I finally go upstairs, I'm not at all sleepy. I look through my old school books trying to find something to read, but fail to get interested in anything.

I get undressed and when I'm in my nightgown, sit in front of the small brown-flecked mirror brushing my hair. By candlelight I look interesting, my face bony and shadowed. A woman very nearly beautiful. I think of Celine's portrait. She said she wanted ten sittings; she's already had seven.

I've still not been allowed to see it. Gwynn says the painting of the dark blue dress is excellent, but that my face and body are rather lifeless. Perhaps that's how she wants to see me: a dummy. I wonder if she's jealous about me? The thought makes me tremble.

*

Last night, I dreamed about the war, a frightening dream which seemed to be full of smoke and rotten smells so that when I woke I had to rush to the window to take in gulps of the cold mountain air. I think I was in the trenches of the last war – what account had I read to make it so vivid: the grey mud, the grey corpses, the rats? – but the wounded man I was fighting to save wasn't Huw, but my father. 'Air,' he was saying. 'Give me air,' and I, with my bare hands, was trying to dig the clayey earth away from him, knowing that he was dying and that I was helpless to save him. My father wasn't in the last war, though Llew, his younger brother was, and died on the Somme in 1916.

I can't eat any breakfast this morning, thinking of the men, the many men so beautiful, who are living my sulphurous dream, with no waking from it. 'Pray for Huw', I tell my mother as she sets off for chapel.

'I always do,' she says, 'And for you, too.'

All day, my dream is more real than real life. I listen to 'Forces Favourites' from some undisclosed place in the South of England. I feel awed and humbled by the bravery of the soldiers, by their cheerfulness as they face the certainty of battle, the possibility of death or mutilation.

I'm sick at heart and full of pity for Huw. But I can't love him.

Chapter Eleven

Today was a dreadful day. Over the week-end, the Deputy Head, Talfan Roberts, had had news that his son, Owen, had been shot down over Germany: missing, presumed dead.

He was a brilliant boy who'd won a State Scholarship to Oxford. I remember him at school. He was the Head Prefect when I was in the First Form, so tall and remote that he already looked like one of the masters. Everyone who knew him liked and respected him.

Talfan Roberts teaches Chemistry. He's not a very good teacher; vague and absent-minded, late for classes, sometimes forgetting them altogether, a bit of an old woman – I suppose he must be well over sixty – terrified of draughts and fresh air. Mrs Lewis, History, is always flinging windows open, urging children to take good deep breaths, while Talfan shudders and complains very loudly of the cold and damp. Everyone has a a a soft spot for him.

We have a service at the end of the afternoon as we always do after the death of one of the old boys and this time even the Third Formers are quiet and attentive.

The Head begins with a very long account of the Russian victories in the Ukraine, the number of miles they've advanced, the rivers they've crossed, the railways they've blown up, the number of Germans they've killed and taken prisoner, and at the point when we're all certain that he's had his much-heralded brainstorm, he stops and explains himself. 'I have to give you all this good news,' he says, 'before I can bear to face what is for me the greatest personal tragedy of the war.' And then he gives a very simple and moving account of his friendship with Mr and Mrs Talfan Roberts and his pride in their son. At one point his voice cracks, he loses the thread of his sentence and has to begin again. He finishes very quietly without his usual burst of rhetoric.

I know I'm small-minded, but when people I despise behave well, it makes me feel really uncomfortable. I expected the Head to bellow and roar about the iniquities of the entire German race, not to speak quietly and poignantly about the tragedy of war.

It's my usual policy never to speak to him except to answer a question, but this afternoon I brace myself to go to his room to tell him how moved I was by his address.

To my embarrassment, Mr and Mrs Talfan Roberts are there with him having a cup of tea. He insists on my joining them and because Mrs Roberts is red-eyed, I start to sniff as well. And then the Head puts his arm round my shoulder and says how well I'm bearing the strain of my husband's absence and Mrs Roberts smiles damply at me and passes me a handkerchief.

Short and dumpy, with little round dimpled face and curly grey hair, she doesn't look cut out for tragedy. Even now she looks bewildered; someone who's managed to mislay her spectacles again, rather than a woman who's lost her only son. Mr Roberts, looking even more absent-minded than usual, pats her hand from time to time.

I'm the first to leave. Mrs Roberts asks me to call on her one afternoon after school and I promise to do so – and perhaps I will.

As I walk home, I feel like an old woman conscious of the frailties of her body; the heart labouring, the thinning blood. There have been many casualties, even in our small community, but I can't seem to accept Owen's death; he's always been one of the golden young men everyone talks about. This time the local papers will be right when they pay tribute to a popular local hero. My eyes are burning. If I feel like this, how can his parents survive? They'll never be the same, they'll never get over it, but how will they manage to get through the rest of their lives? How will they even manage to go home this afternoon and think of getting a meal together?

The walk home – just over a mile – has never seemed so

long. I unlock the front door, put down my bag of books, pick up a letter – for Ilona – from the doormat and lower myself into an armchair, too tired to see to the fire.

I can't face any supper. Ilona makes herself some chips and a fried egg. I take a few chips, to please her, but I can hardly swallow them.

After supper, Ilona brings out her knitting, a coral pink cardigan which she'd started before she came here over a year ago. She's a hopeless knitter and she loses her temper whenever anything goes wrong.

The knitting is just one thing too much. 'Aren't you going out tonight?'

'No, I don't think so. Jack said he might call, but I don't feel like going out tonight.'

'When did you see Jack?'

'He called round in his dinner hour. Why?'

'I was wondering whether he'd seen Mary, that's all.'

'Yes, he did. He stayed in Fronilltyd for three days – in some bed and breakfast place. One day he took her for a three-mile walk by the river, another day to a football match. She's feeling much better and she's got a job in a solicitor's office. The money's poor, it seems, but the work is quite interesting. What else? Carlo has passed on and her father's thinking of getting a fox terrier.'

'You had quite a chat.'

'Yes. We had lunch at Glyn Owen's. Steak and kidney pie. You know, brown bread and onion with Bovril gravy. Quite nice.'

'I suppose he mentioned Talfan Roberts's son?'

'Of course. They were in the same form at school. You can imagine how upset he was. Kept on quoting poetry at me. I didn't think Jack was the type to know any poetry. He's full of surprises, don't you think so?'

For a time she concentrates hard on the coral pink knitting. Once again, I have to show her how to decrease.

'I still haven't had a word from that oaf Denzil.'

'Perhaps he's been sent overseas.'

'They'd have given him time to send a letter. Oh, I don't trust anyone any more, I really don't.'

'You said you didn't care for him, anyway.'

107

'I don't *care* for him, no. All the same, I expect him to send me the occasional letter.'

A knock on the door. 'That'll be Jack,' Ilona says, without much joy.

I can hear her at the front door. 'No, I don't think I'll come out tonight, Jack. I know I said I would, but I've changed my mind. I'm a bit down, to tell you the truth, and so is Rhian. Well, you can come in if you want to, but we're not good company. I'm knitting and she's marking books and moaning.'

'Hello Jack,' I say, as he follows her in. 'Isn't it awful about Owen Talfan?'

'Yes,' he says. 'I'm going to get very drunk tonight. I was hoping Ilona'd come out to keep me company.'

He's wearing a dark suit with a dark, sombre tie. 'You're dressed for a prayer-meeting,' I tell him.

'That's what my landlady said. But I think sinking seven or eight pints will do me more good.'

We're all silent. Ilona takes up her knitting again. 'You deserve to be miserable,' she tells Jack.

I stare at her. I suppose she's angry that he hasn't broken off his engagement to Mary.

'We're both miserable,' Jack tells me.

'You and Mary?'

'No. Ilona and me.'

I look from one to the other for an explanation. Jack studies his black shoes as though seeing them for the first time.

Ilona sighs and puts her knitting down. 'Yes,' she says, 'He's promised to marry Mary Powell at the end of July and I'm having a baby in September.'

We all fall silent.

I feel stunned, quite unable to come to grips with this last shock. 'What a way to let me know,' I manage to say after a few moments.

It's typical of her, though. Not to have involved me in any of the initial doubts and fears; to go through all that on her own, and then to tell me about it as casually as if it's a kitten or a puppy she's decided to have. I feel angry as well as shocked and frightened.

108

'And fancy telling Jack before you tell me.'

'Well, he makes me so mad, that's why. He thinks he's the only one with problems. Anyway, I didn't want to worry you.'

'I thought friends were supposed to share their worries.'

'You've got enough of your own, I can manage mine. I won't be any trouble to you, I promise. I'll be leaving here soon, taking my dreadful secret with me.'

'Don't be melodramatic. You don't have to go anywhere.'

Even as I'm saying it, I know it's not true. My mother-in-law would raise hell if she realised Ilona was pregnant. In her mind it would be as bad as if I was keeping a brothel.

'Have you told Denzil?' I ask her.

'Denzil? *Denzil?* It's nothing to do with Denzil. Do you think I'd want to marry Denzil? I don't want to marry anyone, to tell you the truth. I'll have my Gran's little house when she dies and perhaps I'll open a shop in the front parlour. I can look after myself. Don't waste time worrying about me.'

'You can't be as brave as you pretend, Ilona.'

'Why not? It hasn't come as a complete surprise, girl, has it? It's something I've been half-expecting for years. No-one can go on being lucky for ever. Don't look at me like that, Jack. I've never pretended to be a boring little virgin, have I? If you think I'm common, just walk out and leave me alone.'

'Of course I don't think you're common,' Jack says. 'What's the matter with you? I spend all my time telling you how very . . . uncommon I think you are.'

Is he now hankering after Ilona? He notices me staring at him.

'Have you had a letter from Huw?' he asks me. 'You hadn't heard from him last time I was here.'

Ilona doesn't let me answer. 'Why do you come round here bothering me?' she asks him, real anger in her voice. 'You've got Mary, haven't you? I should think that woman would be more than enough for anyone.'

'Everything is so sad,' I say. 'I've recently had two letters, but nowadays they only make me realise how little Huw and I have in common. 'Is anybody happy? I'd like to think that someone, somewhere is really happy.'

'I'm happy,' Ilona says. 'Honestly I am and I've only just realised it. Yes, I'm happy. I'm twenty-five years old, I've got a bit of money saved and I'm going to have a baby. How bloody marvellous. I've always been a rebel, people have always prophesied that I'll end up badly, so they'll be delighted to be proved right. But perhaps they'll end up envying me. Oh, it's not going to be easy, I realise that. People who find they can't make me feel ashamed of myself will try to make me feel guilty for the baby's sake. "The poor little mite. Have you thought of his struggles, an outcast from civilized society?" I'll have to put up with all that sort of thing.'

'I think the war has made people a little more tolerant,' Jack says.

'Dr Samuel wondered whether I might consider adoption, whether I might consider making a childless couple happy. "Do I look like a Charity?" I asked him. "Do I look as though I care a damn about any childless couple?" He wondered, then, whether I realised how narrow-minded people could be to women in my position. Of course I realise it. Those wives who have such a hell of a life, a houseful of children, no money and husbands who get fighting drunk and beat them up every Saturday night; the most powerful emotion they've got left is anger for any woman who doesn't conform.'

'Marriage isn't always like that,' Jack says. 'It doesn't have to be like that.'

'No, that's the extreme. But even at best, it's an unequal partnership. You're going to get married, or so you say, to a woman you already know to be totally unbalanced. How long is it going to take you to feel enormously proud of yourself and contemptuous of her? Your marriage is doomed before it even begins. What you want to do, Jack, is take stock of yourself and decide what you really want out of life.'

'There are plenty of marriages where it's the man who suffers,' Jack says. 'When a woman constantly belittles a man, *he's* the one bound to suffer.'

When I married Huw I'd hardly considered the problems of marriage. It was simply what two people did, usually when they were in their early twenties; got married and then had children.

'You can't believe any good of any man, can you?' Jack asks. 'You can't believe that I, for instance, have an earnest desire to be a good husband and to make a woman happy. And I feel I stand a chance with Mary. She's vulnerable and insecure and I think I'll be able to restore her self-confidence.'

'No, you won't,' Ilona says. 'She won't respect a man she's been able to manipulate.'

'Anyway, I've already bought her an engagement ring. It would kill her if I broke with her now.'

'Kill her? Great Heavens, why should it kill her?'

Jack looks even more miserable. 'Oh, it's not that I think I'm God's great gift or anything like that. Far from it. But Mary's already suffered enough and it would be another blow wouldn't it? Wouldn't it? What do you think, Rhian?'

'Yes, it would, I'm sure. But I still think it's what you should do. After all, it's what you want to do. It's obvious. You're sitting here now because you want Ilona to go on persuading you to give her up. If you were really intent on marrying Mary, you'd think Ilona was a great busybody and have nothing more to do with her.'

By this time Ilona has started growling at her knitting. 'Look, I'll finish that cardigan for you,' I tell her. 'The part I do will look a bit different because I'm a decent knitter, but the strain of watching you mauling it about is too much for me.'

'Thank you,' Ilona says, handing it over to me as though it were a dangerous animal.

I take the almost-finished left front, undo a few rows, pick up the stitches and carry on. I'm suddenly bored with Jack's problem. I realise how little I care for Mary. We were always considered friends because we were the only two young women on the staff, but I never felt much warmth for her and all I feel for her now is contempt and pity. I must be looking quite fierce because I notice both Ilona and Jack staring at me.

'What's the matter?' I ask them.

'I saw your portrait last night,' Jack says. 'I was having

111

supper with Gwynn and his wife and she showed it to me. It's a good likeness.'

'Is it? I haven't been allowed to see it. Gwynn told me that my dress is good, but that my body is wooden and my face blank. Well, perhaps my face is blank.'

'I'm not saying anything,' Ilona says. 'I'm certainly not going to risk offending you till you finish that cardigan.'

'Gwynn's got his medical next week,' Jack says. 'He's not at all keen to join up. On the quiet, I think he's a bit of a rebel like you, Rhian. He kept saying how he'd like to be English with no doubts about the rights and wrongs of the war. I don't think he'll be a very enthusiastic soldier.'

'I suppose he'll only be a sort of teacher anyway,' Ilona says. 'Something in the Education Corps, a different sort of teacher. He won't be a fighting soldier. Not at his age.'

'He's fit enough,' Jack says, 'and he's not much over forty.'

'I didn't see him in school today. I went up to his room at dinner-time, but he wasn't there. Perhaps he went home.' To my embarrassment, my voice is high and unsteady.

'I don't know. Anyway, he's calling here later on. He's got some holiday sketches he wants to show you. I saw them last night. They're very good.'

He's calling here later on. I want to fling my arms about and shout. I go on counting stitches very carefully.

'I will come out for that drink, Jack,' Ilona says, 'I think perhaps a pregnant woman needs something stronger than tea.'

Oh, bless you, Ilona.

She puts her jacket on and goes to look at herself in the mirror over the mantelpiece. 'Hey, why didn't you tell me I'd got a letter?'

'I'm sorry. I was so upset, I forgot about it.'

'It's from that idiot, Denzil. At last. And just half a page, look. He's hopeless. "We had a terrible journey with lots of – something" – a word I can't read. "Everyone says there's going to be a party soon" I suppose that means the invasion. "I'm quite looking forward to it" What a fool. "I hope it doesn't get too noisy." It will, boy, it will. "If you marry me, I'll come back to effing Wales and find work in those effing

112

quarries." He can't spell quarries after three attempts. "I bet we'll have some good times. What do you say? Love and all that, Denzil." '

'He's going to make an honest woman of you,' I tell her.

'An illiterate barrow-boy from Liverpool,' she says. 'Is that all you think I deserve?'

'You're delighted to have heard from him, anyway. Look at you, grinning away like a cat.'

'Of course I am. We got on very well. I liked him, I certainly didn't want to think he'd forgotten me after a couple of weeks. On the other hand, the last thing in the world I want is to marry him. Get that into your thick skull.'

'He could help you with that little shop.'

'You just want me to be tied up like you are.'

'You're already tied up, my girl. Good and proper.'

While we're teasing each other, I happen to catch sight of Jack who's looking completely distraught. 'Let's go,' he says quietly. 'I really need that drink.'

Gwynn arrives almost as soon as they leave.

My heart is thudding, but I try to remain calm. 'I'm glad you could come. Hasn't it been a terrible day? I tried to see you in the dinner hour.'

'I'm sorry. I felt I had to call on Mrs Talfan Roberts. How are you?'

'Better now. Much better now. Did you have a good holiday?'

'No. Did you?'

'No. How could I be happy?'

'How was your mother?'

'Quite well again, thank you. How is Celine?'

'She's well, too. Have you heard from Huw?'

'Yes. Two letters. He's all right.'

'You're pale. Are you eating properly?'

'I'm always pale. Especially when I'm happy,'

That's as much as we have to say. For the next half-hour we look at each other and sigh. I feel the same peace as I sometimes do when I stare out at the hills.

I don't tell him how unhappy I've been.

He doesn't show me his holiday sketches.

113

Chapter Twelve

This week Gwynn's wife has a throat infection and doesn't feel well enough to resume work on the portrait, so I don't get my afternoon tea with all the sweet pleasure that involves.

I'm hoping that Ilona will suggest a walk to the Ship tonight, but she doesn't. She's in a strange mood; all the pleasure she pretended to feel – or indeed felt – about her pregnancy last week seems to have vanished; now she seems angry and bitter. She's not even hungry.

While writing my weekly letter to Huw, I try to persuade her to write to Denzil.

'Leave me alone,' she says. 'Stop trying to push Denzil at me.'

'I'm not. I'd rather push Jack at you, if anyone.'

She doesn't seem to have heard me.

'Jack is more than ready to fall in love with you,' I say carefully.

She still makes no response.

'Aren't you interested?'

'No. Jack's a fool. A nice enough lad, but a fool.'

'Ilona, have you ever been in love?'

'Yes. But not with Denzil and not with Jack. So shut up about them both.'

'Tell me about it. About being in love.'

'What the hell is there to say? You know exactly what it's like.'

'An ache of pleasure? A torment of delight?'

'Whatever you say.'

'Do you know, Ilona, I was desperately in love with Gwynn when I was sixteen, seventeen. I've never told you that. But I thought it was adolescent foolishness. I never felt anything remotely like it for Huw, so I thought the calm way I felt about him was love grown sensible and mature. How sad it all is.'

'I think I'll have an early night. Nothing depresses me as much as people droning on about love.'

'Take the hot-water bottle, then. There's going to be another frost tonight. Who'd think it was May?'

'All the books and the poems and the songs. Love, love, love. And it wings straight past them like a stone skimming out to sea.'

'Don't forget the hot-water bottle.'

'Go to hell. I like being cold.'

My mother is in the middle of spring cleaning. She's been clearing away my father's books; definite proof, if more were needed, that she intends to marry Alfredo. She's filling a large trunk with all the things she wants me to have.

'Right. These china cows and the set of jugs he had from his auntie. I want you to take them. And the brass candlesticks that came from his grandmother and all his books.'

'I'd like them, of course. I'll treasure them. But what's the hurry? It doesn't make much sense to take them away now.'

'No, I'm sure it doesn't make much sense. Not to anyone but me. I'll be happier, that's all.'

'In that case, I'll get Huw's father to fetch them in his van.'

'Will he come? Has he got the petrol?'

'He's always ready to put himself out if it means acquiring anything for nothing.'

'These things are for you, not for him.'

'They'll be in the family, though, won't they? And Huw is the head of the family. To him, I'm just Huw's wife living in Huw's house.'

'That's how things are. That's how things have always been.' She sighs and sits down at the table opposite me. 'This war is turning everything upside down. Look at you. You're getting used to earning too much money and being your own

116

boss. It's going to be difficult for you to knuckle down to being a housewife. You got married too soon. I said enough. If you were still single, engaged to Huw, not married, and still living in those digs in Iorwerth Place, you'd have more to look forward to and less to give up.'

'You're right. When it comes to handing yourself over to a man, lock, stock and barrel, you certainly need to be sure it's the right one.'

I've gone too far. She sits up straight, her bright blue eyes smiting me. 'You've chosen your man. I'm not talking about that.'

I try to placate her. 'You chose the right one, anyway. Anyone could sense how close you were, how well your marriage worked.'

'It had to work. There was no other way. Knowing that made it easy.'

'I understand that. Even if you'd chosen wrongly, you'd still have had to stick together to make the farm pay. Yes, but the atmosphere here would have been different.'

'We were a Christian family.'

'All right. I was lucky to have been brought up in a Christian family where "love one another" was practised not just preached.'

'I don't know what that means and I don't want to know. I've never wanted to talk about private matters. In this house there was Christian love – and whom God has joined together, let no man put asunder.'

'You think Christian marriage ensures this ever-present flow of love?'

'I'm not as feeble-minded as you seem to think, my girl. Christian marriage is only the first step. The second step is two people's determination to make it work because it's the only choice they've got, the only road before them.'

'Divorce being always wrong?'

'Divorce? Divorce is only for the rich and foolish. Who ever heard of divorce round here – except for Lord Killin who never had anyone's respect in the first place, so had nothing to lose.'

'There are unhappy marriages round here, though, you can't deny that. What about Eben Jenkins and Louisa? They didn't speak to each other for years. Used to leave notes for each other behind the clock. Made their children's lives a misery.'

'There'll always be a few stubborn people who can't pull together.'

'So wouldn't it be better for those people to part?'

'No. Who knows when the day and the hour may come when their hearts shall be reconciled again.'

I let her have the last word. All the same, I've never felt more sure that my life with Huw is over, that I married him without thought, that to remain married to him and have his children would be an act of wickedness and folly. And naturally I'm aware that there's no easy way out. How will my mother take it? Is a woman who leaves her husband even eligible for a teaching job in this part of the world where there are already too many teachers? What else could I do for a living? If only Ilona and I could go away together and start some new life. If we were English it would be easy; English women have such self-confidence.

'Do you remember those two English women who ran that private school in Llanfryn before the war? Betty Price went there when she failed the scholarship.'

'In that big house next to the cottage hospital? Yes. Croft School they called it. The girls wore grey and red uniforms. The fees were very high, they say, and the dinners cost more than dinners in the Dolphin. Anyway, Betty Price didn't learn much for all the good money spent on her. Her mother used to boast about those elocution lessons she was having, but when I asked the girl about them, she could only remember that you had to pronounce Powell like pole. What a lot of nonsense. The name comes from Ap Hywel, so how can you make pole out of that. They'll be telling us to pronounce Hywel like hole next. She's got three or four children now, anyway, so I don't suppose she remembers much about any of the fancy things they were trying to teach her. A very foolish place it seemed to be, run by two very foolish women who'd have been much better off married with children of their own. Private, school indeed. What ever made you think of it?'

I feel I'm in one of those dreams where an avalanche is slowly but surely coming nearer.

'I suppose I'd better be thinking of going back.'

'Yes, I suppose so. I'd better make you a cup of cocoa before you set out.'

'Is Alfredo coming tonight?'

'No, he still can't get out at night. He comes over when he can. I see him once or twice every week.'

'Can I bring Ilona Hughes with me next Wednesday?'

'Of course you can, girl. But I thought she was always out.'

'She's quietened down a lot. She'd like it up here. I've told her about the cowslips in the orchard.'

'I'll make a nice meal, then. Something a bit special.'

'Her boyfriend's been sent away. He was stationed in Tonfaen, but most of them have left there now.'

'This old war! I'm the only one who's got something out of it, it seems to me.'

'And you've only got a Roman Catholic.'

Gwynn isn't meeting the bus. I can't believe it. I ask the driver whether we've arrived earlier than usual but he says no, a few minutes later. I walk as far as the station clock and he's right; it's a quarter to ten.

My heart feels heavy as a stone as I walk home. Why didn't he tell me he wouldn't be meeting me? What's going on? I couldn't go to his house on Monday and tonight, again, I'm not going to see him.

Ilona isn't in, so there's at least a chance that she'll have seen him at the Ship, that they'll have talked together, that he'll have sent me a message; some sort of explanation.

I try to mark some books as I wait for her to come back. 'I really love The Mill on the Floss,' a girl in Form V has written. 'It's one of the books I shall keep for ever, dipping into it every now and then, even when I'm old.'

How could I, my father's daughter, have married a man who doesn't love books? The only books Huw possesses are *The Cricket on the Hearth* – a school prize – *The Rules of Rugby Football* and a hymn book. I didn't even realise that it was important. I didn't think it mattered that he thought Wordsworth was boring and Keats a joke. Dear Huw, Forgive me for being so blind, unable to understand what a child should have understood. I should have known that first time you came down to visit me at college when I'd got tickets for the English department's production of *Duchess of Malfi* and you said over your dead body, and I thought it was amusing. I don't think it amusing now, neither your words nor the determined way you said we'd go to the pictures instead. Why didn't I realise that in letting you decide that, I was already half way to forfeiting my independence? With sadness, Rhian.

I have no-one to blame but myself and that's the most difficult thing to accept.

I don't know what to do. I can't write telling Huw I want to break with him when he's abroad and in danger, but surely to let him think everything is all right between us is equally irresponsible. Will I be able to think more clearly when Gwynn has been called up?

'What's the matter now?' Ilona asks when she comes in. 'Anyone would think that you're the one in trouble.'

Her cheeks are pink from the wind. She's got the sort of face a wicked angel might have, her eyes bright and glittering and her permed hair a frizzy halo round her head.

'I am in trouble. I don't love my husband.'

'Of course you don't. You haven't seen him for three years. No-one can love a photo on the mantelpiece. When he comes back he'll be older and tougher and more experienced, and you'll be older and tougher and more experienced and you'll get on like a house on fire.'

'I don't think so. Anyway, I won't be here to find out. I'm going to leave before he gets back, move right away from Llanfair.'

'No you're not.'

'You don't think I'll have the guts, do you?'

'I don't think you'll be so stupid. Not without finding out what he's like now. He's not going to be the same small-town lad who went away.'

'If he'll have changed at all, it'll be for the worse. I can't think being in the army will improve anyone. You say he'll be tougher, he'll certainly be more insensitive. Think of the things soldiers have to do, the things they have to see. Can those things improve anyone? I don't think so. I know very

120

well that I haven't a hope of any sort of future with Gwynn, but he's made me realise what love could be.'

'Gwynn will never leave his wife.'

'I know that, Ilona. That's exactly what I just said. Why don't you listen to me? Did you see him tonight?'

'No, he wasn't in the Ship. I was with Jack again. There wasn't any beer so we drank lemonade and played dominoes.'

'You ought to marry him, Ilona, just to get him away from Mary Powell.'

'Why should I go round rescuing people? Who do you think I am? The Salvation Army?'

'He's full of promise, somehow. He's developing. He thinks for himself, which is very unusual, especially in a PT teacher.'

'I don't think he will marry her, anyway. I don't see it coming off.'

'He's thoughtful of other people. He's got good manners. I don't mean please and thank you and walking on the outside of the pavement, but the sort of manners that mayketh man.'

Ilona has slumped into her chair, sitting on the small of her back, her legs thrust out in front of her. She yawns very thoroughly. 'Once, when I was seven or eight,' she says, 'a woman gave me a shilling for going to the shop for her. She must have thought it was a ha'penny, but she didn't like to take it back when she saw it was a shilling. That was good manners, wasn't it?'

'What did you do with it?'

'Well, how should I remember? I only remember that feeling I had: half of me thrilled and half of me wanting to give it back to her. I didn't, of course. I didn't get much money. I had an uncle, though, who used to give me half a crown for Christmas and my birthday. I used to have five shillings saved up for the Sunday school trip. We usually went to Rhyl.'

She yawns again, but I don't suggest going to bed. Somehow I'm aware that she's in a warm, confiding state of mind.

'One year I bought a pink chiffon scarf in the Woolworth's there. It was a lovely shade, shell pink perhaps, and it had such a lovely smell. Do you remember how Woolworth's

121

used to smell before the war? Everything bright and new as though there were no such thing as death in the world. Anyway, in the charabanc on the way back, I let a boy fly it out of the window like a banner – it was so beautiful, so soft and shiny. And he let go of it and it blew away. I think that was the worst moment of my life.'

'How in Heaven's name could you have let him have it?' I ask her. With all our worries, she pregnant and I illicitly in love, we're both suddenly full of concern for a sixpenny scarf.

She sighs. 'He was my sweetheart, I suppose. I suppose it was that. I suppose I'd have let him have anything.'

I don't say a word. What is there to say?

'He had my virginity a few years later. I didn't mind losing that half as much.'

A companionable silence descends on us. It seems several minutes before I can bear to break it.

'What happened to him?'

'Don't ask.'

'I'm asking. What happened to him? Where is he now?'

'He married this rich girl. He got her into trouble and they let him marry her. Made him marry her, according to him. Eight or nine years ago now. Oh, Jesus! Things can only get better as far as I'm concerned. D'you know, I'm really looking forward to being old and ugly, and able to be hideously rude to everyone.'

'What was his name?'

'Ifor. Ifor Meredyth.'

'Does he still live in Brynteg?'

'Yes. Well, three miles outside. On his wife's farm. Two children. Could be three by this time, I suppose.'

'Do you ever see him.'

'From time to time. Oh, he tries to keep me interested. Of course I pretend to have got over him, but he's not taken in.'

'And he's the baby's father, I suppose?'

'Yes.'

We sigh like a couple of old women. 'You keep trying to push Denzil at me, but Denzil and I were never like that. We were just mates.'

'I didn't understand. How could I? You've never men-

122

tioned this Ifor Meredyth. I've never heard your voice like that before.'

'Like what?'

'Soft and . . . well . . . a bit sloppy.'

'Soft and stupid,' she says. 'That's me, all right.'

'Does he know about the baby?'

'Yes, he knows. But what can he do about it?'

'I suppose he could leave his wife and set up house with you. If he loved you.'

'Ifor? Ifor doesn't love anyone but himself. His wife is rich, so he's rich. Oh yes, he's somebody in Brynteg; around the market and in the pubs. He's become self-satisfied and important. He's not going to turn his back on all that. Anyway, what about the children? Two little boys, fat as moles, following him about everywhere.'

'Will he help you financially?'

'He'll do what he has to. I'll be all right financially. My Gran's got a bit put by.'

'That's why you left Brynteg, I suppose? Because of him?'

'Yes. Because of him. He thought I should be content with the occasional Saturday night encounters we used to have when he could get away. Well, I wasn't. I started to go around with someone else. To spite him, I suppose. And when he heard about it, God, he was like a madman. Bellowing outside the house for half the night. My father had to go out with a shotgun before he'd go.'

'You had a lucky escape, it seems to me.'

Another long silence.

'No, he was all right, Ifor was. Do you know, Rhian, if I'd been able to marry him, I might have been reasonably happy. I mean that. We'd have had our fights, I know, because we're both of us bad-tempered and stubborn, but we'd have had more good times than bad and a lot of laughs – and that's about as much as you can hope for in this world. And all that prevented it was that rich tart he ran into that Friday night when I'd stayed in to swot for my school certificate.'

'Don't cry,' I say gently, 'please don't cry.'

'Who's crying? Would I cry for bloody Ifor Meredyth?'

'Tears, idle tears, I know not what they mean. Tears from the depth . . .'

123

'And no bloody poetry either, thank you.'

We sit in silence for a little while longer; an occasional sniff from Ilona, an occasional sigh from me. It's long past midnight when we finally go up to bed.

Chapter Thirteen

Gwynn passes his medical and has to join up in two weeks' time. I think he'll go on trying to avoid me now until he leaves home. He smiles quite warmly at me when he sees me in Assembly, occasionally I catch him looking at me from the Art room window when I'm crossing the playground, but he's never in his room when I try to see him in the lunch hour. Perhaps it's for the best as far as he's concerned, but I'm beginning to feel more and more desperate, as though he's trying to deny everything that's happened between us: all the fond words and silences, all the love. I don't feel I can bear it much longer; today I'm too restless even to sit over a cup of tea in the staff room.

In this agitated state; love and uncertainty gnawing at me like hunger, I make the sudden decision to go to his house. Last week he put me off saying that Celine had a sore throat, today I'll pretend to think she's ready to carry on working.

As soon as my last lesson is over, I rush home and put on the blue dress – a dress I've still never worn except to go to their house – and more powder and lipstick than usual because I'm so pale, and manage to get to the house at the usual time. My heart is banging against my ribs as I ring the doorbell.

Celine is quite obviously taken aback when she sees me, but I pretend not to notice, walking into the hall as I usually do. 'I'm sorry you weren't well last week,' I murmur, as casually as I can. She's looking almost as ill as I am. For a moment I feel a pang of pity for her, imagining her worried about Gwynn leaving home. She's wearing a loose, grey dress, a less bizarre garment than usual. I try to smile at her.

She doesn't smile. 'Very well,' she says. 'Come in. Perhaps you should see what I've done. Perhaps it will do you some good.'

I follow her to the studio, disturbed at her words and her manner, knowing now that I definitely wasn't expected, that I'm definitely not welcome. What's happened?

The painting is on the easel facing me. I know it's the painting of me only because I recognise the dark blue dress, the face has been completely obliterated. It looks as though several tubes of paint; green, black and grey, have been squeezed out over it and the resulting mess stirred up together.

Celine doesn't say a word and neither do I. This is no laughing matter: not an artist's playful revenge on work which won't come right, but something different. I feel as though I've been punched in the stomach. I try to say something, my mouth opens but no words come out. There's a rushing noise in my ears.

I look at the painting again, at the swirling green cow-pat covering the face. The light in the room is a strange blue. I gulp air and realise that I'm going to faint.

When I come round, I find Jack standing above me fanning me with a newspaper. I'm lying quite comfortably on the floor, a cushion under my head. Celine has disappeared.

'You're all right,' Jack says. 'You're quite all right. I'm going to open one of the windows now and then you shall sit up.'

I watch him struggling with the window. The portrait has been turned to the wall.

'Where is she?' I ask.

He helps me sit up. 'Well done,' he says. 'Take some deep breaths now. Good girl. Yes, your colour's coming back. Tell me when you feel like getting to your feet. There's no hurry.'

'Where is she? Where's Celine?'

'Gone upstairs, I think. A bit upset. Don't worry about her. Don't worry about anything. Do you feel like sitting in a chair now? That's the way. I'll get you a glass of water. If you feel faint again, put your head right down between your knees.'

When Jack leaves the room, I get to my feet, but have to sit down again very quickly. 'I've never fainted before,' I tell him when he comes back with the water.

'Haven't you? Well, you're quite good for a beginner. Quite promising.'

'Why are you here?'

'I was fetching something for Gwynn. He's in my digs. They've had an almighty row, he and Mrs Morgan. I suppose you know. Do you feel like trying to walk, now?'

'I didn't know. He should have told me. He hasn't spoken to me for days. I only heard about his medical from Mrs Lewis.'

'Rhian, I don't think you're fit to walk home yet, I'll phone for the station taxi.'

'The taxi? Are you sure? Sam Jones will think I've been away for a dirty week-end . . . How long did you say Gwynn had been in your digs?'

'Since Mrs Morgan got the letter. I'll just go to make the phonecall.'

I follow him to the hall. 'What letter? What do you mean?'

He orders the taxi before turning to me again. 'You'll have to ask Gwynn about it. I thought you knew.'

'Please tell me, Jack. Gwynn hasn't told me anything. I only came here because I was feeling so desperate. Jack, you must know how I feel about him. Take pity on me. Please tell me about this letter.'

'Let's go outside then and wait by the gate.'

He holds my arm as we negotiate the steps; I feel as weak and helpless as an old woman.

'Do you remember writing Gwynn a note at the end of last term and asking Mali Vaughan to take it to him?'

'Yes.'

'Apparently she didn't know where to find him, and being more than a bit backward, she put it in her blazer pocket, hoping everyone would forget about it.'

'Oh, God.'

'Her mother found it during the holidays, questioned her about it and in her great wisdom brought it up here last week.'

127

'And Gwynn's wife read it?'

'And Gwynn's wife read it. Yes.'

'I think I'm going to faint again.'

'No you're not. Here's the taxi, look.'

'Whatever did the letter say? I can't remember. "I'm sorry. All my love, Rhian." Only that, I think. I can't remember.'

'Don't rack your brains about it. I suppose Gwynn didn't want to tell you, in case you'd feel guilty.'

'I do feel guilty. Of course I feel guilty. It's all my fault.'

The taxi driver, old Bert Owen, can hardly believe that he's been called out to take us less than a quarter of a mile. To placate him, Jack spends the entire journey talking about the International they'd both been to at Twickenham in 1936.

'No charge, mun,' Bert tells him as we get to the house.

'Have this for a drink, then.'

'Are you sure now? Well, thank you, mun.'

What am I going to do? No wonder Gwynn isn't talking to me. How could I have been so careless?

'Jack, don't come in,' I say when I've unlocked the door. 'Go back to Gwynn's wife. Please. Tell her I'm ashamed of that letter. Tell her I admit to being in love with Gwynn, but that he's not in love with me. That's what she should know. That's all she should be concerned about. Tell her he hasn't been in touch with me for a whole week. Will you do that for me, Jack?'

'She probably won't let me tell her anything. She only let me in before so that I could see to you. She left you in a dead faint on the floor and rushed to the door as though she knew it would be someone with a First Aid diploma, Grade One.'

'Oh Jack, you're the only one who can help me. Please do this for me.' The scent of lilac drifts down from next-door's bush. There's a blackbird somewhere singing his heart out. 'Please.'

I lie down on the sofa, feeling faint again. There seems no way out of this mess. Gwynn has to leave home in less than two weeks ... and how can he leave an estranged wife? I never wanted this to happen, I never wanted to endanger his twenty-year-old marriage and he never, for a moment, let me think that he would countenance it. He told me he loved Celine and that I was, what did he say, the object of his desire. And that was enough for me. How could I have written that silly, careless letter? How could I have sent it to him? Why didn't I realise the danger when Gwynn told me he hadn't received it? I suppose I took it for granted that it would turn up on his desk the next day and didn't even take the trouble to check that it had. What can I do? What if Celine won't see Jack?

There's a knock on the door and I rush to answer it without even putting my shoes back on.

It's the Head. Old Smiley himself. We look at each other warily. I have to ask him in.

'Expecting someone?' he asks as he follows me into the sitting room. – He's never seen me dressed-up before.

I shuffle into my shoes, pull my bag of books off the armchair and ask him to sit down.

'I'll come straight to the point,' he says. 'I received a letter this afternoon from Mrs Gwynn Morgan and in it she enclosed the little note you'd written to her husband.'

'May I see it?'

'Of course.'

He gives me the note and one of his deadliest smiles. 'Naturally I was aware that you and Mr Morgan were spending too much time together. I believe I warned you about it.'

'Yes.'

I read the letter. 'I'm sorry for all the harsh things I said. You're right, I am immature and over-emotional and too much in love and too fearful of your safety.'

It's more revealing than I'd remembered. I put it on the table between us and look up at him.

'I must answer Mrs Morgan's letter,' he says. 'What shall I tell her?'

I watch him looking round the room, taking in yesterday's ashes in the grate, the dust and the clutter. Why should I help him with his reply?

'Mr Morgan's leaving school at the end of this week. May I assure his wife that you undertake not to . . .'

'No. I'd rather you didn't commit me in any way.'

129

Before he came, I'd felt totally in the wrong; now that Celine has made a move, and a rather spiteful and vindictive move at that, I feel altogether less remorse.

'Mrs Evans, I can't have insubordination from my staff.'

'Mr Williams, I'm a loyal member of your staff. I'm a conscientious teacher and I get good results.'

'I don't deny it. But you also involve my pupils in your . . . in your love games.'

Mali Vaughan's little face, her nervous eyes and blank expression, is suddenly before me. 'I suppose I did. I'm very sorry about that. It shouldn't have happened. It won't happen again.'

The Head's eyes are small and shifty, but certainly not stupid. He realises that he won't get more out of me by heavy-handed tactics and I can see him deciding to shift gear.

'Mr Morgan is an excellent art teacher, but as a member of staff he's often been thoughtless and troublesome.'

I meet his eyes, steeling myself for the next gambit.

'I have to tell you that he has repeatedly caused unrest amongst my young women teachers.' He sounds so ridiculously pompous that I have to make an effort not to smile.

He realises that his thrust has missed. 'And now his wife is . . . not so young,' he says, in such a completely different voice that I feel wretched again, tears burning my eyes.

'Mr Williams, I've already sent Mrs Morgan an apology. As you suggest, she must be used to young women falling in love with her husband. I've assured her that, in my case again, it's completely unreciprocated.'

He looks hard at me for several moments. 'Why couldn't you have said so in the first place?' he asks me, his voice still unrecognisably mild.

I take a deep breath. 'I would have, if you'd spoken to me as you're speaking to me now.'

His chest starts to rise again, but he seems to decide that it's not worth the effort. He nods his head at me several times. 'I'll be off then,' he says. I show him to the door and he leaves with another quick nod.

I have the feeling that he's accepted me as a worthy adversary.

I stand for a while, my eyes closed, filling my lungs and soul with the scent of next door's lilac. If Sam Jones knew how much I was taking in he'd charge me for it. It's beginning to rain. There's no sign of either Jack or Ilona.

'So that's that,' Ilona says later when I tell her all that's happened.

'Is it?' I ask her. 'Is that the end of it all?'

'Well, he's off to the army, isn't he? I can't think much else will happen before that. After two or three weeks he'll write to you: a short, bitter-sweet letter. "So we'll go no more a-roving." That sort of thing.

'We didn't even do much roving. I really wish we had . . . you know . . . Since all this has happened. As it is, I feel I'm being hung, drawn and quartered for a lamb. For nothing. If you see Jack tonight, ask him whether he managed to talk to Celine . . . I don't suppose he did or he'd have come back by this time.'

'Sometimes I wonder whether it's Gwynn or his wife you care most about. If Ifor's wife tried to get me into trouble, I'd get someone to throw a brick through her window. Why are you so concerned about Celine? She's had a good run for her money.'

'Ilona, she's getting old. She must be very nearly as old as my mother. I would have done anything in the world to avoid her getting hurt.'

'Except leave Gwynn alone.'

'How brutal you are.'

'I'm a realist, that's all. If you want someone badly enough you've got to sacrifice your scruples. Face up to that.'

'Listen, when you have your Gran's little house, can I come to be your lodger? I'm serious. Perhaps I could get a job in Brynteg. In the elementary school. I can't stay here.'

'You'll change your mind when Gwynn leaves.'

'It's nothing to do with Gwynn. I've made a mistake and I'm just not prepared to live with it for the rest of my life. You're the one who's got herself pregnant, but I'm the one who's trapped. You're not trapped because you don't give a damn for other people. I'm conventional, totally bound by the rules. It's only when I'm with you that I have the courage

131

to break out and think for myself. I want to leave this place. I don't want to live with Huw again.'

'You mustn't condemn a man in his absence. You've just got sick of his parents. They do seem petty and money-grabbing, I grant you, but he may be quite different. *Something* made you fall for him. Perhaps you've simply forgotten what it was. That spark of excitement can't be expected to last three years, but perhaps it can be revived when he gets back.'

'I can't remember any spark of excitement. I only remember feeling safe and comfortable because he was in love with me, pleased that he had a fairly well-paid job with his father, that he went to chapel on Sunday and had no outstanding faults.'

'Not a bad tally.'

'Oh Ilona, I betrayed my upbringing when I agreed to marry him.'

'Heavens above!'

'Don't make fun of me. My mother and father had principles. Money and material comforts were very low on their list of priorities.'

'Rhian, it seems to me that you're casting around rather desperately to find some moral grounds for breaking up your marriage. Where does Gwynn fit in to all this?'

'He doesn't fit in to it. If I move from here, I'll never see him again, I know that.'

'Oh, and you think that will ease all your heartache. I thought exactly the same when I decided to leave Brynteg. I was full of the bravest optimism, thought I was cutting myself off, that I'd be free of him for ever. But believe me, you can't leave it behind you.'

'Won't I ever get over Gwynn? Is that what you're saying?'

She looks at me angrily. 'How do I know? What do I know about anything? Don't make me your guide. You thought your precious Mr Roberts was the one to sort out Mary Powell's problems, but you're not so eager to consult him about yours. Because he'd give you advice you wouldn't want to take, that's why. You want *my* advice because I'm the one who hasn't kept the rules.'

'You're very cruel.'

'You've said that before. Perhaps I am. But at the moment I'm much more clear-sighted than you. You will get over Gwynn. Other people, perhaps Huw, will become important to you again. But you'll never be able to put him right out of your mind, of course you won't. He's a part of your life, girl, a part of your experience. My God, I've seen you coming in here looking like a tortured saint, all pale and glowing, simply because you'd walked up the hill with him.'

I look over at her. I honestly think her eyes have become calmer since she's pregnant. It worries me. Will she become quiet and boring like everyone else?

'You think it's some sort of obsession, don't you?' I ask her.

'How do I know. Love, infatuation, obsession, lust, they're only words. You're the one who studies words.'

We were silent. I thought about words. Yes I studied them, toiled over them, savoured them syllable by syllable, but now I only wanted to get beyond them, to reach the hard elusive truth.

'Christ, whichever it is, it hurts like hell. I can't pretend it's never happened. Love, I mean. It has. And now, oh Ilona, I can't do without it. I want the danger and excitement of it. I'm not going to give it up. I'm simply not prepared to give it up.'

Ilona lets out a long sigh. 'OK. Now you're at least being truthful. You don't really want to run away but to go on facing life here. Plenty of people live half-lives because that's all they can do in the circumstances. Adultery's always had a lousy press, but people don't go in for it out of choice but because it's the only option they have. It wasn't my fault that Ifor married that rich tart, was it? When he was meant for me?'

'I must see Gwynn again before he goes away. I want to . . . oh Ilona . . . I want to make love with him.'

'Of course you do. And you would have long ago, except that he's a nervous old granny. Write to him. No, don't worry, I'll see that he gets the letter safely. I'm not Mali Vaughan.'

'"Dearest Gwynn. Why don't you call here tonight? I can't bear the thought of your leaving me with nothing but

133

words and sighs to remember. With love and lust and obsession and infatuation. Rhian." Do you think that would be clear enough? But Ilona, I don't want to have to beg him to come here.'

There's a knock on the door.

It's Gwynn. Ilona brings him in. He looks shy, a bit of a nervous old granny, I have to admit it.

'I was bringing you a letter from Rhian,' Ilona says, because neither he nor I seem anxious or able to say anything at all.

'You may as well tell him what you meant to write,' she says, nodding at me briskly like a mother trying to persuade her child to recite a verse in chapel.

Gwynn smiles; suddenly not as shy. 'No, I'll speak first,' he says.

Chapter Fourteen

When Ilona finally goes out, we lie on the carpet in front of
the fire, all scruples forgotten. We fit together like two
halves. I cry out with the wonder of it, drown in the depths
of it, the love and lust of it, all, all those kisses. 'That sort of
kissing begins.' Ap Gwilym, the fourteenth century poet knew
far more about it than I did until tonight, those kisses that
course and sing down your body. All this, all this; I can't
believe that something so violent can begin with such baby-
lapping tenderness and end in such peace. My body seems
vast as a cathedral, every cell and bone and muscle and sinew
and blood-vessel and hair consoled and praised and ravished
and comforted and corrupted and blessed.

We lie naked in each other's gaze and it's what I want.
He's very beautiful – the skin of his belly is soft as cream, his
brown eyes have gold flecks in them – and for the moment I
feel beautiful too, soothed and beautiful. And I know that
nothing will ever be the same again. The world will never be
the same. How can I bear all this joy? All the stars and the
sailing moon and the birds at dawn are nothing to me now.

'It was good of you to send Jack to Celine, but, you see, the
damage was already done. She'd already asked me, last
Tuesday when she read your letter, whether I loved you and
I said yes. I couldn't lie, somehow, didn't want to. Oh and
she knew something was wrong even before she got the
letter. All the time we were on holiday, she chipped away at
my defences and I'm glad she did. I thought at first, I'll be
honest with you, that having a fortnight away might help to

135

put you out of my mind, but it didn't. It seemed to bring things to a head.'

'It's been a long time. Since last Tuesday, I mean. I've been very worried. Why did it take you so long to come to me?'

'Oh Rhian, I was sure of my feelings, but couldn't forget the responsibility I had towards you. You're so young. Even now, I know I'm taking advantage of your youth and inexperience. Does that sound patronising? It's not that I'm experienced, I'm not. I've been married for over twenty years and up to now I've never been unfaithful to Celine. I've been tempted before, I admit it, many times before. But before this I've always been able to resist the temptation. With you, I resisted for a day and the next day was as bad as ever and the following day was worse. I couldn't go on.'

'You resisted too long. I thought you didn't care for me.'

'No you didn't. I wouldn't love you so much if I thought you were so foolish and faint-hearted. You knew I loved you. You knew.'

'When you've gone, I'll think this is a dream.'

'No you won't. You'll remember. You'll remember me. And after the war, when I come back, we'll find some way of being together.'

'Where do you go?'

'To London.'

'I'll come to see you. I've never been to London. We'll go to the National Gallery. When I was in the Fifth, doing Art with you, you were always talking about the National Gallery, how wonderful it was.'

'You were lovely when you were sixteen. Cool as crystal. But now you're soft and glowing, "With your nut coloured hair, and grey eyes and rose-flush coming and going."'

'Lovely.'

'It could have been written for you. Hardy. About his first wife, I think.

> *"Where you will next be there's no knowing*
> *Facing round about me everywhere*
> *With your nut coloured hair*
> *And grey eyes, and rose-flush coming and going."'*

136

'Lovely. No, not the poem, but that's lovely too.'

'And this hair, dark and moist. You taste like the inside of a sea shell.'

'I knew it would be like this.'

'One day, I'll paint you like this, so tender and soft and yielding. I can't stop thinking about you. Sometimes you look so cool and composed that I want to make you tremble and cry, so that I can lick away your tears and comfort you. I suppose that's depraved, wanting to punish you because you've made me love you so much.'

'Breaking up your marriage. I told Ilona I'd have done anything to avoid that and she said, anything but leave him alone. She was right. If you hadn't come here tonight I was going to write to you. To make you come to me.'

'What were you going to say?'

'Please come to me because I'm sick with love and lust. Rhian.'

'Lust?'

'Yes.'

'Hussy.'

'Yes.'

Yes seems all I'm able to say as I lie so snugly in the heat of his protection. Yes.

It lasts about an hour, that deep happiness when my feet curled up with delight and the cut-grass smell of his nakedness was in my nostrils.

Then comes the terror of his leaving me. He must leave me. Tonight and again when he goes to London. When I've hardly begun to know the comfort of his lovely body.

'Why are you crying?'

'Because you're not a twenty-year-old Art student. Because I'm not Celine.'

'I'm too old for you.'

'It's not that. It's just that I want your past, all your past. Oh, why am I crying when I'm so happy?'

'Because you're Welsh and we all have this streak of melancholy. We're all trapped in this sense of doom all around us; the barren hills, the terrible mountains, the windswept trees, old castles, old history, old blood gone rusty as

137

bracken. Put out a hand and we feel chill ghosts all around us, ghosts of our defeated armies I suppose. I wouldn't want to live anywhere else. Oh Rhian, I don't want to go away. I don't want to go on teaching either. I want to paint. I want to live with you and paint for you. I want to paint great abstract paintings, charcoal grey and black and rust-red, full of crows and bracken and broken-down stone walls.'

'But what about rivers and lakes and the sea with the setting sun in it? Won't you put water into your paintings? Waterfalls and raindrops and shiny green grass?'

'One day I'll paint you like this.'

'I wasn't happy about Celine's painting.'

'So Jack said. You shouldn't have let it upset you so much. It probably did her a great deal of good. She's very direct, very primitive. She'll be all right, I think. She's got plenty of guts. And plenty of anger.'

I want to ask him whether he still loves her, whether he loves me more, whether he'll love me for ever. I want so much to be noble, or at least decent, but I'm already anxious to extract promises from him.

'When do you have to go? I ask him. The hairs on his chest are almost white. Shall we ever spend a whole night together? 'Are you staying at Jack's tonight?'

'Yes. I sleep on the sofa in the parlour. A lumpy old sofa, too uncomfortable even to sit on. At about three o'clock this morning I got up and lay on the floor which seemed much softer.'

'Must you go back there?'

'Yes. But tomorrow I'll go home. I need to talk to Celine. I must get all this sorted out and settled.'

'You can't stay here tonight?'

'Of course not. I can't risk that. I can't ruin your reputation.'

'You just have. Twice.'

Oh, the gentleness and lovebites and pet-words and long, wet kisses and long, long caresses, the sweet nuzzling, the promises.

I go to bed as soon as he goes, leaving a note for Ilona. 'Dear Ilona. Love Rhian.' What more is there to say?

138

In bed, I feel I'm flowing away very gently like a slowly flowing river.

Chapter Fifteen

My mother arrives here unexpectedly on Saturday morning.
These days she very seldom leaves the farm, so I'm terrified;
convinced that someone has let her know about Gwynn and
me. Oh, and now there *is* something to know about Gwynn
and me!

She's dressed in the bright royal-blue costume she bought
for my wedding and has seldom worn since. It makes her
skin look sallow and changes the shape of her soft body.
Why did I make her buy it? Why did I try to make her look
fashionable? I persuaded her to do so many things which
went completely against the grain. In Tregroes we don't go
in for wedding receptions in cafés, but just have tea and
sandwiches and a slice of wedding cake in the vestry for
everyone who turns up at the service. But Huw's mother
wanted a sit-down meal in Glyn Owen's which meant making
a list of wedding guests and hiring cars. My mother gave in
to everything to make it easier for me, but I know it embarrassed her; the ostentation.

She's out of breath and flushed as she reaches the door.
She avoids my kiss and sits down heavily on the nearest
chair.

'Is something the matter?' I ask her, digging my nails into
the palm of my hand to calm myself.

'I'm afraid so. Yes, Huw's father came up to the farm on
Thursday to fetch those things I wanted you to have and he
saw me with Alfredo. I thought you ought to know.'

She must have heard me gasp. 'Oh, we were only having a
bit of tea, girl, but of course the way a man sits down at a

141

tea table can say it all. I had to introduce them and of course Fredo had to talk a bit of English, which was only polite, but every word he said made it more obvious how things stood and what his intentions were. And Huw's father said not a word in reply, only "Well, I'd best be off then," and backed away like a scalded cat. And he slunk back to his van without even taking the boxes he'd come for.'

'A mean-spirited little man. And probably jealous as much as shocked. You remember how he was always calling on you after Father died? You always insisted it was only kindness, but I knew different.'

'Well, I knew different too, before the end, but that's something else. I never wanted to tell tales about Huw's father.'

After a few minutes she begins to look a little less agitated – she never looks really comfortable anywhere except at home or in chapel – and starts casting an eye over the crumbs on the carpet and the dirty dishes still on the table.

'I've had a lot on my mind,' I tell her, before she has a chance to say anything.

'Of course you have. I know how worried you must have been about me.'

'Don't be silly. It's not you I'm worried about.'

She looks at me sharply, her eyes like blue flames. 'It's not that Gwynn Morgan, Art?'

'He's going to the army at the end of next week.'

What happens next takes me completely by surprise. A sob lurches up from my chest, then another and another. My mother puts her hand over mine and then, of course, I really break down, huffling and sniffling for at least five minutes, squeezing my mother's hand, trying to let her know all the things I can't tell her.

'Well, I'll be off now,' she says as soon as I'm relatively calm again. 'I must let you get on with your housework or you'll be behind all next week. I'll manage to get the half past ten if I hurry. I can't help you with your problem, girl, I wish I could, but I do know that neglecting your work is not going to help you.'

We hear someone at the door. 'I can't think who this can be,' I tell my mother. 'But please wait, because I want to come with you as far as the station. I've got to go in to town this morning.'

It's Huw's mother who comes bursting in, full of her usual self-importance and bustle. She's a large woman, her hand-made dress is cut like a tent and her brown, hand-knitted cap is perched on her head like a little hedgehog.

'Rhian, I saw your mother passing when I was in the queue at Iwan Morgan's and I hurried up to see her as soon as I'd been served – sultanas I was after and I managed to get half a pound. Well hello, Mrs Lloyd, how are you? I thought I'd call round for a few minutes. It's not often you come to Llanfair these days, is it? I must say, you're looking very well. I'm delighted to see you looking so well. Is everything all right? Nothing worrying you, is there? Only seeing you so unexpectedly on a Saturday morning, I wondered whether there was anything the matter, anything I could do to help.'

'Nothing, thank you, Mrs Evans. It's nice to see you, of course, but there's nothing I need at the moment, I'm plodding along quite well. I must let you have some eggs, Mrs Evans, the hens are laying very nicely just now. Pity I didn't bring them with me this morning, but I was in a bit of a rush, somehow.'

'Will you stop for a cup of tea?' I ask my mother-in-law, trying to divert her attention. 'We'll all have a cup of tea. Mam, you can get the quarter past twelve today, can't you?'

'No, I must go, girl, or I'll be trying to catch up with myself all day. I've got to do the flowers for chapel this afternoon, as well as the graves. You make Mrs Evans a cup of tea, Rhian, and I'll take myself off.'

My mother has got to her feet and is looking towards the door with some desperation.

'Only it was you I really came to see, Mrs Lloyd. You see, Bryn was a bit disturbed when he called to see you the other day.' She looks at us in turn expecting one of us to question her. Neither of us does.

'Yes, he was most upset to see you so friendly, Mrs Lloyd, with this Italian fellow you had in the house. I said there was nothing in it. "Don't you worry about it," I told him, "Mrs Lloyd would never do anything to hurt Huw's feelings, she's

143

too fond of him. And besides she's got a very strong sense of right and wrong. She's a deeply religious, God-fearing woman," I told him. "And besides . . ."'

'Why should it upset Huw?' I ask her. 'It doesn't upset me, so why should it upset Huw?'

'Why should it upset *Huw*? Is that what she's asking? What an unnatural wife she is.' She swings her large body round to face me. 'Your husband, Rhian, in case you've forgotten, has been in Italy fighting the Eyeties for a year and a half. Fighting for his King and his Country. Fighting for our freedom.'

'But the Italians are not in the war, now, so they're no longer our enemies. Anyway, Christ says we must love our enemies and my mother is, as you say, a deeply religious woman and she . . .'

'Rhian,' my mother says, 'please don't talk about private matters. I don't like this sort of talk at all. I really must go.'

'And she's going to marry him as soon as the war is over. It's no secret – I intended to tell you, but I didn't see you last week. I've already told Mr Roberts; he's very pleased for them both and he's promised to be one of the officiating ministers at the wedding.'

'That's typical of Mr Roberts. Has he met him, then?'

'No, not yet. But he was asking after my mother, so I told him about Alfredo, told him he was a farmer, and a God-fearing man.'

She gives my mother a look, half pleading and half warning. 'My Huw will never forgive you,' she says. 'In one of his letters he told us that all the Italians are treacherous and sub-human. That's what he said – treacherous and sub-human.'

'But soldiers have to think like that, don't they? It makes it easier for them. They couldn't do the things they have to do against unarmed civilians unless they believed they were treacherous and sub-human. That's the propaganda machine. Alfredo is just a nice, ordinary man. And he's got three young lads, all too young for the army, and he's no idea what's happened to them, hasn't heard from them for almost a year.'

'They asked for it. The Eyeties asked for it. Why did they

join with Hitler instead of joining us? We'd have let them join us.'

'I don't know why. But I'm sure that Alfredo and his sons didn't have anything to do with it.'

'Motherless sons,' my mother says, a catch in her voice.

'What about *my* son?' my mother-in-law asks. 'Don't you have any sympathy for *my* son?'

'I pray for your son every night,' my mother says, quietly and simply 'And now I really must go or I'll miss that bus. Goodbye, Mrs Evans. Goodbye, Rhian. I'll see you on Wednesday.'

I go to the door with her and watch her hurrying down the hill. I feel a great rush of tenderness for her; but if I said anything affectionate, she'd be startled out of her wits. I stand in the sun, listening to the blackbirds for a moment or two before going back to my mother-in-law. Unexpectedly I feel a flicker of affection for her too.

'When I write to Huw on Sunday, I'll tell him about Alfredo. Then it won't be such a shock for him.'

'No, please don't, Rhian. Let him come home safe first.'

I suddenly feel very sorry for her. She's a small-minded busybody, but she loves her son and he's in danger.

'Something tells me Huw is going to be all right,' I tell her. 'I really do believe that. He's a survivor. And when he's back home after going through so much; all the fighting in Africa and Italy and whatever's to come in France, I think he'll be able to take everything else in his stride.'

'I hope so.'

'I hope so, too.'

'I'm glad that lodger of yours isn't here,' she says then. 'That Ilona Hughes. You won't hear anything said against her, I know, but she's too flighty for my liking. She's going around now with Mr Jones, the PT teacher. Leading him astray, I suppose. He used to come to chapel sometimes, but we seldom see him now.'

'He was in the same rugby team as Huw, years ago.'

Her voice softens. 'Was he really? I didn't know that. Perhaps I should get Mr Roberts to have a word with him. Not that *he'd* say much – Mr Roberts won't believe badly of anyone.'

'Oh, these Christians!'

'Don't make fun of me, Rhian.'

For a moment we're almost friends.

When she leaves, I sit with my head on the table and make myself think about Huw, about the sinful way I'm treating him. I promised to love only him, putting aside all others. And after all, I married him of my own free will – if there is such a thing. I think I always knew I should have waited – as my mother wanted me to – but how can you make a rational decision when someone is begging and begging you to get married and he's being sent abroad in a few weeks' time?

I manage to stay miserable for about ten minutes. Then thoughts of Gwynn take over again: the way his eyes darken, the way his lips open a little and grow soft as he looks at me, the beauty of his head and his body and his large strong hands. I know physical beauty is not all-important nor unchanging, but it certainly makes you tremble. I'm trembling now as I think of him, what he can do to me. I'm so lucky; so wicked and so blessed.

He's moved back home now. He and Celine are talking again, discussing the future, trying to remain friends. She said she was sorry she'd sent the letter to the Head, but having done so, felt more ready to forget it, more ready to forgive me. When he comes out in the evening, she doesn't ask him where he's going or whether he'll be seeing me. The French are realists, Gwynn says, ready to make the best of any situation, not the worst. Perhaps she's managed to convince herself that his love for me won't last, so she's able to be tolerant.

In my dreams, she looks white and angry, anything but tolerant. What's to become of us all? She never did me any harm.

The next week passes in a dream. It's perfect weather. After school I walk the three miles over the cliffs to Celyn sands; Gwynn meets me there and we cling together, and talk and talk as though we'll never get another chance.

We walk back in the dark, many hours later, the sound of the sea filling our silences. I can hardly bear it when he leaves me to return home. It's only the thought of the weekend we're going to spend together in London that keeps me sane. We intend to meet on his first twenty-four-hour leave.

I don't even go home on Wednesday; I write to my mother telling her I'll see her next week, letting her draw her own conclusions.

He leaves on the early train on Friday. Naturally, I can't go to the station to see him off, can only listen from my bedroom to the sound of the train taking him away.

Chapter Sixteen

In the past I'd always considered myself conscientious, dedicated, industrious; these were the qualities I admired in others and the ones that had made me a graduate teacher rather than a farm servant or a shop girl. Now something else had taken me over, and it was something very like madness. I was still coping with school, keeping my classes occupied, setting homework and marking it, but deep inside me was a weak, trembling, unstable girl who had lost her lover and was only just managing to choke down a fit of sobbing.

Late every night I walked over dangerous cliff paths the three miles to Celyn sands, which no sane woman would have done at that time, and I'd lie in the places where Gwynn and I had lain together and moan for him and then stand at the edge of the sea and cry out till my throat ached.

One night before he'd left, when it had suddenly turned cold, he'd given me his old tweed jacket to wear; I'd managed to hold on to it, and every evening when I got back to the house, I took it out of the wardrobe, trying to draw some comfort from it, sniffing it all over for some memory of him, sleeping on it at night, rubbing my cheeks on the coarse material until they were sore, shedding so many tears on it that I imagined it smelt of our salt love.

I couldn't bear to sleep in the front room bed I'd slept in with Huw, so I persuaded Ilona to change rooms with me. I was happier, or at least less agitated, in the single bed in the small room overlooking the garden.

I couldn't bear to remember that I was, or ever had been,

married to Huw. It was very difficult to go on having Sunday dinner with Huw's parents, almost impossible to talk to them about him and about our future plans when I knew we had no future together. They, not surprisingly, in view of the imminent invasion and the danger he was facing, seemed able to talk of nothing else. *When Huw comes home. When Huw comes home. When Huw comes home.* And I could do nothing but smile my Judas smile.

Writing to him was getting more and more difficult, too. I filled my letters with trivial news which couldn't possibly interest him, so that I had little space for anything but 'With love from Rhian' at the end. He must surely have realised from those letters that something was amiss.

I wrote to Gwynn every day, though: short letters about kissing and love-making with quotations from Keats and the Welsh love poets. It sometimes soothed me to think other people might have suffered some small part of what I was suffering, though I couldn't really believe it.

The desperate state I was in seemed to isolate me from everyone; even when talking to Ilona or my mother, I could think only of Gwynn. Sometimes his face – his beautiful wide lips, his dark eyes – would appear to me so clearly that it was all I could do not to groan aloud.

One day, though, noticing that the waistband of Ilona's summer skirt was stretched almost to bursting point, I realised that I'd managed to forget all about her problems and felt ashamed of myself.

I turn to her and hug her. 'How *are* you?' I ask her, seeing her properly for the first time for weeks. 'How are you? Are you getting enough to eat, love?'

'No,' she says, pulling away from me. 'Is anybody, these days?'

Then she looks at me, suddenly aware that I'm trying to make contact again. 'But never mind,' she says in a mild, placatory voice which I hardly recognise, 'I've never been used to having enough to eat, have I? Nobody in Brynteg ever had enough to eat. Especially at the end of the week. The end of the week in our house meant cabbage and bread and dripping. And in other houses where there wasn't a keen gardener like my father, it was just bread and dripping.' She drops into a chair, pushes her shoes off and rubs one foot against the other. 'But my father had a nice little garden, fair play to him; cabbages and leeks and carrots ... Only the carrots always had blight and nobody liked leeks ... Well, nobody liked cabbage either except at the end of the week, Thursday and Friday. On Saturday we sometimes had tinned salmon. That was my favourite. What's happened to tinned salmon? You'd think they'd get some for pregnant women, wouldn't you? All the extra I get is this condensed orange juice which is probably all right with gin but horrible on its own.'

I suddenly feel very protective towards her. 'Come home with me tomorrow night. My mother'll make us some pancakes.'

She smiles, then hesitates. 'I'd really like to, but Wednesday is my night for seeing Jack. Wednesday and Saturday.'

'Can't you see him tonight?'

'No. He goes to play cards with Mrs Morgan – Celine – on a Tuesday.'

'Does he? Every Tuesday? What an extraordinary man he is. He used to be so shy of women and now he's engaged to one and has regular dates with two others. Don't you mind his seeing Celine every Tuesday?'

'Why should I mind who he sees? He's just a friend. He means nothing to me.'

'He's a very close friend. You get on well. You're always pleased to see him.'

'I know. It's a nice, easy relationship, but it's not bloody love, is it?'

'Isn't it?'

'You know it isn't. Love is when you're miserable all the time, when you're jumpy every minute he's out of your sight and jealous as hell if he looks at anyone else.'

'Jealousy shouldn't be a part of love,' I say grandly.

'Perhaps it shouldn't be. But it is. You know it is.'

'Women are only jealous because they don't have the same power as men or the same resources. They always have to stay at home instead of being free to go out and do whatever men do, on equal terms.'

'I don't think it's as simple as that. It's only married women who have to stay at home. I'm free to go out and do whatever I want to, aren't I? And take the women in the Forces, don't they have the same power as men? I don't mean about dropping bombs and things like that, but in their private lives? They've got away from home and they can do whatever they like.'

'I suppose they can go out in the evenings and I suppose they're free to mix with men, but it'll take years for them to consider themselves equal. I can't imagine any woman, whether she's in uniform or not, making the first move and asking a man for a date. And while that's still the man's prerogative, the woman is bound to be the passive, dependent partner.'

'I'm not passive or dependent,' Ilona says.

'Well, you're different, I've always said that. Stronger than the rest of us.'

'Don't make fun of me. I've just admitted that I'm jealous as hell. I wouldn't call that strong, would you?'

'If you were married to Ifor, you'd learn to control your jealousy, I suppose.'

'Ifor's wife hasn't learnt much control anyway. She cut up his best suit into ribbons when she found out he'd been seeing me over Christmas. Serves him right. I bet I'd have done the same.'

'I hate the thought of Celine being jealous of me.'

'Oh, enjoy it! You'll be the jealous one next time round. What if he called here and you found him larking about with me?'

'Ilona, has he ever flirted with you?'

'You know he has. It's his way, he flirts with everyone, you'll have to get used to it. Every real man loves women and flirts with them. Gwynn does. Ifor does.'

'Does that mean he'll have affairs with other women? No, I'm serious. It's something I've never really thought about.'

'Perhaps he won't. Not if he knows you really appreciate him.'

'I do, you know I do.'

'I should by this time. You've moaned about it enough.'

We look at each other, give each other those soft, sympathetic, penetrating looks that show we're completely preoccupied with our own lives, our own problems.

'I always feel such sympathy for Blodeuwedd,' I say at last. 'You know . . . the unfaithful wife who was turned into an owl. You must have read the story in school. From the *Mabinogion*.'

'The woman Merlin made out of flowers?'

'Yes. Well, the magician was called Gwydion, but it was probably Merlin under another name. Anyway, she fell in love with a huntsman called Gronw Bebyr – as soon as ever she clapped eyes on him. Great Heavens, he must have been some man. But after all, she hadn't wanted to marry Lleu. He couldn't get a human wife because of a curse his mother had put on him. That's why Gwydion had to create one for him out of flowers; broom and meadowsweet and the flowers of the oak.'

'And he didn't like her?'

'Oh, he liked her well enough. Well, I suppose he did. It just says he slept with her at the wedding feast, that's all it says. But after that, he probably started taking her for granted, going away on visits to friends, and so on. And once upon a time, when he was away from home, Gronw Bebyr arrived on the scene, so lusty and beautiful that she immediately fell in love with him. "There was no part of her that was not filled with love of him." And he felt the same about her.'

'Oh, the meadowsweet and the sweet broom flowers.'

'And he told her he loved her. Oh, and they kissed and kissed. And that night they slept together. And when morning came, she wouldn't, couldn't let him go. So they plotted Lleu's death, which was very wrong of them, of course. But after all, Blodeuwedd hadn't asked to be his wife, hadn't even been consulted. Oh, and it's the same today, women made of sugar and spice, married off in a romantic haze because it's what is expected of them. Women aren't free, they marry whoever asks them, because they're so afraid of the alternative which is being left on the shelf. For a time they might think they're in love. They try to fit into the myth – romantic love, happy ever after – but in a year or two, or even less, they know it was all fantasy and that they've got the rest of their lives to regret it.'

'I don't know anything about romantic love. I don't think anyone could get romantic about Ifor, he's not the right build, somehow. It was pure lust with Ifor. Or impure lust, perhaps.'

'I sometimes think lust is the only thing you can count on, the only thing you can't fake. "There was no part of her that was not filled with love for him." That's the only start for a relationship, it seems to me. Passion may not last for ever, but perhaps life after it is like a summer evening, the blood still warm with the heat of the sun.'

'Who's being romantic now?'

'I'm not being romantic. Passion is real, real as hunger.'

At this point Ilona looks at me with what I might interpret as agreement, even admiration if I didn't know her better. No, she's just hungry. 'All right, I'll make you some chips.' I tell her.

We're friends again.

At the beginning of June, Gwynn is due for his first twenty-four hour leave and I travel to London to meet him.

I'm very excited, of course, but at the same time dreading the journey – a first visit to London – and terrified I won't find him even if I manage to get there. In a way, though, I'm pleased to be undertaking something so difficult; it seems like one of the impossible tasks set lovers in fairy tales so that their love is strengthened and purified.

I have to leave school early to catch the afternoon train. This in itself is difficult enough. 'Will it be possible for me to leave this afternoon at three-fifteen?' I ask the Head, a light sweat breaking out over my body. 'I have to catch the three-forty train to Paddington.'

He scowls at me for a long time without answering, then nods his head. 'As long as you don't make a habit of it,' he says.

'What is there about that Gwynn Morgan?' I hear him ask himself as I leave his study. 'I used to be handsome myself when I was young, but perhaps I always talked too much.'

I race home, change into my dark blue dress, with a pale grey summer coat made by the needlework teacher at school for twelve and sixpence and a tiny pink hat borrowed from Ilona, and set off for the station. I'm so nervous about the journey that I can hardly believe that there's no one there to try to stop me getting on the train. 'Third-class return to Paddington,' I tell Roderick Edwards at the ticket office. 'Huw not home, is he?' he asks politely. 'No, I've got an interview for a job.'

Why did I say that? Perhaps it was at that moment I decided to hand in my resignation at school and move away from Llanfair.

At first the journey is pleasant enough. I've only rarely travelled by train because bus journeys are so much cheaper. I always went to college by bus and it was by bus that we went for our days out by the sea when I was a child.

I only remember one occasion when we travelled by train. It was when we went for a week's holiday to Ogmore-on-Sea. I wonder why we went for a whole week? And by train? Perhaps the harvest had been particularly good that year. I'll have to ask my mother.

A cousin of my mother's, Alun Edwin, a clerk with a timber firm in Llandysul, came to help Dafi Blaenhir manage the farm, arriving a few days before we left, to be shown exactly what he had to do. I think it was the first time I'd met him. He was a small plump man who looked rather like an overgrown child. He had a child's sense of fun, too, almost everything making him laugh, and often till he choked, his shoulders hunching up and his neck sticking out in front of him and moving slightly from side to side like a tortoise we once had. I remember him dressing up in my mother's floral pinafore and giggling like a girl as he swept the kitchen floor and did the washing up. I loved him and sometimes wished I was staying home with him instead of going to the seaside with my staid and serious parents.

It was a good holiday, though, with unexpected treats like tea in a fish and chip shop and a visit to a cinema in Swansea – a first for all three of us – as well as long afternoons on the sands with a new bucket and spade. Chapel on Sunday, of course, but a walk along the cliffs in the afternoon instead of Sunday school.

The train journey, though, was the greatest treat of all, I wanted it to last for ever. The things we saw! How could people read newspapers when there were whole new worlds to see through the windows? And the excitement of the corridor with a WC at either end of it; a basin with brass taps for hot and cold water and a lavatory that flushed. I must have wanted to go at least ten times.

I suppose I must have been about nine that year, a well-behaved child, loved and cherished, always treated with the greatest kindness.

I can't help thinking of the good child I was then, and wondering what my parents would think of the journey I'm making today; its purpose. I'm surprised, myself, at the way I've turned out; a married woman travelling up to London to spend a night in a hotel with her married lover. My mother might sympathise with my having 'feelings' for Gwynn, but she would whole-heartedly condemn my acting on them. So would that kind and good man, Mr Roberts, Tabernacle. The knowledge makes me sad, but I know I'd be prepared to lose everyone's good opinion rather than forfeit an hour of my time with Gwynn.

Alun Edwin died of cancer the following year. My mother visited him in hospital every week – she said he kept the nurses in stitches – but would never take me with her. I haven't thought of him for years. Surely I'm not going to start crying for Alun Edwin? Or for that good little nine-year-old for that matter?

There's over an hour's delay in Cardiff and from there, the journey becomes a nightmare. It's hot and humid and at one point there are twenty people, mostly soldiers and airmen, standing in the compartment, with the corridors even more crowded. They seem much less rowdy than usual, feeling the strain, I suppose, of what lies ahead of them. When I think that some of these tired men, some of them hardly older than schoolboys, may soon be lying wounded or dead in France, war seems an unbelievable barbarity. When a young soldier is pushed against me and apologises, my eyes fill with tears. 'Are you all right, lady?' 'Yes, I'm all right.' 'Is your husband in the army?' 'Yes he is.' 'He may be OK' 'Yes.' We smile nervously at each other.

*

The train is three hours late, arriving in Paddington a few minutes past midnight. I find Gwynn asleep on a bench at the exact spot where he'd promised to be. He opens his eyes as I sit down beside him. 'Good girl,' he says, 'I knew you'd be here.'

I feel very shy with him. He looks tired and almost ugly with his cropped hair and his bulky, ill-fitting uniform. 'You're looking lovely,' he says. 'I was hoping you'd wear that dress, I think a lot about that morning we bought it. It seems like another life.'

'You're not sorry about what happened?'

'No, no. I can't spare the time to think about anything except wanting you, wanting your hands and your lips and your body.'

He doesn't touch me, but my body feels as though he's already inside me. I can hardly stand up for the shock of desire I feel. Is it the same for him? We look at each other in the dim, greenish light of the station, unable to smile, hardly able to breathe.

'I've found us a room in a nice clean hotel,' he says at last, 'and they're keeping sandwiches for us.'

I can't believe I'm in London. The buildings are solid menacing shadows in the darkness. Even in the streets there's a close, acrid smell as though we're still walking in a huge railway station. 'I love you,' Gwynn says.

We find the hotel. It's relatively small and not at all grand as I'd feared. When we sign the register – Gwynn and Rhian Morgan – the tired, blank-faced woman at the desk becomes quite friendly, telling us her husband now fighting in Burma, came from Anglesey. And then, she and Gwynn talk about Anglesey for what seems too long, but afterwards she brings us some lovely hot potato soup to go with our sandwiches, so perhaps it was worth it.

And then she gives us a key and points the way to our room – small and shabby with dark, faded wallpaper and a musty smell – but what do we care. We close the door, set down our small overnight bags and look at each other.

Gwynn is slow and formal, undressing me very slowly and gently, kissing every bone and sinew and fold of flesh until I'm naked and trembling at his touch. 'I have to do this properly,' he says. 'Remembering this will have to keep me going for weeks and weeks.'

'I can't bear it,' I say, overwhelmed by thoughts of a long separation. 'Oh, I can't bear it.'

I drop a tear on his lovely caressing hand and pull him towards me and then formality is forgotten and we're closely and deeply and noisily together, one flesh. Oh, one flesh.

It's the first time we've ever been together in a bed. We try to stay awake, but keep falling asleep in short snatches, then waking again to the warm sweetness and wonder of being together. 'It isn't only lust,' I tell him, at one waking. 'I must tell Ilona. It's tenderness as well. And honesty.' Once, Gwynn wakes and recites a verse he'd found in a book of Forces Writing he'd bought that afternoon.

Heart of the heartless world
Dear heart, the thought of you
Is the pain at my side
The shadow that chills my view.

He can't remember any more except the last line: Don't forget my love. We say this over and over to each other as we wake and sleep: Don't forget my love.

We miss breakfast, staying in that hard, lumpy, lovely bed until the cleaning lady rattles the door knob at eleven o'clock.

When we leave the room half an hour later, Gwynn goes along the corridor to find her. 'Sorry to keep you waiting,' he says, pressing a shilling into her hand. 'I've only got a twenty-four hour leave.'

'That's all right, dear,' she says, winking at him. 'As soon as you called out I was quite happy. Only, last week I had a soldier kill hisself in that room. That's why I was worried, dear.'

Gwynn grips my shoulder and we shiver as we hold each other. That a soldier had taken his life in that little dark room saddened but hardly surprised us; love and despair were so close that day.

'I've written to Celine,' Gwynn tells me when we're sitting over weak tea and grey bread and butter in a café later on.

158

'I've told her she can have the house and the furniture and an insurance policy which will mature next year. When I get back, you and I will move to Lleyn and try to get by on what I can make from painting. Other people manage it.'

'I may be able to get some sort of teaching job.'

'No,' he says, 'you'll be too busy coping with all those babies we're going to have.'

'Will I? Will I really?' My heart thumps against my ribs. 'What a good thing we've both been brought up to rough it.'

'Can you milk a cow?'

'Of course I can. Can't you?'

'No, we only kept sheep. And chickens of course. But I'm good at building sheds and putting up fences.'

'All those manly things.'

'That's right. All those things.'

I rub my face against his sleeve. We sit so close together that our bones hurt. We order more tea and bread and butter and settle on a little whitewashed cottage with three or four acres looking out on Bardsey Island. '*Mae gen i dipyn o dy bach twt,*' I sing to him 'I have a bit of a tiny house, a tiny house, a tiny house. I have a bit of a tiny house. The wind calls round each morning.'

And heigh-ho, the wind and the rain.

We sigh, thinking of hard weather and the lack of money. Two Welsh peasants, our feet firmly planted on stony ground, even our dreams modest.

For the rest of the day we wander about London. We see the Tower and the Thames and many, many bomb sites and then sit in Saint James's Park, kissing when we can, before setting off for Paddington again.

I can't remember our parting at the station.

All the way home, though, fighting back tears and trying to swallow the painful sobs rising from my chest, I keep telling myself: One day I'll think of this as the happiest day of my life.

The Wednesday of the following week is D-Day. Everyone is absorbed with news bulletins. The Head has a wireless in his study and bursts out on anyone who happens to be in the

159

corridor with the latest headlines: 'A hundred miles of Normandy coast under attack' 'A thousand planes in the airborne operation.' 'A thousand troop-carriers in the first blow.' 'Ten thousand tons of bombs and shells.' Vast numbers, huge quantities, cold, impersonal statistics to hide the fear in everyone's heart. I think of the tired-looking lads travelling with me on the train. Perhaps Huw, who may still be in Northern Italy, is not in such immediate danger.

Chapter Seventeen

It's the Headmaster who lets me know. He knocks at the door, Saturday morning, ten o'clock. 'Bad news,' he says. 'Better go in and sit down.'

He follows me to the living room. The walls are coming towards me. 'It's Gwynn Morgan,' he says. 'It's Mr Gwynn Morgan. Killed by one of these new-type bombs on Wednesday night. His wife sent me a message this morning and I thought I'd let you know myself.'

He's sitting in the big arm-chair staring down at his shoes.

'Shall I get you a glass of water?' he asks me, his voice strange, as though full of cold or fever. 'Would you like me to make you a cup of tea? Do you have a drop of brandy? Take some deep breaths. That's the way.'

I don't think I manage to say a word. It's difficult to breathe; the air has become thick and heavy. I can't concentrate on anything but the way he's staring down at his shoes. How well polished they are. I wonder if he can see himself in the shine. I gulp for air.

'The noblest and the best,' he says then. 'This war has taken the noblest and the best.'

He's quiet again, waiting, I suppose, for me to say something or show some sign of life, but I can't respond in any way.

He goes through to the kitchen and brings me a cup of water. I grip it tightly and look into it. There's a tea stain at the bottom of the cup and another about half an inch from the top. When he goes I'll rub them with a pinch of salt.

'Mrs Morgan had a letter from his CO. Death was instanta-

161

neous, that's what he said. Instantaneous. The whole canteen was wiped out. Fourteen soldiers killed. All new recruits. All fine men.'

His words came from a great distance. When he's gone, I'll clean all the cups; put some salt on a rag and get all the stains off. I'll clean everything.

'I must go now. Why don't you drink some of that water? It would do you good. Or will you make yourself a cup of tea? I must go now. I must call on Mrs Morgan to offer her my condolences.'

I try to get to my feet.

'No, no, please sit down, Mrs Evans, I'll let myself out. I wanted to tell you myself. Killed by one of these new type bombs on Wednesday evening. Very bad news. Sorry to have to give you such very bad news.'

Sorry to have to give you such very bad news. Even after he's gone, the words skate about crazily in my head. Such very bad news.

He's only been away seven weeks. We hadn't even had our week-end together. We were going to meet in the Cotswolds in three weeks' time and have two whole days, two long nights, together.

Such very bad news.

We had so little time.

What shall I do now? Such very bad news. I tilt the cup in my hand and let the water trickle very slowly onto the carpet and watch the dark patch spreading. Darkness. Darkness spreading.

Some time later Jack lets himself in. He squeezes my hands, makes up the fire but doesn't say a word.

Then Ilona is back from the Post Office and we have the first of many, many cups of tea. Such very bad news.

'You don't feel like screaming?' Ilona asks me. 'We wouldn't mind, would we Jack? It might do you a lot of good.'

I don't feel like screaming.

'A long walk? A nice hot bath?'

'I'll be all right. I don't want anything.'

162

There, I've spoken. It's like trying to speak underwater. Jack and Ilona look at each other triumphantly as though all their problems are over.

'Now you can go, Jack,' Ilona says briskly. 'Jack's got a cricket match to umpire this afternoon. He'll be back later.'

Some time afterwards I can hear her in the kitchen making herself a meal. She thinks I should tackle a little something. A boiled egg. A poached egg. A scrambled egg. What about a small piece of toast. Potato mashed up with milk and butter. Potato with buttermilk.

'No thank you.' 'No thank you.' 'No thank you.'

'Another cup of tea, then.'

'Where will the funeral be?'

'Back here, I suppose.'

'In Llanfair?'

'I suppose so.'

'They'll bring him back here?'

'They'll bring the body back. Yes.'

'I don't suppose I'll be able to go to the funeral?'

'Of course you will if you want to. All the teachers will probably be going, perhaps the whole school. I'll certainly be going. All his friends will. You can go with Jack and me.'

At about seven o'clock Ilona makes me some *te sincin*, slightly burnt buttered toast cut up in strong tea. The butter glistens on the surface of the tea like oil on a puddle of rain. My grandmother used to have it for supper when she'd taken her teeth out. Even without her teeth my grandmother had a lovely smile. And a lovely delicate smell, too, like cedar wood or old silk.

Ilona lets me feel her baby kicking; a tiny movement, faint as the pulse in a thrush's throat. Nothing can comfort me.

The day draws to a close. I feel that I am dead. When I crawl into bed my eyelids drop heavy as pennies on my smarting eyes. All, all is lost.

I sleep deep as a stone in a pond and wake to the knowledge of my burning loss.

163

I can't summon up the energy to go to chapel. To tell the truth, I don't much want to hear Mr Roberts with his long, ardent prayers for the return of peace and sanity. As far as I'm concerned, the whole world can burn to a cinder now.

I'm still in my nightdress when my mother-in-law comes up in the early afternoon. 'Good gracious, girl, whatever's the matter? Have you got the flu, or what? Why weren't you in chapel this morning? You knew we were expecting you for dinner. And me with a nice piece of best-end in the oven. I'd have thought you'd at least have had the good manners to let us know you were ill.'

'I'm not ill. No, I'm just sick of everything, that's all. Sick of sermons, sick of lamb and mint-sauce and Sunday school and hymns and anthems and psalms. Sick of everything.'

'Rhian, whatever is it? What's got into you? Whatever's happened to you? Is your mother all right? Is is something I've said? Is it something to do with Huw or what?'

'No. It's nothing to do with you or Huw or my mother. I'm sorry to have upset you. I just couldn't drag myself to chapel this morning, that's all. My mind is sick, that's all.'

Ilona comes in from the garden, a small bundle of broad beans in her hands.

'This is Ilona Hughes. My mother-in-law.'

They look at each other with little nervous smiles. I tip my head at Ilona. 'Give her the beans, love.' I've come out in a sweat and can't think of anything else to say. I want my mother-in-law to go.

Ilona hands over the beans, the smile hardening on her face.

'Well, thank you very much, I'm sure. A little boiling of beans will be very welcome, I'm sure. Quite a nice size, too, fair play. Nice full pods. Well, I'll go, then. And I can only hope you'll be better soon, Rhian. What can be the matter with you, girl? I can only hope you'll come to your senses soon.'

'Haven't you heard about Mr Gwynn Morgan?' Ilona asks. 'Killed by one of those flying bombs on Wednesday evening. We've all had a terrible shock, but he was a special friend of Rhian's.'

'Mr Gwynn Morgan? No, I hadn't heard about Mr Gwynn

164

Morgan. There was nothing about him in chapel this morning. Well, he wasn't one of our members, was he? He turned Catholic, didn't he, with his wife? And he's been killed, has he? Well, that's a great pity indeed. Dear, dear, I heard he'd joined up.'

She perches on the arm of the chair, staring at the beans, but thinking of other things. After a moment or two she looks up at me with narrowed eyes. 'But I'll tell you one thing,' she says. 'If you don't pull yourself together, girl, there'll be talk of you and this Mr Gwynn Morgan. I'll tell you another thing, married women are not supposed to have special friends, especially when their husbands are overseas fighting for their king and country. And another thing, my son wouldn't be very pleased to hear about this sort of carry-on, not coming to chapel and sitting around all Sunday morning and being sick of this and that.'

'I'm sorry. I'm very sorry.'

The room becomes even more tense. I suppose my apology is almost a confession of guilt, I don't think she'd expected it.

'I'll go,' she says quietly. 'I suppose I'd better go.'

'It was better to have it out,' Ilona says smoothly. 'She'll probably hear rumours and speculation and now she'll be able to check them. I can just hear her, can't you? "Are you trying to insinuate that there was something wrong in the relationship between my daughter-in-law and Mr Gwynn Morgan? They were friends and colleagues, nothing more. And I'll tell you another thing, there's something very sick about anyone who can cast aspersions on those who have made the Supreme Sacrifice." Great Heavens, she's a pain.'

'She's Huw's mother.'

'She didn't deserve those beans, anyway. To think of the way I've been coddling them, watering them every evening and singing them lullabies.'

'My mother's got plenty of beans.'

'Well, don't forget to bring some back with you on Wednesday. Only, I hope your mother doesn't put too much manure on them. It does something to the taste, I don't care what anyone says.'

*

Will I go to see my mother on Wednesday? Will I go to school tomorrow and for the rest of the term? Will I go on breathing and drinking cups of tea and shoving food into my mouth and going to bed and getting up, my body like some horribly efficient machine, built to last? The thought of the rest of my life stretching out before me in a long, long procession of empty days and weeks and years makes me groan.

All day long I sit in my nightgown, shifting around from chair to chair, sighing and groaning. My mouth feels as though I've eaten metal polish, my feet are swollen, like an old woman's. Ilona tells me about a woman in Brynteg who developed dropsy after her husband died. Because she couldn't cry, her tears flooded her body and eventually drowned her heart. The people Ilona knows in Brynteg! She says they're descended from a tribe of night-worshippers.

The next day, I manage to go to school and to take my classes. My teaching is completely mechanical; words I've used many times before flow out of my mouth in what seems an appropriate sequence and my pupils take notes, stare about them, mumble messages to those sitting nearby in quite the usual way. I begin to think I can count myself among the walking wounded.

In the afternoon, though, Arthur Williams in 2A manages to ground me again. He's developed a great shambling calf-love for me because I ask after his father who's still in prison. 'Miss,' he says, 'isn't it terrible about Mr Morgan, Art? I was watching you in Assembly this morning, Miss, when the Head told us about him getting killed, and you went as white as a potato. It's not right is it, Miss? Old men like Mr Morgan having to go and fight for the English? It's not right, is it?'

'No, it's not right,' I say, sitting heavily at my desk, the drift of my lesson lost in the blackness in my head.

He prompts me. 'Dafydd ap Edmwnd, Miss,' he says. 'How his poetry compares with Tudur Aled's.'

'Thank you. And don't interrupt me again, Arthur.'

'No, Miss.'

The two girls in the front desk smirk at one another.

Does the whole school know what I'm going through?
Does it matter?

The Head summons me to his room at the end of the afternoon. 'Funeral on Wednesday,' he says. 'Two-thirty in the Catholic church. The school will be dismissed at two-fifteen. Of course all the staff will want to go, black arm-bands are all that will be necessary. That's all, I think, Mrs Evans. Oh, and Mrs Evans, I just want to say that I'm not disappointed in you. Full marks again, Mrs Evans. That's all.'

I look him straight in the eye. 'Thank you for coming up to tell me on Saturday.'

'That's all right, Mrs Evans. Sometimes I can be quite human, can't I?'

I learn the difference between grief and grief. When Gwynn and I had to part – and it was a parting full of sorrow for his absence, anger that he'd had to go and fear for his safety – my heart seemed to be agitated by quivering cross-currents, an extreme disquiet that I thought might kill me if it went on too long. When I knew he was dead, it seemed as though my heart was muffled and buried. I could feel black dust and choking darkness. It was like being already dead.

I keep on remembering poor Marged Rees whose young husband was thrown from a horse and killed and who'd gone out every morning for years – at least six or seven years – looking for him, pulling at people's sleeves and asking 'Have you seen Elis?' 'He was killed, Marged fach,' someone would tell her, 'and you bought a black coat and had him buried tidy and decent in Bont.' And then she would remember and go to the churchyard and spend the rest of the day there in all weathers. When her mother died a few years back, they had to take her to the asylum in Carmarthen but she doesn't speak at all now, according to the one or two people in Tregroes who still visit her. I keep on remembering her. Marged Rees. No-one could do anything for her, though everyone tried; the doctor and the minister and the district nurse and all her neighbours.

*

The funeral isn't as bad as I'd feared; in fact the desolate music and the unfamiliar Latin words give me a small measure of comfort. Ilona has had time off from the Post Office and I'm sitting between her and Jack.

Celine, in black from top to toe, manages to look both dignified and dramatic. Her face, behind her velvet hat's black veil is luminously white. I suddenly see her naked; sensuous and white. She and Gwynn were married for almost twenty years, slept together for almost twenty years. I'm ashamed of the rage of sexual jealousy I feel. In a church, too, and during a funeral service. Tears rise to my eyes but before I can blink them away, Ilona hisses something in my ear. I turn towards her. 'Mary Powell,' she mouths. 'What the devil does she want? Tell Jack she's here.'

I catch sight of Mary at the opposite side of the church and point her out to Jack. As I stare at her, she catches my eye and I can feel a stab of hatred coming from her. And I'm suddenly aware that it was Gwynn she was in love with and that her spite against me wasn't because I was angry with her about Alun Brooke, but because she suspected or had found out that Gwynn was in love with me.

For a moment I feel sorry for her. Gwynn had once taken her home for Sunday tea because she was lonely and shy, and she'd fallen in love with him. And all the nonsense about Alun Brooke had grown out of that.

Poor Mary Powell with her round face, her shapeless body and her awkward ways. How lucky and blessed I was to have been loved back. I'd lost him, I'd lost him, but I'd never lose the knowledge of his love.

I love you, I whisper to him in the dark, incense-smelling church. *I love you. Don't forget my love*.

When the service is over, I break away from Ilona and Jack, determined to confront Mary Powell.

I come across her almost at once and manage to turn her from the path to the patch of grass between the church and the priest's house. She's wearing a short black coat which is too tight for her and her face is the colour of porridge. My sympathy towards her has gone.

'You were in love with Gwynn Morgan weren't you?'

A tear trickles down her nose. 'What if I was? What's it to you?'

'I'll tell you. He's dead now and no-one can claim him, but I won't have you ruining Jack's life. You don't love Jack. You only need him to soothe your pride – I know you don't love him.'

She looks bewildered, as though she's trying to place him. 'But I don't want Jack,' she says at last. 'I've had some money come to me from my mother's brother and I'm going to Cambridge to study Law. It's nothing to do with you, but I wrote to Jack last week to break off the engagement.'

'Did you? I hadn't heard that. I'm sorry I said what I did. But you're doing the right thing, believe me. You'll do well in Cambridge.'

For a moment we look at each other with something approaching kindness. Then the moment hardens. 'You were just making use of Jack,' I tell her. 'It wasn't right.'

'I suppose you think you're blameless,' she says venomously.

'No.'

'I know about you and Gwynn Morgan. I used to watch you going up to the Art room every lunch hour and I knew quite well what was going on. And you a married woman with a husband on active service. And he married too, and both of you entrusted with shaping the lives of innocent young people. It was disgusting. You had sexual relations together, didn't you?'

'Yes, we did as a matter of fact.' What makes me admit to it? Pride? 'Yes, we did.'

Her face seems to disintegrate. 'I don't ever want to speak to you again,' she says. 'Let me go. You're disgusting you are. I'll tell you what you remind me of. My step-mother's got a rose in the parlour in a glass vase. A very beautiful red rose it looks, but that's only the half of it. The other half is the thick, ugly stem in the water, a vivid green with great thorns like beaks sticking out of it. That's you, that is. Oh, you're pretty enough, but cruel and evil as well. And you weren't the only girl he was after. You know that, don't you?'

My blood is boiling now. All I want to do is hurt her. 'I

know he was never after you anyway. He invited you home to tea once because he felt sorry for you, because you were so lonely and pitiful. And you made trouble for him, telling everyone he'd taken you out for a birthday celebration. He didn't even know it was your birthday. He was certainly never after *you*.'

'I don't ever want to speak to you again,' she says, 'I'm going straight to the station to get the next train home. I intended to have a few words with Mrs Morgan, but I can't face her after this.'

'She'll survive that.'

Ilona is suddenly at my elbow. 'Yes, his wife will survive that very well. We'll all manage to survive your departure with great fortitude, so don't delay it on our account. Come along, Rhian.'

'You're a fallen woman, Rhian,' Mary Powell says, ignoring Ilona and looking at me with round, frightened eyes. 'I'd never, never have believed it. I thought you were only flirting with him, and that was bad enough.'

'For pity's sake, don't let that crazy woman upset you,' Ilona says as we follow the crowd to the churchyard.'

'She hasn't upset me. She's written to Jack, releasing him from the engagement, so I suppose I can forgive her anything. I wonder why he didn't tell us.'

'He told me, but it didn't seem important. All I've been able to think about is you and Gwynn.'

But of course, Mary Powell's words did upset me. 'You're a fallen woman, Rhian.' Those frightened, accusing eyes. I was even more upset though by the way I'd attacked her.

Chapter Eighteen

Days pass, as they do. The summer term is always too full, but I suppose the extra work involved in getting the Fifth and the Upper Sixth ready for their examinations means I have less time to brood. I don't mean that I'm beginning to recover, but beginning, perhaps, to get over the shock and to be reconciled to my enormous loss.

I start going to chapel again, smiling carefully at Huw's parents but avoiding them after the service. It surprises me that my mother-in-law is able to let things ride; she's usually a great one for Having Things Out. She's built that way; thirteen and a half stone of well corseted flesh with – on a Sunday morning – a straw hat on the top.

I get three letters from Huw in less than a week, all written, I think, before the invasion, but I can't answer them. Even the short, uncommitted letters I've been writing for the last few months now seem too false.

Eventually I decide to tell him the truth. Too much has been hidden from too many people; suddenly I feel the need to proclaim my love and my loss. My dear Huw – I underline the 'dear,' feeling very tender towards him as though he's a character in a story, someone rather young and innocent who impulsively married a foolish, worthless girl. I tell him about my passion for Gwynn and how I succumbed to it, admitting to breaking every marriage vow and giving him permission to feel free of me. He can divorce me, I tell him, when he comes home. I promise to give up the house and furniture and to make no financial demands on him. I'm quite sure he'll never forgive me, but I hope he'll eventually recover his trust in women and find somebody else. It's quite a long letter, stilted, but still moving. I cry a lot over it.

But I find I can't post it. I feel sure that he must be in the fighting by this time and I can't take the risk that getting my letter will make him even a jot less determined to survive.

What I decide is to take the letter to his parents, telling them what's in it, explaining that I'm letting them decide when to send it to him because I feel that they are now his next of kin.

I know that I'm going to hurt them badly, yet as I walk down the hill to their house I'm feeling almost peaceful, almost serene. It's been raining and I get a sense of well-being from the cool, damp air. The pavements are full because it's a Saturday morning but I feel detached from everyone. Two girls from Form Five call out to me and I smile at them, but hardly knowing who they are and hardly caring.

The mood lasts. I say what I've planned to say quietly and firmly, almost as though I'm only delivering a message from someone else, as though I'm not really responsible for any of it.

I haven't given any thought to their reaction. My mother-in-law stops unpacking her shopping basket and sits down at the kitchen table, too stunned to speak. She's never thought that I'm the right person for her son; she'd have much preferred a frivolous, gossipy little town girl, someone who'd be running to her three times a day for advice and help, but now she's thinking only of Huw. She opens her mouth but immediately shuts it again. She picks up the letter as though she can hardly bear to touch it. She doesn't raise her eyes to look at me.

My father-in-law reminds her that he's come in for his lunch and that he hasn't got all day. She turns on him. 'Yes you have,' she says. 'You're staying home this afternoon.'

It's only then that he realises the seriousness of the situation. He sits down, too. 'But I always work till four on a Saturday,' he says truculently.

I repeat that I'm sorry for the way things have turned out.

'Didn't we give you everything you wanted?' he asks me, managing, as ever, to reduce life to the most basic level.

172

'You've always been very generous,' I tell him. 'But from now on I'll be giving you Ilona Hughes's rent and paying you the same amount myself.'

It was the right thing to say; he nods his head and grunts a bit. 'That seems fair,' he says.

My mother-in-law though, is still silent; not being so mercenary, she's not so easily appeased.

'I have to go now.'

As I close the back door behind me, I can hear her anger against me beginning to break out. I go and walk by the sea which is blue and still.

I wish I could think of that visit as a great ordeal, but I can't. I suppose I was carried along by the knowledge that I'd feel less stifled, less hypocritical after writing to Huw and handing over the letter, and this proved true. After that Saturday morning, I really felt I could breathe more easily. I felt I'd only done what I had to do; what my life had been leading up to.

A few days later I write a letter of resignation and take it to the Head. I tell him about the letter I've written to Huw, tell him that I intend to burn my boats and move to North Wales with Ilona.

He's silent for a moment or two, his face blank.

'How about your mother?' he asks at last. 'How will she feel about your moving away?'

'She'll be all right. She'll be getting married again as soon as the war's over. She'll be all right.'

'Well, then, I can't object, can I? I'll be sorry to lose you, that goes without saying. I've got nothing but praise for your teaching. You can depend on me for a decent testimonial.'

'Thank you.'

'And perhaps I ought to tell you something else, now that you're leaving us.'

I look at him quickly and wait for what's coming. He always enjoys his power to surprise. 'I never really blamed Gwynn Morgan,' he says. 'How could I?'

I try to smile, to acknowledge whatever affection or admiration he intends, but I can't manage it. I sit opposite him, my eyes red, my throat sore, but feeling his sympathy.

'No-one will talk to me about Gwynn. Everyone is too embarrassed. If I were his widow, people would be willing to talk about him and it would keep him alive for me.'

He clears his throat. 'He came to see me before he left, told me how things were between you, how you were going to move away together when he came out of the army.'

'He told you that!'

'You're surprised. Well, he was on my staff for almost twenty years, you know. I suppose we were quite close in a manner of speaking – that is to say, I never interfered with his department and he kept out of my way. A good working relationship. We weren't friends exactly, but we certainly weren't enemies. Anyway, he told me about his plans for the future, how he was going to try to make a living from painting.'

'Did you try to dissuade him?'

'Oh yes, I thought it my duty to try to dissuade him. I didn't mention his private affairs, you understand, but I did remind him about his pension and all that. But he said . . . '

'What? What did he say? Please tell me.'

'"Bugger the pension," were his actual words. An inelegant phrase, I thought, but expressive enough. "Bugger the pension." Yes.'

'And was that all?'

'That was all. He was sitting . . . no, he was standing, but with his foot on the rung of that chair, and at that point, he shoved his hand out towards me, we shook hands and then he left.'

'Thank you.'

The Head gets up, shaking his head like a dog that's been out in the rain. 'He left some of his drawings in the Art room,' he says. 'I thought I'd get Miss Simpson to mount some of them for the Prize Day exhibition, but if you'd like one or two, perhaps you should have them.'

Without further word, he marches me out along the crowded corridor and up the two flights of stairs to the Art room, the chop and cross-currents of voices dying out as we progress by.

I haven't been in the Art room since Gwynn left at the end of last term and I have to battle with a flood of memories. If the Head had said anything to me in those first moments, I think I'd have burst out into a noisy bout of crying.

But he doesn't. He turns his attention to small, grey-haired Miss Simpson, Gwynn's replacement, who's mixing paint for her afternoon classes.

'Well done,' he says. 'All preparation completed before the bell is my fundamental rule for all practical classes. I hope you're not mixing too many colours, though, Miss Simpson. Three colours are quite sufficient for any piece of work these days. *Five!* Miss Simpson I'm afraid you haven't learned to husband your resources. The war may last another six months, you know, or even another year. In the meantime, three colours only and much smaller sheets of paper, Miss Simpson. Please don't forget.'

Miss Simpson, realising how lucky she is to get even this temporary post, smiles as he bullies her. The bell rings for the beginning of afternoon school. 'We won't disturb you for long, Miss Simpson,' the Head says. 'Mrs Evans and I are here to decide what to do with Mr Morgan's paintings. I'm sure you'll see to it that your class – 4B isn't it? – doesn't disturb us.'

4B crowd in with their customary bang and flourish, see the Head and start twittering like a classroom of small birds. Miss Simpson has backed her small frame into a corner, but by this time I'm feeling well enough to frown threateningly at them, and slowly they lapse into silence.

The Head takes out the portfolio of drawings and watercolours: landscapes and seascapes; some very delicate, some bold and dark; about a dozen altogether. He spreads them out on a table at the back of the room.

'Which would you like?' he asks me.

'I'd like them all.'

He looks at me sullenly; they'd certainly have made an impressive show in the Hall on Prize Day. But he gathers them up carefully, replaces them in the portfolio, hands it to me and marches to the front. 'Thank you, Miss Simpson. That will be all.'

The swell of voices gathers again before we've reached the top of the stairs.

'I must go to my class. Thank you, Mr Williams.'

'I shall expect very hard work from you, Mrs Evans, for the rest of this term – exceptionally hard work and some spectacular examination results. By the way, I don't think Delia Morris is coping too well at the moment. Is she perhaps spending her time around the town cafés in the evenings? If I were you I should have a talk with her. Is it more encouragement she needs or more homework?'

He knows everything about everybody, but at the moment I don't hold anything against him.

'I'll speak to her. I'll sort it out.'

When I get home I pin the drawings and watercolours up around my small bedroom and they bring me a measure of comfort when I pace about at night.

On the Wednesday of that week – and for the first time since Gwynn's funeral – I go home to Tregroes.

Huw's parents have called on my mother and told her about my letter to Huw: I'm for it.

Adultery, she says, is not a nice word. I agree with her. 'It's certainly not one of my favourites,' I say, 'but compared with *death* for instance, I find it relatively undisturbing.'

She inclines her head a little, accepting my rebuke. 'I was sorry to hear about Mr Gwynn Morgan,' she says.

'You can call him Gwynn, Mam. He might have been somebody else's husband, but he was my lover and we were going to live together.' The sob in my throat almost chokes me.

'How could you have lived together, girl? He with a wife and you with a husband. Where ever could you have lived? Who would have wanted you as neighbours?'

'We were going to go away together. We were going to have children together.'

'Heaven help us! Illegitimate children they'd have been. What ever would your father have said?'

'He'd have been very distressed, I know.'

'I would have been very distressed, too. So would Fredo. But don't cry, girl. It didn't happen.'

'I wanted it to happen. I wanted to live with him and have his children. More than anything in the world. That's why

I'm crying. Because I loved him with all my heart and soul. As a woman is supposed to love a man.'

'As a wife is supposed to love a husband.'

'Yes, that's how I loved him. As the hart panteth after the water brooks.'

'Blasphemy, now. Taking the Lord's name in vain.'

'I don't mean to be blasphemous. I know too much of the Bible, that's my trouble, it comes into my head unasked. As the apple tree among the trees of the wood, so is my beloved among the sons. I sat down under his shadow and his fruit was sweet to my taste. He taketh me to the banqueting house and his banner over me is love.'

'Don't cry, girl, don't cry. I won't say anything else, I promise you. He's dead, poor man. It's over. And I suppose you might change your mind about Huw after a while. That's what I told his parents, anyway. I don't know whether I believe it or not.'

'No, I won't change my mind. I've given in my notice at school and I'm applying for a post in Caernarfon so that I can live with Ilona.'

'With Ilona Hughes? Is she going back home, then?'

'Yes. She's got to look after her grandmother who's had a bit of a stroke. And I'll get some lodgings nearby. It'll do me good to get away from Llanfair.'

My mother looks shaken but doesn't try to dissuade me. 'Well, don't stay away too long, girl. I'll miss you, you know that.'

'I'll get back every holiday.'

'You'll pine after your little house.'

'No. It was Huw's house, his father's house, his grand-mother's – but not mine.'

'You'll take your father's books with you?'

'Of course I will, and all the other things you gave me. I'll have to start packing before long.'

'Everybody on the move! Fredo is going to Italy quite soon.'

'Before the end of the war?'

'Italy is on our side now, it seems, and the Italian prisoners of war are going to be repatriated. When there are ships available, they say, but when will that be? It's very hard on him, poor man. He hasn't heard anything about his sons all this year. Huw's father was tamping mad about Fredo too. "That Eyetie" he called him.'

'He probably thinks we're both loose women. What does it matter? What does anything matter?'

But I suddenly think of Mary Powell at the funeral. 'You're a fallen woman, Rhian,' and feel hot and angry again. And ashamed, too, I suppose.

After supper I'm too restless to sit long. I walk up the hill with great angry strides waiting for the evening to pass. No one will be meeting me from the bus.

My mother is listening to the wireless when I get back; fierce fighting continuing in Normandy with the Allies making steady advances along the Cherbourg peninsula. Huw could well be in the thick of it. I can't pray, but I cross my fingers for him.

'I must go, Mam.'

'I'll come a step or two with you. Come, Floss.'

Hewl Fach is ablaze with wild roses and honeysuckle, their scent as sweet and delicate as though there were no such things as war and death. I take my mother's arm and when the bus comes I can hardly bear to leave her.

Next morning the Head isn't in Assembly. Talfan Roberts, Deputy Head, scrapes his throat and reads, rather haltingly, a long passage from Deuteronomy, tries but fails to lead the hymn singing, drones out the announcements, then walks out, having forgotten to dismiss us.

'Where's the Head?'

No-one seems to know. We all half-expect him to burst through the door – he always bursts through doors – but he doesn't.

'Right,' Jack says, bounding on to the platform, 'Everyone turn. Now walk quietly to your classrooms. Lead out, Form Six.'

'Has he been called up, Miss?' a little lad from 2C asks me. 'If he was in the Army, Miss, would he have to take orders?'

'That's enough, Owen. The Head doesn't have to ask your permission to take a morning off school. He's probably got a committee meeting.'

'Can we have a holiday, Miss? Can we have a quiz? Can we have a spelling bee? Oh, not lessons, Miss. Not today, Miss.'

It's strange without him, peaceful but oddly disturbing at the same time.

'Where is he?' I ask Talfan in the lunch-hour.

'Don't know. He had someone to deal with, that's all he told me, and Heaven help him or her, whoever it may be. Anyway, I shall have a nervous breakdown if he's not back by tomorrow. Everyone seems to think I'm supposed to be in charge. Up to now being Deputy Head has only meant having tea with the governors once a month – and that's bad enough.'

In fact, the Head is back before the end of the afternoon. I know, because I'm called to his room.

'Sit down, Mrs Evans. Right, I won't beat about the bush. I've been to see an erstwhile colleague of yours, Miss Mary Powell.'

'Really. How is she?'

He gives me a long, baleful look. 'I didn't go to enquire after her health. No, I went because she'd sent me a filthy, anonymous letter.'

He passes me a letter, a thick white envelope, the address in bold black capitals. My hand shakes as I open it.

I think you should know that one of your staff, Mrs Rhian Evans, is an adulterous woman not fit to be in charge of innocent young people. One who knows.

I manage to keep my voice fairly steady. 'How did you know it was from Mary Powell? It's postmarked Shrewsbury.' *How she hates me.*

His eyes flash at me. 'How did I know? How do I know who locks the girls in the changing room? How do I know who chalks dirty words on the blackboard? Because I've made it my business to know these things. I know my pupils. I know my parents. I know my staff. Because I've made it my business to know them. There's not much that John Cynrig Williams doesn't know about his school.'

He sits back in his chair as though expecting a round of applause.

179

'What happened?' I ask quietly. *I can feel her hatred crushing me.*

'What happened? I took her to the police station and got her to sign a confession. A bit brutal you think? Well, I can tell you one thing: kindness is rarely any use when dealing with the writers of filthy letters. Perhaps you'll be a Headmistress one day, so it's as well I should give you the benefit of my experience. Any more questions?'

'Will they make any charges against her?' *She hates me, but I can't blame her.*

'They won't clap her in prison, if that's what you mean. No. But they have her confession. She's not daft, she'll think twice before writing any more nasty little letters. I would have got another confession out of her to show Jack Jones except that I've washed my hands of that unfortunate business.'

'She's released him from their engagement.'

'What? She has? Why doesn't someone tell me these things?'

'I thought you'd have made it your business to find out.'

'Very good. A quick stab below the belt is an excellent tactic. You're learning fast, Mrs Evans. You'll be a credit to me, yet.'

'Her mother died in an asylum.' *But I still attacked her in the churchyard.*

I've taken him by surprise again, but he quickly recovers. 'So? Her mother died in an asylum. Does that give her licence to spread filth amongst people?'

'No. But marching her to a police-station might be considered a little harsh under the circumstances.' *But no more harsh than my harsh words.*

'So what exactly would you have done?'

'I've no idea.' *I was certainly never charitable towards her.*

'Oh, I'm sure you'd have been very kind, very understanding. But as I've said, kindness doesn't work with poison letters. You may go now, Mrs Evans. Oh, and by the way, you'll be receiving a letter of apology from Miss Powell. Needless to say, it won't contain a shred of genuine remorse, but writing it may have done her some good.'

'I suppose you suggested that?' *Was anyone ever kind to her?*

'Suggested it? I stood over her while she wrote it.'

I get up to go. 'Thank you, Mr Williams.'

'Oh, I enjoyed it. The break from routine was very pleasant. And, look, I've even made you smile.'

Chapter Nineteen

At school I try to appear normal, pushing my grief further and further down inside me like someone trying to pack too much shopping into too small a bag. By the end of the day I'm exhausted with the effort and drag myself home to bed, where I lie flat and quite still till Ilona gets back from work. Crying would do me good, I know, but the pain has become hard as granite, I can't cry.

The summer evenings are lovely. Sometimes Ilona and I go to sit on the sea wall to watch the setting sun – we've had a month of superb sunsets – but somehow we always end up thinking and talking about the war. I suppose it would be worse if we were on the South coast facing Normandy, but since the invasion, the war seems very close, even here. We're told on every news bulletin that our losses are fewer than expected, but people are still living in fear of that telegram from the War Office. I know I am.

'Do you pray, Ilona?'

'Good Lord, no. I gave that up the day they took my tonsils out. I was about eleven, I think. I'd stayed awake all the previous night praying and praying that I should be cured without an operation. Well, it didn't work, did it, so that when I came round from the anaesthetic it was without tonsils or God. And to be truthful I've never missed either.'

The air is rinsed after the light rain. The sky is a clean, bright pink.

'I think there is a God, but perhaps the only valid prayers are those for greater understanding.'

Ilona's eyes are direct and a little too sharp. 'Greater

understanding of what?'

'Of His nature, the nature of His love and mercy. If we could understand, perhaps we could accept. I can't seem to understand or accept Gwynn's death.'

'Of course you can't. He was killed by a bomb. Who can accept bombs? There's precious little of love and mercy about bombs.'

Ilona, bright about lots of things, is seldom at her best when it comes to theological discussion. I only manage to peer through the glass darkly, but she seems intent on looking the other way.

I decide to change the subject. 'I feel really guilty about school. I can't seem to rouse myself from this apathy. I don't seem to care about my exam results or my reports. I don't care about anything.'

'Why should you? You've already worked too hard in that school. Don't give it another thought. Oh, you'll be much better at the end of term. When we leave this place, you'll have other things to think about, other people to meet and make friends with. I'm longing to get away.'

'It's all right for you. You're going home to your family and soon you'll have a new baby as well.'

'But my family will really take to you Rhian, because you're so genteel. They're a rough lot, my family, very impressed by quiet people who don't drink or swear. And as for the baby, you shall take it out for me every afternoon. Ifor's getting me a new pram.'

'Will you be seeing a lot of Ifor? Will people know it's his baby?'

'I suppose so. I suppose it will look like him; fat with sandy hair and a big lump of a nose. Jesus, what do I see in him? He's bad-tempered and ugly and unreliable. Why are women so stupid? By the way, I saw your mother-in-law in Finch Square this afternoon and she smiled at me quite kindly. What can it mean? Is she plotting something?'

'I really don't know. She baffles me; I expected all sorts of trouble from her, but she's been almost too quiet. And I expected Huw's father to try and turn me out of the house, but not a word. I can't understand it.'

'Perhaps they're counting on you changing your mind, so

that they'll be sitting back ready to forgive and forget.'

'No, I'm sure they could never forgive me. And I think they must have sent Huw the letter I wrote, because I haven't heard from him for three weeks now. Oh, I hope he's safe. I'll feel so wretched if anything happens to him; responsible, somehow.'

'Great Heavens, girl, you can't hold yourself responsible for a war. Have some humility. Pull yourself together. You'll be thinking you're God next. Like your Head.'

'He doesn't think he's God. Just a minor saint. Saint John Cynrig Williams . . . You know, I used to hate him, but I'm getting quite fond of him now that I'm leaving. I'll miss him when I go. And I'll miss Jack, of course.'

'I'll miss Jack, too. God, if I was anything like sane, I'd marry him.'

'Has he asked you to?'

'About a hundred times. He's coming round later on to make it a hundred and one. Hey, we'd better go home or we'll miss him.'

'Poor Jack. He hasn't had much luck with women.'

'He has. He got away from that dopey Mary Powell and very soon he'll be free of me. That's wonderful luck. Who'll he be after next I wonder?'

We don't get back until half past ten. Ilona doesn't seem too concerned that she's missed Jack.

'Do you think I look pregnant?' she asks me as we're clearing up before going to bed.

'Well, you don't stick out in one big lump in the front. You could be just fat, I suppose. I mean, fatter than you were. Why?'

'I heard Myfanwy Jenkins whispering something to Katie Lloyd this morning, both of them staring at my belly. I suppose they know. They pretended to believe me when I told them I was having to go back home to nurse Nain, but I don't suppose they did.'

'Do you mind?'

'No. As long as Jack's name isn't dragged into it. I wouldn't want them to think badly of Jack. Perhaps I shouldn't go out with him from now on.'

'Oh, stop being so conventional. Why shouldn't people gossip? There's precious little entertainment these days. Give them something to enjoy.'

The next evening, when we've just finished washing up, there's a knock at the door and Ilona goes to answer it. I'm hoping she and Jack will go out for a walk and a drink, because I've got some reports to write.

'It's Gwynn's wife,' Ilona says, rushing back into the living room looking wild and flustered. It's Mrs Morgan– Celine – shall I ask her in?'

'You'll have to, I suppose.'

I stand up too quickly and feel dizzy. I haven't seen her since the funeral. I straighten my hair in the mirror. I look terrible, my eyes are suddenly burning and my lips feel parched.

'Come in.' My voice sounds high and unnatural. 'Won't you sit down? Would you like a cup of tea?'

'And a raspberry bun?' she asks dryly.

'You never liked raspberry buns,' I reply, as smoothly as I can, 'so it's just as well that I haven't any.'

'I won't have tea either, thank-you. It will be a very brief visit.'

She's dressed in a plain black dress with a pearl choker round her neck. She's lost weight and looks older than she did, but very smart, very French. I remember Gwynn telling me that she never went out of the house without an hour's preparation.

I wait for her to continue. I run my tongue round my lips. I can't think of anything to say.

'I called because I heard you were leaving Llanfair.'

I clear my throat again. 'This is my lodger, Ilona Hughes. This is Mrs Morgan, Ilona.'

'Yes, we introduced ourselves,' Ilona says. Even she seems subdued. She sits in a chair opposite Celine, as though to keep an eye on her.

'I was grateful to you,' Celine says, 'for being so calm and discreet at the funeral. It might have been very different.'

'I'm sure you'd have coped with anything.'

'No, I don't always manage to keep my head. As you

know. How is Jack? He still calls, but we play cards, we don't talk. Is he still involved with that hysterical woman? That Mary Powell? I don't ask him.'

'No, that seems over. He's quite well I think. He may be calling here soon, he and Ilona sometimes go to the pub together.'

'To the Ship? You don't go with them? Why is that?'

I shrug my shoulders. Why has she come? What does she want?

'Are you very un'appy?' she continues.

'Of course I am. How can you ask?'

'He told me about your plans.' I can see a muscle move in her throat.

'We had plans, yes.'

'He was going to leave me, but I still wish he was alive and not dead. Do you believe that?'

'Of course I do. You loved him.'

'Do you think love lasts, then, even after – even after one has been rejected for another woman?'

'I don't know,' I say miserably. 'But I should think it might. Especially a long-standing love. You were married for twenty years. You've got twenty years to look back on.'

She's looking at me, not angrily, I think, but sadly. 'Every 'appy memory has been destroyed for me,' she says. 'I wanted you to know that. There's nothing left for me, nothing at all. I wanted you to know that. I wanted you to know how much of my life you've ruined.'

'She knew what she was doing,' Ilona says. 'She did it with her eyes open – because she couldn't help it. Sometimes it's like that. Sometimes you don't have a choice.'

I feel as though I'm fighting for air. 'I had no choice,' I say, echoing Ilona's words. 'I can't tell you I'm sorry, because though I am sorry – very sorry – for what I did to you, I know I'd do exactly the same again. I don't regret it. I can't.'

'And I can't forgive you,' Celine says. 'I'll never forgive you. I can't.'

'I don't expect you to.'

We look at each other for a long time in a sadness which is almost despair. I find myself wondering whether I'll ever see her again. She never did me any harm.

'He loved you,' I said. 'I know he loved you. He told me so when we first became friendly. He said he loved you and that I was someone he couldn't help . . . desiring. Later on, though . . . it was the war, perhaps. If he hadn't been going away, I don't think we'd have become so desperate. I don't know. I'm not trying to excuse myself.'

'No, I didn't think you would. I gave you that much credit. I wish I could hate you, but I can't. I found you good company. It was kind of you to sit for me, though I suppose you did it to be with him.'

'I suppose I did. Yes.' The room is swaying.

'I can't forgive you,' she says. 'But I don't 'ate you.'

She suddenly gets up and thrusts out her small, soft, almost boneless white hand at me. She was always very formal, shaking hands at the beginning and the end of every painting session.

'Will you go back to France when the war is over?' I ask her.

'No, I'll stay here.'

'Won't you be very lonely?'

'Yes. But I'd be very lonely anywhere.'

Ilona takes her to the door and when she's gone, I fall into a rage of weeping, crying passionately, bitterly, painfully, until I have hardly any strength left to draw breath.

Jack doesn't call until after ten and when he does, it's to bring bad news: Mary Powell has been found dead, drowned in the river Irfon near her home.

'We went for a long walk by that river,' Jack says. 'Do you remember, Ilona, I told you about it? When I was there in the Easter holiday. It was a lovely day, too, the sun shining very brightly, but cold at the same time, a lovely day for walking. And we talked about swimming – isn't that strange? – and I promised I'd teach her to swim in the summer. She'd have been a fine swimmer, she had good strong shoulders on her, but she said, no, she'd always hated the water, the cold violence of it. What a tragedy. D'you know, I can't believe it. I still can't believe it. The cold violence of it, that's what she said. I can't believe . . .'

He's talking so fast and furiously that I have to interrupt

him. 'She must have fallen in. She was probably watching out for something, a kingfisher or an otter, and lost her balance. I've almost done it myself. And if she couldn't swim, she'd have panicked, and the current in a river can be really treacherous.'

'You can't fall into a river,' Jack says.

'What are you talking about? Of course you can. Don't you think anyone has ever fallen into a river?'

'Small children perhaps, but not adults. Not unless they're completely drunk, anyway. No, a human body has natural balance. You can lean over really far, but the body's centre of gravity stops you falling in.'

'What nonsense. That's just theory, Jack. It's nonsense. People fall into rivers every day. And they drown, too.'

'Don't argue,' Ilona says. 'There'll be an inquest, let's wait for the result of that. We've all had a shock and we all feel guilty. I know I do. I only met her once, but nobody disliked her as much as I did. I thought she was a rotten cow and dangerous as well, and I said so over and over again. And if I turned you against her, Jack, well, I'm sorry, but I still think I was right. I'm not going to start whitewashing her because she's committed suicide.'

'So you think it was suicide?' Jack asks. 'So do I.'

'It may have been,' Ilona says. 'Let's wait to see what the inquest says.'

'Well, I don't think so,' I tell Jack. 'Look, she'd been left this money – two or three thousand pounds, Mrs Lewis told me – and was all set to start a law degree in Cambridge. What a great opportunity for her. She'd have been looking forward to it, she was that sort. She was very ambitious. She had a very good brain.'

Ilona looks unconvinced by my argument. 'Anyway Jack, remember that it was she who broke off the engagement, not you. You've got nothing to blame yourself for. You were always kind to her, soft as butter, as you are to everyone.'

'But deep down, she knew I wanted to be free, she must have known. I couldn't be the same towards her once I'd got to know you. She must have known.'

'No she didn't,' I say. 'She wasn't the perceptive type, she had a good brain but no sensitivity. With Cambridge in front of her, she probably couldn't be bothered with you, she probably thought she could do better. Oh, that's being mean and small-minded again, I know, but I'm sure it was something like that. Look, it's very sad. Let's agree to feel very sad because she's dead, but let's not go on and on about feeling guilty. It won't do anyone any good.'

'I do feel guilty, though,' Jack says, 'guilty as hell, if you want to know the truth. I thought I was in love with her and found out I wasn't.'

'I'm going to bed,' I announce, getting to my feet. 'I'm worn out.'

'Gwynn's wife has been here,' Ilona says. 'The poor girl's had enough trauma for one day.'

'Good Lord,' Jack says, 'Mrs Morgan here? What did she want? Was she abusive?

'No,' Ilona says. 'She was quite civilized. All the same . . .'

'All the same, I'm worn out.'

When I'm in bed, I hear them going out. It's a mild moonlit night and a walk will do them both good.

Poor Mary Powell. I want to stop thinking about her, but I can't. If she did drown herself, it might have been for Gwynn's sake rather than for Jack's. Could she have had it in her to kill herself for love? I almost envy her.

The next day the Head calls me into his study again. He made a brief announcement in Assembly about Mary's death, and I imagine he wants to know whether I'll be willing to represent the school at her funeral. I intend to decline.

'Sit down,' he says in his gruffest voice. 'Well, what have you got to say to me? It was all my fault, I suppose, is that right?'

For a moment I'm too bewildered to speak.

'Marching her to the police-station is how you put it, if I remember. Rather drastic was how you described it, I think. Rather harsh.'

'Oh, I see. So you're another one who wants to be held responsible for Mary Powell's death. Is that it?'

'Certainly not. I'm merely giving you the opportunity of telling me what you think.'

'I think she was in love with Gwynn Morgan and became overwrought when he was killed. I think Jack Jones and Ilona Hughes my lodger, and you and I and possibly her step-mother were no more than small irritants. We didn't do anything to help her state of mind, but we didn't cause it. That's my opinion.'

'I was simply an irritant? Marching her to the police-station and standing over her while she wrote to you would have affected her as much as a gnat bite, is that what you're saying?'

'Or a grain of dust in the eye. Yes, that's what I think.'

He grunts and then stands up. 'Now then, who do you think I should send to the funeral? Talfan and you have had too much of funerals, and so have I. What about Mrs Lewis, History? Handsome woman. Looks well in black. Yes, I think we'll decide on Mrs Lewis. Will you send her to me, please? So I've dwindled into a mere irritant, have I? Well, well, well. A gnat-bite. Well, well.'

What I can't get out of my mind is the way I attacked Mary on the afternoon of the funeral when she must already have been feeling so desolate. 'He was never after you, anyway.' How could I have been so insensitive and cruel? If anyone should feel guilty, I should.

'How did Miss Powell come to drown, Miss? Was she out swimming?'

'No, she fell into the river.'

'Praps she was pushed in, Miss?'

'No, I don't think so, Alfie. Nothing like that.'

'Praps she committed suicide, Miss?'

'No, I don't think so. Look here, do you think we could possibly start the lesson now?'

'Only I wish I hadn't complained, Miss, that time she clouted me. She left soon after, didn't she? I never had much of a headache, Miss. Not really.'

'Look Alfie, however Miss Powell drowned, whether she committed suicide or not, had absolutely nothing to do with you. All right? Nothing. Her fiancé was killed out in Burma

191

if you want to know the truth. Alun Brooke his name was. He was a Second Lieutenant in the Intelligence Corps. All right? It had absolutely nothing to do with you.'

'I've forgotten my homework, Miss. Is that all right, Miss?'

Chapter Twenty

On the last day of school, I'm called forward to the platform during Assembly, praised for my hard work and dedication and presented with a black fountain pen and propelling pencil.

In private, afterwards, the Head tells me that it's now my clear duty to look ahead to a new and exciting chapter of my life; new challenges and new responsibilities, then descends from the high ground by giving me a photograph of Gwynn taken on a school trip to London in 1936. As I leave his study, he leans forward as though to kiss me, but recovers himself in time and frowns fiercely at me instead.

I don't have much to pack; two suitcases of clothes, a trunk of books – mostly my father's, – and a cardboard box full of china and linen, yet it seems too much to take by train. Ilona has roughly the same amount; fewer books but more clothes.

'Ifor can come down to fetch us at the weekend,' she announces one morning after reading her letters. 'He's got a new van and he says it won't be any trouble, he can tell his wife he's going to look at some sheep. What day shall he come? Saturday or Sunday?'

I have a moment's panic. I've managed to get a good post in the Grammar School in Caernarfon and decent lodgings in Brynteg, about half a mile from Ilona's grandmother, but now that the move is imminent, I'm full of pain and misgiving. All my most precious memories are tied up in Llanfair; in this house, in the Art room at school, in the Ship, on the hill, on lovely Celyn sands. How can I leave? On the seafront, by that wall outside the Infants' school, leaning against those railings, the richest moments of my life occurred. Should I be trying to forget them? What would be left? Only something thin and dark rattling about in the emptiness.

I take some deep breaths. 'Sunday, then. Then I can go home again on Saturday. I think my mother would like that.'

'Try not to be upset, Rhian. Damn it, girl, you're not going far.'

'It *is* far. North Wales is like abroad. I won't even be able to understand people talking.'

'You've understood me.'

'You're a very simple person.'

'Look, would you like me to come with you to your mother's? You talk such a lot about her and I've never clapped eyes on her yet.'

'No, I don't think so, thank you. She'll find out soon enough that you're pregnant, but I don't want to overwhelm her with the evidence.'

'Is it as obvious as all that?'

'Well, it's not written all over your face, but once the eye travels downwards . . . yes, it's fairly obvious.'

'No wonder Jack and I are getting funny looks in the Ship. I really shouldn't be seen with him now.'

'They probably think you're married. You look like an old married woman.'

'Old now, as well as simple.'

'And rather fat about the middle.'

'Well, what do you expect? I am seven months pregnant. Do you know, I worked out that I probably conceived on Christmas Eve. Rather nice, I think.'

'Yes. *So hallowed and so gracious is the time.* But doesn't that make you eight months pregnant?'

'Does it? Well, it doesn't mean much. First babies are usually late and I suppose it will come when it's ready. I'm in no hurry.'

'I suppose your grandmother knows about the baby?'

'Of course she does. She doesn't mind at all. Her first was born out of wedlock. Isn't wedlock an awful word. Fancy being locked into a marriage.'

'I don't know that I'd mind it . . . if it was to the right person.'

'I'd mind it. I'd rather be tied to a shop. There *is* room for another shop in Brynteg, Nain says. When she was a girl, her mother had a bit of a shop in the front room, faggots a penny each and rice pudding, ha'penny a portion. I think I'll go in for newspapers and tobacco, something for the men. Cheer up Rhian. You'll love it in Brynteg, I promise you.'

As we'd already said our goodbyes on Wednesday evening, my mother's surprised to see me again and concerned that my new landlady might be worried at my change of plan. When I tell her that I'm staying with Ilona's grandmother for the first few weeks, she's happier and immediately fetches me some eggs and a fruit cake for her.

She's very busy and as usual shrugs off my offer of help – 'I'll be longer showing you what to do, girl, than doing it myself' – so as it's a warm, cloudless day, blue and gold as far as the eye can see, I decide to walk over the fields to Tregroes; a sentimental journey, I suppose, and foolish too, as my spirits are already low, my heart heavy.

The birds have stopped singing, though the hedges are still full of summer. The last of the honeysuckle has a heavier, more pungent smell than it had a month ago, and the wild roses have grown high into the trees. In the distance, the wheat is a beautiful blushing yellow.

I come to the elementary school I attended until I was eleven, an uncompromising granite building with slate roof and tall narrow windows, overlooking the lovely hills on one side and on the other, the steep valley. Our headmaster was a small frustrated man, unhappy in his marriage, it was said, certainly no longer interested in teaching. He spent long stretches of every day staring out of the windows on the valley side, as though that way lay escape. He was often moved to tears by some incident in a book we'd be reading as a class, he'd bite his lip, blow his nose and sigh, then set us some written exercises and resume his position at the window. He was never unkind. In a community beset by innumerable instances of real poverty, his was, I suppose, the poverty of a life without love. I think of Mary Powell; the poor girl is always in that deep green, gloomy place at the back of my thoughts. 'Suicide while the balance of the mind was disturbed,' the inquest said. She would have done well at Cambridge, but it was love she wanted; and lacked. Jack has been dreadfully upset by her death; we've seen very little of him in the last few weeks.

A short walk and I'm at the chapel where I was christened and confirmed – and married, too, though I try not to think about that – instructed and bored for many, many hours, where I made up rhymes and stories to pass the time, sang and prayed, day-dreamed about boys, searched the hymn-books for passion and the Bible for dirty verses and occasionally tried to understand something too difficult to understand, about God.

I can remember the first time I was taken to evening service instead of being left at home with my grandmother: my delight at seeing the moon and all the dazzling company of stars when we came out. I suppose I must have been about three then. I can remember, a few years later, the agony of being called forward to the Big Seat to receive some prize or other and wishing hard that I wasn't so clever.

I look through the tall windows at trees and hills I once knew so well I could draw them from memory. I can still recall in the greatest detail the different bald or balding head of every deacon in the Big Seat. I can still remember vividly the large mild face of the half-idiot man who brought round the collection box, even to the wiry hairs inside his moist red nostrils. I can remember the thorough way the precentor – song-raiser in Welsh – cleared his throat while the organ played the introductory bars of the hymn. I can remember the lovely tenor of the minister's young son and the trembling contralto of the minister's wife. I remember looking at my slightly budding chest, wondering if I would ever have a great imposing bosom like hers, which fell away like a ski-slope before her. Chapel three times on a Sunday is guaranteed to turn you into an acute observer if not a Christian. I think I could still reproduce every knot and grain of the pitch-pine of our pew and the one in front.

I remember my father's funeral, the minister's text, 'And on the column was the work of flowers,' the chapel crowded to the doors. I remember my father. I walk over to the churchyard to look at his grave, beautifully cared for by my mother, a bunch of tea-roses spilling their white and yellow petals onto the ugly granite chippings. '*John Trefor Lloyd, Buarth, Tregroes. Born 12 January 1892. Died 7 September 1940. A true and faithful servant unto His master.*' I never liked that inscription, the way it confined him. I wanted something altogether larger: farmer, poet, philosopher and faithful servant unto His master, but my mother considered that over-reaching and vulgar.

I can't leave without pausing at a weatherbeaten old gravestone at the far end of the churchyard.

In memory of
The children of David and Letita Thomas.
They died as follows:
John, 14 May 1872, aged three years.
Mary Ann, 15 May 1872, aged six years.
David, 16 May 1872, aged five years.
Hewell, 22 May 1872, aged three months.

As usual the starkness of the wording blurs my eyes; no fine Victorian sentiment recording the resignation of David and Letita to the will of God, only cold anger at the fever or famine which had so ravaged their family. *Un dlawd yw fy nghenedl i.* My nation is a poor one.

Gwynn's village, Nantgoch, ten miles away, is much the same; a small farming community, a chapel society with concerts and singing festivals the highlights of the year, a strange old language, one of the oldest in Europe, binding people to their ancient pre-Christian roots when giants walked the hills and the birds of Rhiannon sang.

I shall find the same sort of people in North Wales, I know that. Though the men work in quarries and the women are tougher and sharper, according to Ilona, they have the same background of chapel and music and books.

All the same, these are *my* acres.

I walk back to the farm through fields of ripening wheat; my mother, like everyone else in these war years, growing cereal crops in little steep fields which have always in the past been laid to pasture.

*

'I'm not happy about you going away, girl.'

'I know you're not, Mam. But try to remember that I'll be with friends and that I've got a decent job and a good salary.'

'Yes, teaching is a decent sort of job, I'll grant you that. A good teacher can help and inspire a lot of children, I know that. Education has always been important in this country. But what is a salary but money, and don't expect me to judge anyone by that standard. Old Benny Brynhir half-starved his men, they say, and he died leaving thousands. Money is nothing but a curse to the ungodly . . . But I know you didn't come here for a sermon. And in any case, I have no right to preach to you.'

'Of course you have. Every right. You've always done it and you always shall.'

'No, no. I'm a sinful woman.'

'If you're sinful, Mam, Heaven help the rest of us.'

I look at her fondly, but see at once that she's trying to tell me something.

'Fredo managed to get out of that camp last night. He hadn't been able to come here for almost a fortnight. It was quite late. We were . . . Oh, I can't begin to tell you what happened. I can't believe it myself. It was . . .'

'You needn't tell me, Mam. I know what you mean, don't distress yourself.' I try to take her hand but she pulls it away. 'But how can you possibly think it was sinful when you're going to get married? When you'd have been married already if it were possible.'

'Oh, that's the oldest excuse in the world, girl. "We were going to get married." "We were saving up for a ring." "We were waiting for a house." I'm a sinner, Rhian, and so is he.'

'Mam, you haven't had time, yet, to get it straight in your mind. Go to chapel tomorrow and think about love and hate, which of them is good and which of them is evil. You and Fredo are harming nobody by your love. Gwynn and I were, I admit that. Our love may have been a sin, it probably was, but only a hypocrite could call your love a sin, and Christ hated hypocrites more than anyone. You know that.'

'I know the Bible, my girl.'

'All right. Then tell me where exactly it says that two good, unselfish people who love each other, shouldn't . . .'

'That's enough, Rhian. There's no need to go into details
. . . I know what you mean.'

'Mam, you two are not even committing adultery. Oh, I
can surely say that word because it's in the Bible, Exodus
Chapter Twenty. Listen, which commandment have you ever
broken?'

'I've coveted a great many things, girl.'

'Only necessities that we couldn't afford.'

'An inside tap, for instance.'

'An inside tap! Oh, I'll pray for you. She's coveted an
inside tap. Dear Lord, please –'

'Don't Rhian. Don't take the Lord's name in vain.'

'I will if it makes you see how foolish you're being. You're
as good as any mortal being can possibly be. You don't even
have any *little* sins like being lazy or greedy. You get up
before six every morning, you work hard as a beast of
burden all day and you give Gino and Martino your sweet
ration. You go to chapel at least twice every Sunday and
drive us all mad with your old hymns. You live a perfect life.
Except . . . well, perhaps there is one thing.'

'Yes?'

'Perhaps He will think you rather ungrateful.'

'Ungrateful?'

'You should be thanking Him, I think, for this beautiful,
loving Italian He's sent you.'

'Rhian!'

'I'm not going to say any more, I'm not going to preach.
But that's my considered opinion. Ingratitude is a sin. You
should be thanking Him: Dear God, from whom all blessings
flow.'

'Well, I don't know where you get your ideas from, Rhian,
I'm sure.'

When I get back to Hill Street, Ilona is lying on the floor with
a cushion under her head. 'I've started having this damned
baby,' she says. 'Oh Rhian, I'm in labour and it's agony and
you must get hold of the midwife. Oh, Jesus. Oh, help.'

My heart thumps against my ribs. 'Are you sure? You said
September. You've always said September and it isn't August
yet.'

'Oh Rhian, I'm frightened. This wasn't supposed to happen till I got to Brynteg. Oh, God, here's another bloody pain. I've been having them since five. Where the devil have you been? I thought you'd be back on the four o'clock. What happened to you? Where have you been?'

'I'll have to get someone to stay with you while I run down to fetch Lydia Owen. What about Mrs Jones, next door?'

'Oh God no, not Mrs Jones. Rhian, I think I'm dying and I don't want to die with Mrs Jones. No one should have pain like this. Oh God, I'm swelling up with it – my belly feels like a wardrobe. Tell me what to do.'

I don't know what to do. She's gripping my hands so hard that I can feel her pain. Nothing has prepared me for this. I know that quantities of boiling water are needed at a confinement and stacks of newspapers and two or three pudding-basins, but what one does with them I can't imagine. I've never had anything to do with babies. I've seen calves being born, but cows are such placid creatures. Even when things get very bad they only stare at their heaving sides and wait.

I manage to free my hands, straightening out my fingers one by one. 'I won't be a minute,' I tell her, 'Stay where you are a minute.'

I dash out into the road. Arthur Williams, the great lumbering boy whose father is in Swansea jail, was out there earlier, whooping back and forth on his man-sized bicycle.

He's still there. I shout to him and slowly and apprehensively he comes up the hill towards me.

'Arthur! Hurry up, Arthur! Can't you see I'm waiting for you?'

'What is it, Miss? I'm not doing any harm, Miss.'

'Do you know Iorwerth Place, Arthur?'

'Yes, Miss.'

'Not Iorwerth Terrace but Iorwerth Place.'

'Yes, Miss.'

'I want you to take a letter to Mrs Owen in Iorwerth Place. I think it's the second house after the Red Lion, but you'll have to ask.'

'Yes, Miss.'

'She's a midwife. You know what that means, don't you?'

'Yes, Miss.'

'It's my lodger, Arthur. She needs Mrs Owen urgently.'

'You needn't write a letter, Miss, I'll get her for you. "Mrs Evans's lodger needs Mrs Owen urgently" And I'll show her the way up here, Miss. You needn't bother with a letter.'

'It's a matter of life or death, Arthur.'

'Right, Miss.'

He was on his bike and flying down the hill before I'd got back to the door.

'I've sent someone for Lydia Owen. Can you try to get up?'

'No, of course I can't.'

'I'll help you. I'll pull you up. She'll want you on a bed, I'm sure. Anyway you'll be much more comfortable. That's it. Oops-a-daisy. That's better.'

'She's not married, I take it,' Mrs Owen says as she takes off her coat.

'No.'

'Pity. Not that it makes any difference to this part of things. It's character that counts in this part.'

Oh Lord, not that, I think to myself as we hear Ilona groaning upstairs.

'I managed to get her into bed.'

'Did you put newspapers over the mattress?'

'Is that what the newspapers are for?'

'Well, we won't have much time to read them, girl, will we?'

There's another awesome groan from Ilona.

'Mrs Owen, she's in such pain. It can't be right.'

'She'll be better as soon as she sees me. Old Lydia may not have a pretty face, but . . .'

'It's character that counts.' I finish her sentence for her, trying to hurry her upstairs.

'And forty years experience,' she says. 'That's what they see in my face. Forty years of easing babies into this nasty old world.'

'Well, come now, you're not too bad, are you? We're going to give you a lovely bath, not too hot, not too cold, and it'll make you feel ready for anything. It's such a pleasure to bring a baby into a house with a bathroom, it makes it so much easier for the mother. A bath is the most soothing thing at this sort of time. My job would be child's play if every house had a bath and an inside lav.'

I escape to run the bath while Ilona is telling Lydia that having a bath is the last thing in the world she intends to do, that she might as well try to persuade her to have a dip in the sea while she's about it. She's still refusing to contemplate the idea even as Lydia is helping her into the bathroom, telling her how well she's doing and what a pleasure it is to see such a fine-looking body.

I think her body looks terrible, as though it might burst open at the navel at any moment. What if the baby was born in the bath? Would it drown? I wonder if Lydia Owen's been drinking. She looks half-drunk, but then she always does.

'I think she'd like a nice cup of tea now,' Lydia says after about fifteen minutes during which time Ilona has been soaking in the bath, steadily cursing and groaning, 'because we've got quite a few hours wait. After I've got her out of the bath and comfortable, I'll be off home to get my ironing done. I'll be back around midnight.'

'It's going to be quite straightforward,' she tells me as I show her out some time later. 'Everything is perfectly normal. We'll have a beautiful baby here before morning service tomorrow.'

'Shall we have a game of cards while we wait?' I ask brightly as I go back to the bedroom.

'Get out of this room and stay out.'

She does seem more comfortable after the bath, better able to bear the pains, though they gradually come more often and last longer. After each pain I sponge her face and arms with cold water and tell her how brave she's being and then wait for her to start groaning and shouting and swearing again.

Lydia Owen comes back at midnight as she promised, and the baby, a lusty boy, is born at twenty to two, the time in between being both frightening and thrilling.

At only an hour old the boy is already sucking, a remarkable feat according to Mrs Owen and there's a rich birth smell which I recognise from the farm. By three, Lydia has left and there's such a weight of peace in the room that I want to fling open the windows to share it with the sleeping town, with the world.

I think about my birth on Fair Day when neither the doctor nor the midwife could be contacted, so that an old long-retired nurse had to be brought by horse and trap from a nearby village. 'Of course, you were born by the time she'd arrived, your grandmother had done everything for me, well, she'd had nine children hadn't she, and there wasn't much she didn't know, but old Nurse Oliver stayed the night anyway and made herself useful getting some supper for your father.' Every birth has its own importance, its own history. I realise that Ilona and I will talk about this one while we both draw breath.

At five, Ilona wakes and feeds the baby again. 'Isn't he absolutely gorgeous. Look at his little ears. Look at his eyebrows.' I can hardly believe it's Ilona talking. She's suddenly become heavily maternal, but I don't suppose for a minute it will last. 'Don't you think you'd better get some sleep now?' she asks me with a sweet solicitude I've never before heard in her voice.

'No, I'm still too excited. I'll wait now till Lydia Owen comes again at nine. Perhaps I'll go to bed for a few hours when she leaves.'

'In that case do you think you could do me a big favour? Do you think you could possibly go to the kiosk to make a phone call for me?'

'Whoever's going to be awake at this time of morning?'

'Ifor will be. If you go now, you'll catch him before he goes out milking.'

'Yes, all right.' I can hardly refuse. 'What exactly shall I say?'

She looks sideways at me. 'You'll think I'm being very unreasonable,' she says meekly.

'You? Never! How could I think that?'

'The thing is, I don't want him to come here today. I don't want to see him. Could you tell him not to come? I'm not supposed to ring him except in an emergency, but this is very important isn't it? To stop him coming down all this way.'

'Yes, of course. But I don't see why he shouldn't put himself out a bit.'

'Only, I don't want to see him, Rhian. Isn't it strange? For the first time for ten years, I feel free of him. Absolutely free.'

'It's having the baby. Some spiders are the same.'

'Yes, but it's not that. I know you won't understand this, I hardly understand it myself, but I'm not in love with him anymore. Not a bit.'

'Oh.'

'You see, Rhian, I think I've fallen in love with someone else . . . I think I've fallen in love with Jack.'

My mind is spinning. 'Have you? With Jack? Well, I'm very pleased. Naturally, I'm very pleased. I think it's very suitable and sensible.'

'It's nothing to do with being suitable and sensible.'

No, of course not. It wouldn't be. 'What exactly happened?' I ask her.

'It was just . . . well, it was when we said goodbye yesterday. He was going home and I went to the station to see him off. Just for old times sake. We've been good mates for the last few months. And, do you know, he kissed me.'

That seems as much as she's going to say. 'Oh,' I say again.

'Yes, he leaned forward and kissed me. It was the first time he'd ever kissed me. And it was one of those kisses that start something. Oh, don't look at me like that. Close your mouth. You know exactly what I mean. We couldn't even get close because of the baby, but there was something so loving in the way he was looking at me; you know, something very strong and very tender at the same time. And I wanted him to stay so badly. And when the train left, I was so furious that I'd let him go without saying anything, that I walked right up to Beacon Point to try to calm myself and that's when the pains started.'

'And you still feel the same today? About Jack, I mean. You still . . . '

'Yes. Listen, I've fallen in love with him. I don't fall in

204

love with people very often – hardly ever, in fact. It's always been bloody Ifor.'

'Well, Jack is certainly in love with you.'

'Is he? Oh, but he won't want anything to do with me now. Not when he sees me with a baby. Oh yes, he knew it was there inside me, but now that it's born, he'll see me differently. Men are very changeable.'

'So different from us,' I murmur, but my sarcasm is lost on her.

'I'll tell you what, I'll adopt this one and then you'll be free again.'

The boy is in my arms, looking with great concentration at a spot somewhere beyond my left shoulder and gripping my finger. If only I'd conceived when I was with Gwynn: I'd willingly put up with every slander and hardship to be in Ilona's place.

'Give him to me. I don't even want you to take him out of the room.' Her voice plunges. 'Oh, look, I think he recognises me. Oh, his eyes are so dark. Like damson jelly. Great Heavens, aren't I lucky that Ifor won't want a share of him.'

'He's got a son already?'

'Two. He'll be glad to get shot of this one. And he'll be glad to get shot of me, too. He couldn't quite let me go, but I think I've been a burden to him for years.'

She seems relatively untroubled at the thought.

'Is that Ifor Meredyth? This is Rhian Evans, Ilona's friend. She's had the baby ... Yes, early this morning. And the thing is, she doesn't think you should come down today. In fact, she doesn't really want you to.'

'I see,' he says, slowly and carefully.

'But she'd like you to go to her grandmother's to let her know that she won't be with her for another two or three weeks. To explain to her. She'll be writing to her, tell her, to let her know how she's getting on.'

'I see.'

'They're both well,' I tell him, beginning to feel that he isn't going to ask.

'I'm very pleased about that,' he says. 'Very pleased. Tell her I'm very pleased about that.'

He has a slow, lazy voice. I can see him vividly; a sensuous, well-fed, well-to-do farmer, used to his own way and his own importance at home, in the pub and in the market.

'I will. Look, I'd better go back to her now, she's on her own. You will go to her grandmother's?'

'Yes indeed.'

'Boy or girl?' he asks, then. 'Her grandmother will want to know.'

'A boy. A seven pound boy.'

'Very good,' he says. 'Very good. And I suppose she gave you a pretty bad time, did she?'

There's a sort of lazy indulgent affection in the question, but I can't let it pass. '*She* had a pretty bad time, if that's what you mean,' I say sharply.

'Oh yes, I know about these things,' he says. 'Look, why don't I come down later on today in any case? For a visit, like. I've made all the arrangements now, got the wife's cousin in for the milking tonight. I could still come, you know.'

'No, I don't think she'd want that.' I take a deep breath and look out at the sea. 'You see, things are changing for her. Well, in fact, things have already changed for her. I'm sure she'll be writing to you later on. To explain everything – you know what I mean.'

'I see,' he says again, catching my drift at once. 'I see.'

There seems both regret and relief in his voice; though perhaps I'm sensing only what Ilona has already told me.

'Well, tell her I've been to the solicitor, will you? Tell her she'll be hearing from him. And tell her –'

The operator comes on the line. 'Your time is up caller. Do you wish to pay for further time?'

'No thank you,' I say firmly. 'Well, goodbye, Mr Meredyth.'

'Tell her to ... to get in touch with me.' His voice has taken on a measure of urgency; I smile at myself in the little mirror over the phone as the operator cuts us off.

I stand for a minute looking out at the sea emerging from the darkness; little shivering silver plates on the olive green darkness. It must be beautiful to see the sun rising over the sea, but here we have the blaze of red and gold only in the evening. At daybreak, the sea begins to gleam very gradually with a light which seems left over from the previous night's excesses, cleansed and calm and very peaceful.

My eyes seem full of sand. I shall write to Jack later on today when I've had some sleep. I feel too light-headed at the moment to tell him all that's happened since he went away.

Chapter Twenty-One

As Ilona had promised, life becomes a little easier in North Wales. Now that I no longer live in Huw's house surrounded by his family, his friends, his neighbours, I certainly suffer less guilt.

Now I have only Gwynn's death to contend with and though this is an immensity of loss which I can only think of in Biblical terms, immeasurable like the love of God, it's no longer a bitterness which burns my throat every time I swallow. I'm getting used to it, I suppose, getting used to feeling half a person leading half a life.

Starting a new school means hard work and discipline. Every day I feel that I'm sitting an examination; studying the paper, tackling the first question, completing it, ticking it off and going on to the next, not allowing my mind to stray for a second.

My digs, with an elderly widow called Lily Thomas, are clean and quiet. She brings my evening meal, simple but adequate, into the chilly front room which is my sitting room, and exactly half an hour later takes away my empty plates and cup and saucer, spreading the green baize cloth back over the little table so that I can get on with my marking. The highlight of the evening is when she taps on the door to invite me to the kitchen to listen to the nine o'clock news. As soon as it's over, she goes up to bed, but I'm allowed to sit up and read in front of the kitchen fire – almost out by this time – until ten. If I stay a minute after, she taps gently on her bedroom floor to remind me of the electricity I'm using. She's a tiny woman and she creeps about the house in carpet slippers, as though her chief aim in life is to disturb the air as little as possible.

I don't go to Ilona's very often because her grandmother has taken a dislike to me, insisting that I'm the district nurse coming to take her away, whether to the asylum or to the workhouse she doesn't say. I'm not even allowed to nurse the baby.

He's thriving in spite of that. Ilona has named him Thomas Gwynn – Gwynn so that I leave him my money, she says – but he's called Tommy and it suits him; he's plump as a little bird.

I was afraid that Ilona would find it too difficult to break away entirely from Ifor Meredyth now that she's back in Brynteg, but she never sees him as far as I know. She gets money from his solicitor every month and says it's all she wants from him.

To my great disappointment, Jack has written to her only once; a short letter, friendly enough, congratulating her on the baby's birth, but making no reference to the letter I sent him. I go over it in my mind, wondering if I was direct enough. 'She's become very fond of you,' I'd written, 'and she was upset that she'd let you go on the train without managing to let you know. Why don't you come to see her before we go to North Wales?' Surely that was plain enough. He'd certainly seemed in love with her, so what had happened?

'He's met someone else,' Ilona says if I mention it to her. 'Why shouldn't he? Why shouldn't he find someone attractive and easy-going? After all, he's quite a catch, he's got a good job and he's fairly good-looking. Why should you think a bad-tempered, unmarried mother is all he's fit for? He's probably interested in that woman they appointed to your job. I've stopped thinking about him long ago.'

Ilona's grandmother is a small, fierce-looking woman with dark skin and yellowish eyes. She's nearly bald so she always wears a knitted cap even in the house, and whenever I'm there pulls it down over her eyes and goes to sleep, her chin on her chest. She's eighty-eight. Ilona is worried because she hasn't made a will. She's always said that her cottage is for Ilona, but with no legal proof, Ilona's afraid that her eldest sister, who has three children and an errant husband, may decide to claim it. It's a very old cottage, dark and tiny, the windows no bigger than pocket handkerchiefs.

My mother writes me a long letter every week. There's heavy fighting again in Italy, between the Germans and the Allies this time, and Fredo is very worried for his sons. Someone from her chapel ran in to Huw's mother in Llanfair and was told that Huw is in the thick of the fighting, probably in Holland. My mother begs me to write to him, but somehow I'm not able to. I'm pleased, of course, to have news of his safety, but I can't write to him.

Mr Churchill says the war will be over by next summer.

I go home for Christmas: a ten-hour journey it turns out to be, three crowded short-distance buses with long waits in between.

I have a really deep and dreamless sleep in my own little room and wake refreshed and ready for anything. Which is just as well because in the middle of the afternoon a telegram arrives for me: 'Please return. Nain serious stroke. Ilona.'

'Dear, dear, what a pity,' my mother says, starting to pack my things again, taking it for granted that I'll be going back immediately.

'But it's Christmas Eve tomorrow. I can't leave you alone for Christmas.'

'I won't be alone, though, girl, not exactly. You see, Fredo is allowed to be here for the day. Yes, they're not nearly as strict as they were. His chaplain has been to see me, you know, and we had a long chat about religion. He'd never heard of the Congregational sect, mind, but I explained how it meant all the people in the congregation being equal before God with no bishop or senate and he said it wasn't so different from their religion, except of course for the Pope and the cardinals and the bishops. But it's the same laws of Moses, he said, and the same Christ the Saviour, so that we mustn't let small differences stand in the way. So I think I'm doing right, aren't I, and I'm sure your father would say the same.'

'I'm sorry not to see Fredo. I've brought him a Christmas present, look. Two pairs of hand-knitted socks. My landlady knits. They smell awful, but it's only the oil from the sheep.'

'They're beautiful. They'll last for ever, too.'

'And I've brought you some material for a new costume, a ready-made blouse, new gloves and a new hat.'

'Good gracious me! And whenever am I going to wear all this finery, girl, at my age?'

'I thought you might have a wedding to go to, some time next year.'

'Oh dear, dear.' And she blushes like a girl.

Next day the buses are even more crowded with people travelling home for Christmas, but apart from me, everyone seems happy; the war news is good, food more plentiful this year and the weather is sunny and bright. When I arrive in Caernarfon, the last bus for Brynteg has already left, so I have to take a taxi: another fifteen shillings on top of the bus journey.

I find that the old lady is in a coma and not likely to recover consciousness. Ilona is weeping; the tiny house is crowded with relations, all weeping. And I'm so tired and angry that I was called back that I start weeping too. It gets later and later. No one think of leaving, no one thinks of going to bed. We take it in turn to make sandwiches and cups of tea, endless cups of tea. At midnight someone switches on the wireless and we hear the bells chiming for Christmas and almost immediately Ilona's mother comes downstairs saying, 'She's gone, she's gone,' and we all troop up to see her and start weeping again.

Then everybody sits round the fire drinking whisky and telling wildly disrespectful stories about the old lady who seemed to have lied and cheated her way through life in great style. Nobody had ever got the better of her, it seems. They can hardly believe that she's dead now, silent and defeated. They drink to her memory until it's time for Tommy's first feed.

We spend a strange Christmas Day. The family has left, but in the afternoon we have a visit from the minister, a very shy young man who assures us of Christ's welcome in Heaven for Theodora Owen, the stray sheep, the beloved sinner, and then has a piece of my mother's cake and dandles Tommy on his knee.

Ilona and I are too tired to cook either dinner or supper, but we light a good fire and watch Tommy kicking on a rug and have sandwiches again. In the evening we listen to a ghost story on the wireless and then we're almost afraid to go to bed because of the dead woman upstairs. We're really ashamed of ourselves in the morning.

Greta, Ilona's eldest sister, agrees to forfeit her claim to the cottage on condition that she has the twenty-seven pounds in their grandmother's Post Office book and the other sisters and sisters-in-law settle for a pair of jugs each from the dresser.

Ilona invites me to be her lodger next term and I accept.

After the funeral, I go home again for the last week of the holiday.

My mother tells me that Jack called the previous day, wanting news of me. 'Yes, he trudged up Hewl Fach in all that snow we had yesterday and when he realised you'd had to go back to North Wales, he returned on the next bus, wouldn't even stay for a spot of dinner. He seemed very disappointed, girl. A nice man, I thought him, and so did Fredo. He told me to tell you that he's applying for the deputy Headship, now that Mr Talfan Roberts is retiring. Perhaps that's all he had to say – but I don't think so, somehow.'

'He's got my address in Brynteg, he can write to me if he wants to.'

'They still miss you at school. Mr Cynrig Williams is giving the woman they appointed to your job a hard time, it seems.'

'He gives everyone a hard time.'

'There's no need to bite my head off, girl. What's Mr Jones done to offend you? I thought you were friends.'

'Let's not talk about him, all right?'

My mother's prepared a beautiful dinner to celebrate the New Year: a roasting fowl with potatoes and sprouts and all the trimmings, followed by the Christmas pudding which Fredo, who'd tasted some the previous year in camp, had insisted should be kept for me. The table is beautiful: the lace tablecloth, made by my great-grandmother and shown in the Great Exhibition in 1851, two tall red candles in a pair of heavy brass candlesticks which are always on the table for any celebration but never lit, and the best dinner service, a wedding present, grey leaves on a white background, which comprises in all thirty-six plates, four meat plates, two tureens with covers and two gravy boats with ladles, which no one but my mother has ever been allowed to wash or dry.

'Is it still complete?' I ask my mother, 'this dinner set?'

Other families might boast a wireless set, an indoor lavatory or the electric light; we had a complete dinner service.

'No, not now, girl. I broke a plate on the day of your father's funeral and then poor old Davi Blaenhir broke another as he was putting it away for me.'

'Nothing lasts for ever.'

'Nothing lasts forever except longing.'

I sing the old song as she brings the dinner to the table:

'Derfydd aur a derfydd arian, derfydd melfed, derfydd sidan,
Derfydd pob dilledyn helaeth ond er hyn, ni dderfydd hiraeth.'

Nothing lasts except grief.

The start of a new year makes everyone introspective, I suppose, and I can't help being aware of how much I've changed, of how bitter I've become. Whenever I read a newspaper these days I'm on the look-out for those paragraphs describing personal tragedies: the young couple killed on their honeymoon, the soldier killed on the very day his girlfriend accepted his proposal of marriage, such happenings seem to help me feel reconciled to my loss, whereas any picture of sweethearts reunited and looking at each other with love and longing makes my loneliness more terrible to bear. I'm ashamed to be so self-absorbed.

'It's a wonder to me, Rhian,' my mother says, 'how you can be so unselfish. There you are, spending your hard-earned money on an outfit for my wedding, when your own life is in tatters. Well, you take after your father, he was just the same. Your father could always rejoice in other people's good fortune, even when we were scraping round for ha'pennies. I only wish I could be that sort.'

'So do I. I'm not like that, I can tell you. Of course I'm happy about *you*, but I don't care a jot about anyone else.'

'No? What about that Ilona? Aren't you feeling annoyed with Jack Jones because you think he's letting her down? To me, he seems very sensible, thinking things through before committing himself. It's not his baby, you told me that.'

'People can be a bit too sensible.'

'Really?'

'As Christ said.'

'*Christ*?'

'When they were complaining about that poor widow who'd spent all her money on the precious ointment for his head.'

'I know the Bible, my girl.'

'Don't be too sensible,' he told them. 'Follow your instincts a bit more. Bend with the wind. And thus ye shall enter the kingdom of Heaven.'

'Rhian, that's a very free interpretation of the Scriptures, it seems to me.'

It proves difficult to tell Mrs Thomas that I'm leaving her. 'And there was I thinking of you as a daughter,' she tells me in her timid little squeak of a voice. Anyway, I order a pram suit for Tommy, bobble hat, double-breasted coat and leggings with feet, so she forgives me and says I can call in any time for a cup of tea.

At the beginning of term, Miss Perkins, our Headmistress, breaks her leg on the slippery pavement outside school and we have a peaceful couple of weeks before she returns, more short-tempered than ever.

During a snowy period at the beginning of March, when the buses can't get through to Brynteg, I have to stay two weeks at a boarding house in town and I'm so lonely that I cry myself to sleep every night.

The day I get back to Ilona's, I find that she's had a letter from Jack asking her to marry him. 'How wonderful,' I exclaim. 'Oh, I *am* pleased.'

But she's furious with him. 'I'm all right now. I've got over him. I've got over him and bloody Ifor Meredyth too. I'm really happy, if you want to know the truth, all the bother over with. I'm looking forward to spring-cleaning Gran's bedroom and whitewashing the house and the shed and digging the garden and planting potatoes and onions. All right, it might seem strange to you, but I'm looking forward to it. I'm all right now. I've got a bit of money saved and with what you give me for your keep and what bloody Ifor Meredyth gives me for Tommy, I'm doing all right. How dare he spend six months summing me up, weighing me up. If he'd written asking whether he could come on a visit, it wouldn't offend me so much – it wouldn't offend me at all, it would show he missed me and wanted to see me again and maybe start something. But to send me this proposal of marriage, making it so cold and business-like. He doesn't even say he loves me, only that he doesn't think he's good enough for me, that he's hesitated so long, aware that he isn't good enough for me. Of course he isn't good enough for me. What man is ever good enough for a woman? Women are always tougher and braver and much nicer as well. But I was in love with him last summer and I'd have had him then, given half a chance. But how do I know it wasn't my body leading me astray? When your body is being flooded with all these maternal feelings, how can you be sure of anything. Perhaps all I wanted was a daddy bear with me in the cave, something like that. Anyway, he's bloody well had his chance, mate, and now I can't decide whether to send him a postcard with a very short scathing message or not reply at all for six months. What do you think?'

I don't say anything. I've felt disappointed in Jack, goodness knows, and I don't think he's being honest even now. I think his long hesitation is because he's not certain he can cope with Ilona. He's nervous of her, not because she's unconventional and an unmarried mother, but because she's not the type to give him the whole-hearted approval he's always looking for. He needs someone to boost his confidence and he realises that Ilona is too honest to give him any reassurance she doesn't feel.

'You're not really interested, are you?' she asks me after a few moments.

'Of course I'm interested. I don't feel able to advise you, that's all.'

216

'Oh, get on with your marking. You simply don't care about my problems.'

We sit in silence for the rest of the evening, each of us sighing from time to time. She goes to bed much earlier than usual, complaining of a headache and looking martyred.

I can't sleep and at two o'clock I hear her moving about so I go to her room to see if I can get her anything. She's sitting up in bed suckling Tommy and looking remarkably contented. 'Perhaps I ought to write to him,' she says quietly. 'He must mean something to me or I wouldn't get so angry, would I? I'm certainly not going to marry him, but I wouldn't mind spending a weekend with him now and then. I don't suppose I'm really cut out for a nun, am I? Being without all the fuss and bother has been very peaceful, but perhaps there's plenty of time for that later on. Oh, for pity's sake, say something, Rhian. Don't just stand there, your feet cold as clams on that lino. Come under the quilt for a bit.'

'Write to him. Say you feel very annoyed that he thinks you'll marry him as soon as he snaps his fingers. But say we both miss his company and that he can come up for a day in the Easter holidays.'

'The Easter holidays? In a fortnight's time? Well, perhaps so. Yes, perhaps I'll send him a short letter, a cold and careful few lines.'

It takes her three days to get the letter written to her satisfaction and he comes up the following Saturday.

He's changed, I think; he seems older and more self-confident. He's got the deputy Headship, he tells us; perhaps that's made the difference.

He's annoyed when I suggest taking Tommy out for a walk in his pram. 'I'm not a schoolboy here for a quick kiss and cuddle,' he says, 'I'm here to talk and listen and make plans for the future. I suppose you know how Ilona feels, Rhian, so stay and hear how I feel. I'm thirty-one now, and I take a serious view of the world. Perhaps you think that five and a half years of war haven't affected me, because I've been lucky enough to be out of the fighting, but you'd be wrong. I've suffered as well. Three of my closest friends have been killed. I've read accounts of horror and torture. Have you seen the pictures of those people who've been rescued from the concentration camps? They've made me realise that Gwynn was right not to listen to you, Rhian, when you tried to persuade him to be a conscientious objector. God knows, I hate Churchill's non-appeasement policy, but the cruelty of that pales beside what the Nazis have done. I'd be proud, and so would Gwynn, I'm sure, to be a member of the Allied Forces now. I suppose you think all this isn't relevant to a relationship between a man and woman, but it is, I think it is. We're all part of the society we're living in, and I want to make my contribution to the rebuilding process. For a start, I'm out to change the school. The Head knows I'm not going to be another Talfan, ready to put up with anything for an easy time. And I've got plans for the community, too, seeking election to local government as my first step. I've got work to do and I want a wife to help me, not some frivolous girlfriend.'

I think Ilona and I are equally astonished to hear him speaking so passionately. But I can't really think of anything but his reference to Gwynn – I'm quite overwhelmed by the realisation that he may be right. I can't help re-living the quarrel we had, the letter of apology I sent him, the trouble it caused when it got into Celine's hands. That's all I can think of. I need to consider it all, all the implications. I suddenly want to be out walking on the moors in the wind, the grim peaks of Snowdon all around me. I need to be alone.

'You two have a lot of talking to do,' I say at last. Ilona doesn't seem able or willing to say anything.

At the sound of my voice, though, she pulls herself together, walks up to Jack and slaps him hard across the mouth. 'Marry someone else,' she says, 'save the world with someone else. Don't bother me again.'

He grabs her hand and looks as though he's about to retaliate.

'Stop it, stop it,' I shout, tugging my coat from the back of the chair where Jack's sitting and rushing out, slamming the door behind me.

I walk in the bitter March winds, going back, step by step, over my quarrel with Gwynn, our reconciliation, all the passion of our short time together and my scorching loss. I can't bear the thought of going back to Ilona's cottage. I don't want to go back anywhere.

I must be several miles from the village when the storm blows up. I shelter in the hedge, not knowing where I am or which way to go. As the snow covers me, I think of Gwynn and me last summer on Celyn sands, how he used to lie on top of me, shutting out the world.

I'm rescued next day by a party of local men. For a time I'm fully conscious, aware for instance, that it's Ifor Meredyth who's carrying me, growling and cursing whenever he loses a foothold. The drifts are twelve foot high; everything is white and hard and glittering.

When Ilona lights a fire in my little bedroom, the flames terrify me.

I develop pneumonia. For days I'm delirious. Often I'm in the snow, searching for Gwynn and crying because I can't find him. I hear Ilona telling Dr Jenkins about Gwynn, how he was killed by a flying bomb after only six weeks in the army.

He takes hold of my hand. I try to focus on him; he's a large man, elderly and gruff. 'You must leave the dead in peace,' he tells me. 'You're on the mend. It's your life that matters now. You've been given a second chance.'

'I don't want it.'

'You do. Millions have died but you were saved. Strive to deserve it. *Live*.' His grip on my hand makes me cry out.

'Leave the dead in peace. Live.' His words echo at me through the tunnel of my fever. 'You've been saved. *Live*. Leave the dead in peace.'

Slowly I begin to recover.

When the weather breaks, my mother comes to see me. She makes me some chicken broth and says that Tommy has a better notion of eating than I have.

I've forgotten Tommy. When they bring him to see me, I hardly recognise him, he's grown so big. He doesn't recognise me; when I try to hold him he struggles and cries. He can say mama, mama.

Jack comes to visit. He and Ilona seem shy and awkward together; he says it's because they feel guilty about me. I was

219

gone for hours, it seems, before they noticed. I feel that they're making plans to get married but neither of them will admit it.

Ifor Meredyth comes to see me, grunting as he climbs up the narrow stairs. He seems very proud of me, keeps saying I'm doing very nice. Apparently ewes often panic when they're separated from the flock, whereas I bowed to fate and conserved my strength.

'What strength?' Ilona says crossly. 'She's weak as a white mouse. Feel her wrists, they're like sticks. Do you want a cup of tea?'

'No, I'd best be off. I don't want to be in trouble for nothing, do I? You've got another bloke, I hear. Well, it's time to settle down, isn't it? Feel the same myself. Time changes and we change with it, more's the pity. The little lad's getting on champion, anyhow. I'll fetch him a pet lamb next year, he'll like that. Good about the war, isn't it?'

'What about the war?' I ask Ilona, when she next comes up with Bovril and offers of an egg.

'It's over. Mr Churchill is going to make a speech at three o'clock this afternoon. I'll bring the wireless up if you promise not to get too excited.'

The war is over; all the bloodshed and destruction. The church bells ring out and later that night we watch bonfires on the hills, even as far as Anglesey.

'Will you phone my mother-in-law to ask after Huw?' I ask Ilona the next day.

'Do you think I should? She may read into it more than you intend.'

'It doesn't matter. I must know that he's all right. It would be such a load off my mind.'

'Do I tell her you've been ill?'

'I suppose so. It might make her feel kinder towards me. I wish my mother was on the phone . . . I wonder when Fredo will be going back to Italy. She'll be so lonely. I wonder if he'll come back?'

'Of course he will.'

'I don't know. He's got another life in Italy, hasn't he? His three sons and all his relatives. His farm.'

'He'll come back to your mother.'

I get up to sit in the small armchair Ilona has put by the window. My legs buckle under me as I try to walk. I can't think when I'll get back to school; Dr Jenkins says not until September. I open the window and watch Ilona walking back from the telephone kiosk. It's a sweet spring day and Tommy is sitting up in his pram waving his arms. Ilona smiles up at me and nods her head. Huw is safe and well.

Huw is safe and well. Gwynn is gone, and all his beauty, but the war is over and I'm alive. And for the first time for almost a year I find myself glad to be alive.

Postscript

It's the middle of August, 1945, two weeks after America dropped its atom bombs on Hiroshima and Nagasaki and Japan surrendered.

Today I got a letter from Llanfair. It was from Mr Roberts, the minister of Tabernacle, and he tells me that Huw, who has recently returned from Germany, would like to see me again. Apparently he was bitterly angry with me for several months and determined to get a divorce as soon as the war ended. But after the last few months in Berlin, witnessing so much destruction and grief; bombed homes, bereaved parents, orphaned children, my infidelity seemed to lose its sting, and since he still has some affection for me, he wonders whether we can meet to discuss the future. He's changed, Mr Roberts tells me, older of course, but more mature too.

I shall write back to say I'd be pleased to meet him. I owe him that much.

Ilona and Jack are getting married next year and are buying a house in Llanfair.

Fredo has not yet returned from Italy. He discovered that his eldest son had been killed last year in a bombing raid on their village. Their house is intact, but he still has a great deal of work to do on the land before he can leave. He promises to be back before winter.

My mother has learnt the Lord's Prayer in Italian.

Celine has returned to France.

Gwynn is dead.

Now read an extract from Siân James's

stunning new novel, *TWO LOVES*...

Though Ingrid Walsh had been enthusiastic about her work – the first person for a long time – Rosamund was far from happy after she'd left. Ingrid had seemed to feel she was some sort of freak. Had she really opted out of life? 'How could you have given it all up?' she'd asked, more than once. 'All the excitement; being young and in the centre of things?' Was her life so abnormal, then? Until recently, Rosamund had thought of herself as fairly contented; she had a son whom she adored, a very supportive mother living nearby, a lovely house and almost enough money.

Her painting wasn't much more than a hobby, she'd always realised that, but it gave her a certain amount of satisfaction and enough money for treats – extravagant Christmases and holidays abroad. She exhibited twice a year with a local art society and always sold three or four paintings.

It was true she didn't have much of a social life; she was invited to certain functions, the occasional party, but had never enjoyed standing about with a drink and a plate of indigestible food, making small-talk. And none of the men who'd shown any interest in her had seemed worth pursuing. A few years ago she'd met a young doctor at a charity ball; he'd persevered in his attentions for a while, but they had little in common. Going out with him often seemed rather an effort even though her mother was always ready to babysit, and after a few months' desultory courtship he'd stopped ringing her and later phoned to say he'd got engaged to a nurse at the local hospital. She'd run into them soon afterwards. His fiancée looked about eighteen, was very glamorous and had succeeded in bringing him to life as she herself had never been able to do.

Rosamund was slightly peeved at being supplanted, but only her mother was really disappointed: 'He was so fond of you, dear.'

'Joss didn't like him,' Rosamund had said firmly. 'He had no rapport with children, so it wouldn't have done, would it?'

Joss adored Thomas, not that that made any odds, because he wasn't available; less so now than ever.

Rosamund sighed. Thomas's son, Harry, had been Joss's best friend since they were in nursery school together, so of course she and Thomas had been thrown together for years; he was always around, returning Joss from their house in the village or fetching Harry from the schoolhouse. They were comfortable together, liked each other, got on well, and three years ago had become lovers. Neither of them had planned it, but after it happened, it had seemed natural, almost inevitable.

She sighed again. He was also very nice-looking. She wished that didn't make as much difference to her as it did; it seemed the trait of a very superficial person.

Thomas's wife, Eliza, was a career woman who seemed to have little time for him; that's why Rosamund didn't feel as guilty about their relationship as she otherwise would. Occasionally she fantasised about his leaving Eliza and coming to live with her and Joss, but knew it was impossible because he was a devoted father – with three sons of his own – and a dutiful husband. He was husband material, warm and loving rather than exciting. Whenever they were able to snatch an hour together, she felt, not dazed by love, but comforted, more reconciled to life, more completely human.

It had taken her some months to realise that it was much easier for her than for him; he was the one torn between two women, two lives. She started noticing the deep frown lines between his eyes when he got out of her bed and the way he held his body as he got dressed, his elbow tight in against his ribs as though deeply uneasy by what he was involved in. He was a nicer person than she was.

And then the previous year, Eliza had become pregnant again. Rosamund was surprised and rather shocked when

Thomas broke the news to her; she'd somehow assumed that they didn't have sex together, though Thomas had never said so. She'd suggested at that point that they should give up their affair, but they hadn't, though their meetings had become more infrequent. And they'd hardly seen each other at all since the baby was born the previous month.

Then just over a week ago, she'd called on Eliza, taking her a present for the baby. She'd felt uncomfortable about going, but thought it might seem strange if she didn't, since they were neighbours and their children friends. Also she was longing to see the new baby.

She didn't know Eliza well, or particularly like her; she seemed to have no time for those she obviously considered lesser mortals. At one time Rosamund had felt slightly aggrieved to be so often asked to pick Harry up from school and to keep an eye on him until his father fetched him at five or five-thirty. Especially since Eliza seemed to assume that she couldn't possibly have anything more important to do, and never phoned to thank her. She'd never bothered to find out what exactly Eliza did as a business consultant, but it was probably very high-powered and certainly well-paid; the family had a large new BMW every year and the children had every conceivable gadget and a roomful of computers, which wouldn't have come from Thomas's salary as science master at the local comprehensive.

'Do you want to come in?' Eliza asked her after opening the door, almost as though she was delivering pamphlets rather than visiting a new baby.

'Please. If it's convenient, I'd love to see him. I've brought him a little sweater. I'm sure he's got dozens, but this one was so pretty. Joss thinks he's wonderful. What are you calling him?'

'We haven't decided yet.'

'May I see him? I hope he's not asleep.'

Eliza looked at her wearily and pointed to a chair. 'Sit down, won't you. Look, I don't feel like making small-talk, but now that you're here, I'd just like to ask you to lay off my husband. All right?'

'To lay off your husband,' Rosamund repeated, shocked to the bone by Eliza's attack. 'But you've always said . . . I mean,

Thomas has always said that you didn't mind his spending some time with me occasionally when you're working.' She glared at Eliza. 'And you're always working,' she said, unwilling to take all the blame. 'I mean, Thomas and I are friends. I mean, I don't see him very often, hardly at all these days. I mean . . .'

'I admit to treating him in rather a cavalier fashion, I know I cut him out of my life to some extent, I know I didn't give him enough time and attention, but—'

'A man needs time and attention.'

'All right, I've admitted to being negligent. I don't blame you for trying to take him away from me – he's an attractive man – but now I want him back. It's as simple as that.'

'Have you given up your job, then?'

'Yes.'

'I see.'

'So what's your answer?'

Rosamund took a deep breath. She wasn't prepared to accept Eliza as the wronged wife and herself as the intruder; it was far more complicated than that. 'I'll have to discuss it with Thomas – he's got a part in all this. I don't want to make you a promise I can't keep.' They looked hard at each other. 'Do you love him?' Rosamund asked.

'Of course. He's my husband.'

'That sounds a bit glib. What if I love him, too? I'm certainly very fond of him. I'm always very happy to see him.'

'You're just happy to be fucked. Because you haven't got anyone else.'

Rosamund looked straight into her eyes. 'Have you? I answer your questions. Why don't you answer mine?'

'He's my husband and the father of my children and I want to turn over a new leaf and be a good wife and mother. I want us to be a proper family again. And if you have any decent feelings you won't stand in our way.'

'Does that mean you love him? That's what I want to know. That's what I asked you.'

'I certainly don't love anyone else. Though I admit to neglecting him, it was never for another man – there's never been another man – it was only for my work.'

'And I expect your work will take over again quite soon.'

They were interrupted by a sudden cry from the pram standing outside the French windows, not the first shaky bleat of a new baby on waking, but a sharp wail of pain, a cry to be immediately attended to.

Eliza fetched the baby, put him over her shoulder and patted his back. He grew quiet.

Rosamund was surprised again at how small new babies were. She wasn't able to see his face; Eliza seemed determined to keep his back to her, but the little body cocooned in its white cotton blanket seemed too small to be living a separate life. She suddenly decided that if she was about to give Thomas up, she'd like to be pregnant first. 'I'd love a baby,' she said. And was surprised at how fretful she sounded.

'They're nice little things,' Eliza said, her voice milder.

And then she must have realised how lucky she was, or at least how strong her position, because she took the baby from her shoulder, loosened his shawl and showed him off to Rosamund. His face was red and stern and his hands were little trembling claws. 'Oh, he's beautiful,' Rosamund murmured, her voice hushed as though in a church.

She hadn't expected Eliza to breast-feed in front of her, especially as her breasts were rather slack and tired-looking, white with greyish veins. It made her look weak and vulnerable instead of sophisticated and powerful. Rosamund felt pains in her own breasts, almost as sharp as when Joss was newly born. 'I'd really like a baby,' she said again.

'Well, you certainly can't have Thomas's; that would be most unfair. It's bad enough for him already. He's very worried about giving you up.'

So it was already arranged? Rosamund felt she should at least have been consulted.

TWO LOVES is now available in hardback

from Piatkus Books

The very best of Piatkus fiction is now available in paperback as well as hardcover. Piatkus paperbacks, where _every_ book is special.

The prices shown above were correct at the time of going to press. However Piatkus Books reserve the right to show new retail prices on covers which may differ from those previously advertised in the text or elsewhere.

Piatkus Books will be available from your bookshop or newsagent, or can be ordered from the following address:
Piatkus Paperbacks, P.O. Box 11, Falmouth, TR10 9EN.
Alternatively you can fax your order to this address on 01326 374888 or E-mail us at books@barni.avel.co.uk.

Payments can be made as follows: Sterling cheque, Eurocheque, postal order, (payable to Piatkus Books) or by credit cards, Visa/Mastercard. Do not send cash or currency. UK and B.F.P.O. customers allow £1.00 postage and packing for the first book, 50p for the second and 30p for each additional book ordered to a maximum charge of £3.00 (7 books plus).

Overseas customers, including Eire, allow £2.00 for postage and packing for the first book, plus £1.00 for the second and 50p for each subsequent title ordered.
NAME (Block Letters) _____
ADDRESS _____
_____

I enclose my remittance for £_____
I wish to pay by Visa/Mastercard Card.

Number ☐☐☐☐☐☐☐☐☐☐☐☐☐☐☐☐
Card Expiry Date _____